A Champion's Heart

By Piper Huguley

A Champion's Heart
A Born to Win Men novel
By Piper Huguley

Liliaceae Publishers

Cover by Teresa Sprekelmeyer
Editor: Felicia Murrell

Books by Piper Huguley

Home to Milford College series
The Lawyer's Luck
The Preacher's Promise
The Mayor's Mission
The Representative's Revolt

Migrations of the Heart series
A Virtuous Ruby
A Most Precious Pearl
A Treasure of Gold

Novellas:
"A Sweet Way to Freedom" in The Brightest Day
"The Cowboy's Christmas" in Christmas in America
"The Washerwomen's War" in Daughters of a Nation

Dedication

An author once told me not to put my work out there unless my heart was part of the story. At the time I heard those words, I was a scared aspiring author who had to bring her young son to her workshop because I could not find a babysitter. She did not know in that moment, less than three months from her death, she gave me the strength to finish this story. Thank you, Dee Stewart. This one is for you.

To J.A.

I hope you have found the peace and fulfillment you were always looking for.

Acknowledgements

Many people believed in this story, but the special ones are: Barbara Sue Andrews, the Boston Brides Immersion class of 2015, Heidi Cullinan, Mari Christie and the Golden Heart judges of historical romance in 2013. Blessings to each and every one of you.

CHAPTER ONE

Pittsburgh, Pennsylvania - 1935

Asking for money should be a sight more easy than fighting for it.

Because asking wasn't getting. And he needed money to keep fighting.

1935 wasn't no easy year for anybody. Money was hard to come by just now, even with the rich numbers man, Jay Evans.

Fighting was all he knew, and he was good at it. Good enough for a Negro like him to get in the ring with a white boxer. That's where the real money was. He could make much more than enough for a room and eats for a week. He could make enough from one fight in one year, but only if he were able to get a fight with a white man.

Small streams of sweat started a pathway down his back in the small closed office. Where did that come from? February in Pittsburgh meant cold, not hot. He always had a hard time controlling his sweat. It was how he knew he was in the right profession. People didn't expect boxers to control their sweat.

'Cepting for Delie.

She always say, "You sweat as much as a sooey pig stuck in a sty unable to get out."

"Not sooey, Delie, sow."

"Whatever. I can't keep all the farm animals straight."

"You brought up on a farm."

"That doesn't mean I have to know the animals' names, Champion. Sheesh."

Delie. The lingering memory of his childhood sweetheart warmed the pit of his stomach.

Please, God, let her be all right.

More sweat rolled down his back, but he welcomed it. The memory of her cinnamon freckles against her golden brown skin filled him full like his mama's rice pudding with cinnamon dashed across the top. He hadn't had none of that pudding in seven years, the same amount of time he hadn't seen Delie. His beautiful sunny, funny Cordelia Bledsoe. The last good thing in his life.

And he had been fool enough to let her go.

The warm thought of her made him forget how hungry he was.

A slight cough caused him to stare into the stern countenance of Jay Evans, who had entered the cold room from outside, shaking the snow off the shoulders of his well-tailored suit. Hadn't seen no numbers man this well turned out since he started fighting back in '28. Money troubles impacted the numbers racket, but not Jay Evans.

He stood straight ready to meet his fate. The numbers man's handshake, firm and solid, made him feel good in return. He spoke up as his mama taught him to do. "Mr. Evans. Thanks for meeting with me."

"I appreciate you waiting and coming through the snow. Pittsburgh is not very cooperative this time of year, I am afraid. It hasn't snowed all season. Now, here it comes when folks want to start thinking about spring. How can I help you today?" The man's deep voice had a tinge of an accent that Champ couldn't place. Jay Evans didn't sound like any Negro he had ever heard before.

"Sir, I'm a fighter and—"

"You mean a boxer?" Jay Evans sat himself down. His elegant countenance belied how broad his shoulders were. Here was a man who could take care of his own if need be. Maybe even having a fight or two of his own.

"Yes, sir. I fight—"

"Box," Jay Evans insisted. "It's your chosen profession. It's who you are. You need to speak about your profession with pride, not as if it just happens to be something anyone could do."

Yeah, a new way of thinking about it. He made a lot of sense. "I box. I have a 60-2 record and I want to move up to better stakes."

"An ambitious boxer." Jay Evans noted and crossed his legs. "Nothing wrong with that. A nice idea at these times."

"Yes, sir."

A stirring outside interrupted their discussion.

Jay Evans went out to the outer office and Champ faced the desk again, praying.

Gotta calm down. Stop sweating. He seem nice. Maybe he'll give me the money. Please, Father God.

Jay Evans reentered the room. "I apologize, Mr. Bates. My wife is here to take notes for me today since my daughter who usually does it isn't well."

Champion could sense a lighter feminine presence in the room. He stood to meet it. Turning around to meet the woman, he was knocked out by a sucker punch to the gut. The sea turned in his stomach in that second.

"Nettie Bledsoe."

Nettie's eyebrows came together in the same stern expression she fixed on him when he and Delie got into bad mischief, like when they were eight and went skinny dipping in the Bledsoe's creek.

She was not excited to see his face, for sure. "This is the boxer you were planning on backing?" Oh yeah. She sounded like, 'I'm gonna tell Mama'.

"You know my wife?" Those broad shoulders of Jay Evans's were now set in a more defensive position. Champ knew he better explain. And quick.

Nettie was quicker. She always did have a silvery tongue. "Champion Bates is from Winslow." She lowered her head. "He and Delie were—"

"Engaged." Champ jumped in. Time for some fancy footwork.

Nettie raised one of her stern eyebrows. "Engaged. Hmm. He abandoned her at the train station leaving my baby sister to wait all night long since she didn't know he had taken an earlier train somewhere else, leaving her far behind."

Another punch to the gut. That wasn't exactly how it happened, but he could see how it appeared from Delie's side. The hungry, scraping feeling in his gut turned up and sounded a loud, long rumble into the silence of the empty room.

Because of what he had done, his fighting chance slipped away. He didn't know anyone else to ask. Jay Evans had been his last shot.

"How's all of the family?" Champ tried to be merry.

Foolishness. Nettie was not as easily charmed as other people, not after what he had done to her sister.

Jay Evans's face wore an intractable expression. "We should all sit down and catch up." He gestured to his wife. "Garnet, I will need you to take notes."

Oh my. He called Nettie by her real name. A sign of a fight coming for sure, and if Champ knew anything, he knew when a fight was coming.

Nettie said nothing to her husband, but her own shoulders were set. She jerked herself around and sat down, taking up her pen and notepad with a set line on her lips.

Champ drew out a breath.

Jay Evans still believed in him. The chance was still there. Nettie wouldn't answer his question about the Bledsoes, but he still had a chance. "I want a match with Jim McGill."

Jay was the last one to sit. He whistled. "A tall order."

Nettie put down her pen and closed her notebook. "Then there is no need to discuss this further."

"Garnet, I need you to make note of my explanations to Mr. Bates here." Jay gestured to him with an elegant hand.

"Jay, I—"

"Ephesians 5 verse 22 to verse 33." Jay spoke through stiff lips to Nettie, nodded at Champ and waved his hand to continue.

A little laugh stirred inside of him. What happened? This numbers man just quoted the Bible at Nettie. Nettie, who knew the Bible better than anyone.

Her lips firm, Nettie took up her pen and notebook again poised to write.

"McGill is white, but if I could buy my way in… They might respond to green money."

"Oh, I know, Mr. Bates. But if I buy your way in, you'll have to win. Tell me something. Are you a Christian?"

Champ had not stepped foot into a church since he left Winslow, but he wasn't about to reveal his attendance record to this bible-quoting numbers runner. "I believe in God, sir."

"A godless man who boxes. Well." Nettie patted her marcelled hairdo.

"Winning is what I do, sir," Champ spoke up for himself in as confident a tone as he could. "If you get me the match, I'll win."

"That's more what I like to hear. How long would you need? How much to train?"

Here it was. Champ pulled a paper from his pocket, smoothed out the wrinkles in it as best as he could and handed the paper to Jay Evans. "I would like to have the match in March or April."

"One to two months. Hmm." Jay took the paper and inspected it. "Planning on eating red meat?"

"Oh, no. I mean… I don't have to."

"You have to. We got to build you up so you can win." Jay gave the paper to Nettie. Champ's heart beat even faster. "Make out a draft to Mr. Bates for twice this amount."

He could not refrain from standing. "Thank you, Mr. Evans."

"I may check in on you once a week to see how the training is going. I'll let you know if I am able to secure the match."

He shook Jay Evans's hand and walked out to the front office with Nettie. Her heeled shoes beat a tattoo on the floor as she walked to a small desk. She opened several drawers and closed them firmly, still keeping her lips taut.

Nettie's eyes did not flinch. They must be doing very well for Negroes. Good for them. But what about Delie? Was she still down in Winslow? Was she okay?

"Is Delie okay? Is she married?" Champ gripped his hat as he spoke to her, trying hard to be friendly. And charming.

She must be okay. She wasn't trying to tough it out during these terrible times. Good. He had what he wanted. If they had married as naïve eighteen year olds, things would have been different and he could never, ever have taken her joy from her. He would rather die than see her bent and broken. Leaving her had been the right thing to do, even if she and all of the Bledsoes hated him.

"Do not suppose that because my husband is giving you money for this half-cocked scheme of yours that you can think to ask me questions about my sister. I do not approve of boxing. It is against what God wants us to do to live in peace with our fellow man. But I do as my husband tells me."

She was the one people thought would never marry. Isn't life something?

Nettie opened the draft book and paused before it. "Do you even have a bank account?"

Champ shook his head. What bank trusted Negroes these days? Anyway, he had heard that banks were not good things before the markets fell and was glad he didn't have his little bit of money in one. "No, ma'am."

"Wait here."

Nettie went back into Jay Evans's office, leaving Champ with a sinking feeling to match the sharp pains in his stomach. He had not yet had breakfast. Or dinner the night before. He couldn't rightly remember the last time he'd had a meal. Now this woman kept avoiding his questions about Delie.

She came back clutching some cash bills and handed them to him. "This is 1/3 of the amount you asked for. If you come back in two week's time, we will give you the next third and the last third two weeks after. At least, if you come back in two weeks, we can tell you more about where the match will take place."

"If he can get it." He put the money away in a deep pocket.

"Have those Sundays at First Water taught you nothing? Speak unto the Lord and He will make it mighty. If my husband bothers to invest in you, it is because the Lord makes it so. You should attend our church to find out more about God's will. But I think you're just interested in the money."

"Times are hard, Nettie. I need money to train."

"Hmm." Nettie handed him a card. "This is a doctor's office. Make an appointment to be checked over."

Champ's heart skipped a beat. Then two. "I can't go to no doctor."

"If you want money next time, then you will. Make sure to buy some beef and fix it to build yourself up. Go to the doctor. He'll give you vitamins and make you ready. If you are going to be a warrior for God, you have to be healthy in the temple God gave you."

"Yes, ma'am."

"We'll know if you do. The doctor is my brother-in-law."

Punched again. That's why Nettie had said nothing. Delie was married. *Oh, God, why did you forsake me?* "Delie's husband?"

Even as he said the words and watched Nettie walk back around the desk to sit down, he tried to calm himself. *Everything will be okay. The world ain't ended.*

But it had. Delie had married…a doctor. Who would find out he wasn't healthy and everything would be over. No more fight.

He swiped his palms across one another and stood a bit taller despite the stitch in his side. Well, at least Delie had enough to eat and a warm place to sleep at night. He had been right to let her go. He could put up with the pain in his stomach and his heart. A fighter—a boxer—endured pain most of the time anyway. For seven years, he had done without his funny, sunny Delie. He could endure more if he had to.

Nettie's coal black gaze trained on him, measuring him, judging him. He thought out of all the Bledsoe sisters, she would have been the most understanding, but he guessed not.

"Ruby's husband. You were very little, I guess, when he came down to Winslow and he and Ruby had to leave town. My…a little more than twenty years ago."

Relief, sweet and blessed, washed through him. He had to sit down. So he did. "I remember Mama speaking on that doctor." He looked down at the card to read it. The words swam before his eyes. "Morson," he said slowly.

"Right."

"I will. Thank you." Champ turned to go. The money felt like a weight in his pocket. He had a lot of work to do.

Nettie's words floated out behind him. "Delie never got over being abandoned. It would be impossible for her to trust any man again enough to marry."

Was it possible to feel joy and sorrow in both hands at one time? Champ would have stopped walking, just enough to take in Nettie's words. However, his heels were light as if he could do anything. No, this was the fight he had been looking for.

He could fight, and he would. And, when he got the kind of paycheck he had chased for seven years, he would go back to Winslow to Delie.

Why wait? He could go now and train down there. He would be able to see those pretty freckles one last time before he couldn't see them anymore.

And make sure she still loved him as he loved her.

Yep, he was going to Georgia. To fix the biggest mistake he had ever made in the twenty-six years he called his life.

Winslow, Georgia – a few days later

The cold of her own sweat always woke her.

Delie shivered and tried to pull the quilts closer around herself to warm her body, but the bed sheets were practically soaked through with more sweat. She stood and let the coolness of February meet her body. *Please, Lord, I have to go to the bank in the morning. I can't catch a chill right now.*

She shook her head again to clear the fog-laced dream from her mind. Some help. The after effects of the dream, the same dream she had every few months or so, always stayed with her for a long time after. Nothing to do but wait it out.

She took up one of her mother's pieced quilts, one of the wedding ring ones from her hope chest and wrapped it around her body. She walked in it, like a young queen, out onto the wraparound porch and stared out into the chilly Georgia night.

She cleared her throat. The dream was so vivid. She would be hoarse in her voice from yelling at Champion, just flat out yelling at him for leaving her behind and not taking her with him as he ventured out into the world.

Each time the dream ended, she thought she had been drained of moisture. But no, she was always wrong. Hot, silent tears always streaked down her face. And today was no exception as the hot salty tears slid across her hated freckles. Why, after seven years, did her heart still hurt?

When she was younger, she asked her brother-in-law who had lost his leg in the Great War if he missed his leg. She had waited to ask him her inappropriate question when no one else was around to tell her about how inappropriate it was for her to ask it. She had known the answer before Asa told her his simple two-word answer, "Every day."

And while she still had her limbs and at least some good sense about her, she knew what he meant. It was the same way she missed Champion. It made her so angry he was out in the world, boxing and doing fine without her. Every now and then, his mama would let her know just how so.

Seeing Champ's mama triggered the dreams more often than not. It would be good and fine to get away from Georgia, Winslow and First Water Christian Church, in that order, if only she could. She would love to escape Mrs. Bates's smugness about her son so Delie couldn't get "her claws into him."

She longed to retort she was not a bear. But saying that aloud was one of those inappropriate things she should think and not say to the uncharitable woman who would have been her mother-in-law if Champ had been man enough to elope with her almost seven long years ago.

"Mama Dee?" Small footsteps shuffled onto the bare, cold floor. Delie turned to face little Bonnie, who was four. Most in the orphans' house called her Mama, but only Bonnie and one other called her Mama Dee. "You having that bad dream again?"

"Yes, pet. Come and sit with me."

Bonnie came to her and Delie wrapped the quilt around them both. "Don't you know there is no boogey man, Mama Dee? You got to get your rest."

Bless this child, God. Don't let her know the boogey man is real.

And tomorrow, she would go and face him. The boogey man. The bank, which would surely tell her the requests for money would be denied. She was crazy to hope anyone would give her any more money to support Negro orphans, they would say. Nobody wanted those kids. Everyone thought they should stay abandoned.

But she would go back into downtown Winslow and offer up the one thing she had one more time. The farm.

At least they had the farm, even though it was becoming run down. No one else around these parts had it as good as they did. As the former teacher for First Water school, these four children were the ones left, two sets of siblings. Their parents sent the children to school one day and while they were getting an education from her, left them behind.

She snuggled closer to Bonnie, "I can rest easier now that you are here."

Bonnie patted her knee with a confidence only youth could provide. "You deserve better."

Delie wasn't going to argue. The little girl slumped on her as she did her best to get the rest she knew she deserved. Champion Bates was always mighty hard to get off her mind after her dream. Seven years in the wilderness. *Please, God, please help us to find a way to security and safety.*

And help me get Champion out of my heart.

Amen.

CHAPTER TWO

Delie tried not to mind that the dress she had to wear to town was already five years old. Emerald, her older sister, was a master at repair. She should have been grateful for the way Em added collars and cuffs to make the dress appear new. Her cloche hat had been turned over and inside out and the gray velvet nap was starting to show bare spots of wear. Em had cut the edges of the cloche down until it looked like a little gray saucer perched on top of her freshly waved black hair. Thank goodness for Em's training as a Madame Walker hairdresser as well. Delie still looked well turned out at the height of the depression.

"Try not to speak out of turn, sister." Em said in her gentle way.

"Why does everyone act as if I have a bad temper?"

"Because you do."

"I'll say what I have to. This town owes more to these kids than shutting down their only school and not providing any support for them. I'll take this to President Roosevelt if I must…or Eleanor. She'll listen."

Em patted her hands. "Just take care, Delie."

"I will. Just watch the children." Delie squeezed Em's hands reassuringly and left through the front door.

Delie stepped a gray-heeled foot onto the big porch. She smoothed down her legs with a big dab of Vaseline, hoping to make her cinnamon-brown legs look smooth and not just shiny. She had no money for stockings. Stockings were a foolish choice when the children needed to eat oatmeal or Post Toasties.

The children were outside having their morning constitutional. "You all be good, you hear?" Delie minced down the walkway and turned away from the front gate, determined to walk to town in her gray heels. Thank goodness it was February. Any other time of year, there would be a lot of red dust kicked up onto her slick legs. She had a red undertone to her cinnamon-colored skin, so it might be complementary, but dusty legs were not flattering.

By the time she got to town, her feet were killing her and she didn't feel so cute with her gray fox wrap. She stopped several times to rub her feet back to feeling, even as she prepared the words she would say to tell Mr. Hank Johnson what she needed.

She really didn't look forward to talking with him. The hungry, intense look in his eyes said if she did him a good turn every once in a while, he would probably give her the money. He was married to blond Mary Hastings, Delie's playmate before she became Champion's playmate. She tried to tell Mary about her husband, but they were too far away from their days of playing dolls together. Maybe Hank could be guilted into it and give her the money without too much fuss. It was wrong to lust after his wife's former playmate.

Everyone in Winslow, especially Hank Johnson, assumed because she was still single at the ripe old age of twenty-six, she was dying to have some itch scratched, but that wasn't the case. She sat down on the bench in front of the bank and tried to make it look as if she were waiting for the bus. It would be improper for her to rub her feet in town, but she had to rest her feet.

The old Logician bus lumbered down the street to the hotel. The twice a day appearance of the bus was a reminder that Winslow was still a place where travelers could stop and get something to eat before they crossed the border into Alabama. The hotel had a policy of not serving Negroes, so Delie strained her neck to see if any Negroes got off the bus.

The Bledsoe farm used to be the stopping place for Negro travelers. After Mags moved North, her family stopped the service, but Delie liked to let folks know where they could get a good meal in town so they didn't have to go into the hotel dining room, get their food and eat outside. Her feet stung as if there were razor blades stuck between her toes. But it was God's work to be charitable, so she started to cross the dusty street in Winslow as the bus pulled off on its way to Alabama. She stopped in her tracks.

Only one Negro, a man, had gotten off of the bus. He faced the hotel, and the first sight that hit her eyes was his delicious looking backside. Delie fanned herself as she crossed the street. Maybe she did have an itch.

His fine backside was encased in some nice new clothes, a rarity these days on a Negro man. He wore some silky-looking cuffed-off black pants with some city slicker type shoes and his shoulders,

Delie could see from the middle of the dusty street where she stood, were very broad. She doubted this man could walk through any doorframe straight on. "Lord, have mercy," she whispered.

That was wrong of her. She should not have called on the Lord in vain, but when she saw those shoulders, she didn't know what else to say. From the back of his head, covered in tight jet-black curls, she knew he was a Negro. Best to do the Christian thing and let him know what he should do to get a good meal. "Mister." Delie approached the man. "They don't serve our kind in there, you know? You can go to Mrs. Saunders over in Mill Town and she can feed you a good meal if you are hungry. She won't charge much."

Delie's ankles were never very strong, but they went and collapsed on her when the man turned around. Champion Bates faced her, with glasses on. With glasses? Since when? Her heart thudded in her chest very hard. The gray fox head on her wrap nodded up and down like it was alive and well again.

Champion gripped her by her arms to prevent her from falling down. The electricity between them when he touched her was even stronger today than when he had left her behind seven years ago. How was that even possible? "Cordelia May Bledsoe."

Her head swirled at his strong, sure masculine voice. When he left Winslow, Champ's body was thin, short, and small, like a banty rooster. Out of that slight, strong body came an impossibly deep voice…then.

Now, hearing him say her name sent shivers up and down her spine. A man's voice boomed out, not a boy's. She held her breath as the understanding came. He had been a boy…then. And, she had been a girl. He had abandoned her because he was a child, not yet ready to take on a man's responsibilities. Now, he was grown up. His shoulders were proof. And just what was under that jacket? *Stop it, Cordelia May.* Lord, have mercy. With great effort, she pulled her arms away from his searing touch. "What?"

"You know I can eat at my mama's house if I'm hungry."

"Of course. I just didn't know…"

His slow smile was the same. The smile crept across his tan features at a slow snail's pace. "You didn't know who I was, did you?"

"I don't identify people from behind." Delie snapped with some of that temper Em had warned her about. Em would not begrudge her now…maybe. Especially since she wanted to die remembering how she just now thought about his backside.

"Well," Champion's gaze up and down her gray swathed body was just as slow and appraising as his grin had been, even through the strange glasses. "If I had seen you from behind, I would have known you, Delie May." His brown eyes took in every single part of her, from her gray fox wrap to her hips down to her slicked up Vaseline legs and scuffed gray Mary Jane heels with the razor blades she was sure was stuck inside of them.

"You look different, Champion. That's all." Delie squared her shoulders, trying to look as if she didn't care. And she didn't. Did she?

Dear, God. Delie asked a little forgiveness for calling on the Lord again. Champ was going to step closer to her. *No, don't let that happen. Step away.* But, she couldn't. Her feet would not move. It was those hidden razor blades. People called them heels. "I ain't changed, Delie May. Guess you have. Mama say you a fine college lady now."

"I have my degree, yes." Delie put her defense for herself into her words, so he could not see her gray fox head moving.

"And you a teacher?"

"I had our old school. Yes."

"My my. Somebody like you wouldn't want to be bothered with a sweaty fighting man like me."

Her mouth went dry at the very thought of what he was talking about. Bothered? Hot and bothered? A trickle of sweat made itself aware down her back. *Please, God, help me.*

An itch crawled up her legs. Hadn't that itch gone away years and years ago? *Hold on.* She cleared her throat, "We were just children then, Champion. Playing children's games."

There. Yes. Good work, Delie. She was a grown-up teacher. In control. For the first time in her life. "Hmm. Those weren't children's games, girl. That was grown up stuff."

Delie's knees turned to jelly. "I don't remember what you are talking about."

"Yeah, you do." Out of the corner of her eye, she watched as his large man's hand looking more like a paw came near her cloche. He touched a wayward curl of her hair. How had it escaped the cloche, giving him the means to touch her? She would speak to Em about her hairdressing skills.

"Well, it was wrong." Delie willed her feet to move away from his hand. *I got to think of something, anything, other than that mistake we made.* She shifted. "I was giving myself to the man I thought I was going to marry. I was wrong about that."

"Were you?"

"I was," she said firmly. "I came over here to help a stranger. I've done my Christian duty. I'm going to continue on my way and conduct my business at the bank. Champion."

"Delie."

Now, she had to go back across the street on her pained feet, in those heels. With Champion staring at her. From behind. What was more daunting? Delie moved her lips in prayer. God heard her. Nettie had always told her God heard her prayers and she had no choice but to believe her big sister. *Get me across the street, God. Let me not make a fool of myself.*

Thankfully, God stayed by her side and was with her as she walked across the street with purpose and Bledsoe dignity. She stepped up onto the sidewalk and headed into the door of First Georgia Bank. The bank was the only business in town a Negro could walk through the front door of. As she closed the bank door, heads snapped up to look at her. Hank Johnson made his way toward her, showing her his desk, ready to help her…for a price. "How is Mary?" Delie hoped to head him off at the pass. "She's expecting again, isn't she?"

God had stayed her hand, helped her across the street and away from the temptation that was Champion Bates. There was no reason to believe he was going to leave her now. *Thank you, God.* As Delie prayed, she found renewed strength and purpose in facing the oily Hank Johnson, who she knew would turn down her request for money. It was well, though. God was with her, as always. Just as Nettie said.

Back when he had to pick cotton in the fields, Champion remembered how dry the bolls were when they came off in his hand. Always, the cotton required a sacrifice. Blood. The crisp snappy cotton hulls were sharp and pointed and always demanded a price of the cotton picker. Some blood always came off on the bolls when they were picked. It didn't matter how hard or long the drivers demanded they "pick clean", some blood would come away with it.

Watching Delie walk across the street with her womanly shape and clean fresh scent acting as a complete and total deterrent to his life's plans, he understood anything worth having required a blood sacrifice. Cotton was the prize, but picking it required blood. Sacrifice. Could he win Delie again? He had come down to Winslow to train and to see his mother. He had been away for far too long, but she would be glad to see him. Who would fix his steaks while he trained? His mother would be happy to do that for him. But maybe, Delie…

But there she was, taking her fine self into the bank. Why was she going there? What Negro had anything to do with a bank, in the South, especially these days? Not here anyway, which is what made Jay Evans's bank operation so remarkable. No, in Winslow, this was Paul Winslow's territory, even though he died five years back. Champion picked up his suitcase and sat down on a bench in front of the hotel. Unless he was told to move on, he was going to wait right here for Delie to get out of the bank and find out what she was doing in there.

Not even the latest his mama had written to him about her gave him a clue as to what she was doing in the bank. When he had left, her parents and sisters were so alarmed at her behavior at near eloping, they got together the money to send her away to high school and college in Atlanta, at Spelman. She had been gone from Winslow for four whole years. Only seeing fit to come back three years ago when first her mother and then her father died, leaving Em all alone on the farm.

Champion crossed his legs. That was a puzzle. In all of their talks, Delie always talked about getting away. And, she had. Atlanta was certainly better for Negroes than old poky Winslow. So why had she come back? To teach school? There were other places a young Negro woman could get a job teaching. Why bother?

The door to the bank swung open. Delie came out, closing the clasp on her gray purse. She turned to the left and then to the right. He stayed in her sights as she turned back and forth. Champ gave her a little wave with his hand. She paid him no attention as she went two storefronts away from the bank where the general store used to be, emblazoned with the U.S. Post Office seal on it.

Champ stood, picked up his pasteboard suitcase and walked over to wait for her in front of the post office. Through the windows, Delie retrieved her mail and opened a letter to read from it. Delie ripped it up and put the torn pieces of paper into her purse. She knew better than to litter in this town. She gazed outside and their eyes met once again.

Champ waved at her and gestured for her to come out. She did. "Bad news?"

"You could say so."

Instantly, Champ was concerned. "What was it?"

"It was a letter from Nettie warning me you had been by Jay's bank."

"Why should she warn you?"

Delie stopped short. He could see her mentally rubbing her ankles to think about it. "If you don't know, then don't count on me to tell you."

She kept walking and Champ knew, because he knew her, her feet hurt her something awful. Delie would never, ever wear clothes to make her uncomfortable. They had always laughed about how she looked wearing girl clothes. Delie only ever wore overalls. The only time he remembered her wearing a dress was at their graduation party. Her dress was all white and sparkly. She wore a big feather in her hair, which Em had made sure was silky and pretty. They had danced the night away.

She was like a graceful gazelle, a thing of rare beauty. He longed to possess it.

And he had.

Then she went back to wearing her overalls and laughing and he loved her even more. "Stop, Delie."

She kept going, not listening to him. "I have to get back home and talk to Em."

"You won't make it on those hurt feet. Should I carry you?"

She stopped. They stood at the edge of town about to take the long road back to the Bledsoe farm, which used to be all country. Now, more farms cut up the long road. It sure looked different than when he left. "You're going to carry me, along with your suitcase?"

"If you need it. It would help my arms some."

"Help you? To train, as Nettie was saying? For your fight?"

Champ nodded. "Yeah. I could carry you on back to the farm and get some training in at the same time."

"If carrying me meant doing you a favor, Champion Jack Bates, I would rather not. I'll walk by myself, thank you."

"That's mighty mean of you, Delie."

"I'm feeling mean after a visit to the bank. If you don't like it, go on to your mama's and get your meal you wanted."

"What did they say?"

One thing Champion never, ever expected was for Delie's eyes to tear up. Crying was for sissy girls, Delie always said. Life was a golden treasure. She had nothing to cry about. As the baby of the family, she always got whatever she wanted.

"They said, I mean, Hank Johnson. You remember him? He said nobody wants those Negro children, not even their parents." She whipped open her gray purse again and pulled out a paper. "I can fill this paper out and get fifty bucks per kid to leave Winslow with the children and never return."

Champ stood there, shocked. Not at what Hank Johnson had said. His comment was typical Winslow and now old man Winslow was dead, someone around here had to step into his shoes as the town's head honcho. Delie had children on the farm. Delie? Had children on the Bledsoe farm? "How many are there?"

"Five. Most of them were my pupils at First Water Grammar School. Some of their parents dropped them off at school and never came back for them."

Champ ran his fingers over his hair. Abandonment happened more and more often nowadays. "So, what you are you going to do?"

"I'm not going to forsake them or give them up. That's for sure. They've been through too much." Ah, yes, there was the strong, stubborn Delie who would rise up and then settle right back down again. And seeing her, as he knew her, his heart rose up. He determined she would stay proud. She had to.

"If you need help, I can do it."

"You?" Delie stopped, tottering a little bit. He grasped her by the elbow again, an instinctual reaction. He did not want her to fall, and yet, he could not help but touch her. A pleasant sensation went up his hand through his arm at touching the gray fabric, which kept Delie's arm nice and warm.

She, however, seemed to be aware he was experiencing a pleasant feeling and was determined to stop it. Sorrow filled him at the thought of Delie hating him. He didn't want to think that she could hate him, but clearly, she did. He had blocked it out all these years, too much of the strong fighter to face his emotions for her and now here it was, the consequence of his rash actions.

"Yes, me."

"Since you have been seeing to yourself for all of these years, let me let you in on a few bits of information. Children need someone they can rely upon. It is enough these children have been abandoned by their families, the very people they thought they could count on for whatever reason. And now, you come along just because you have some training money in your pocket, thinking you can do them some good. No. No, thank you. Go on and train. Sculpt yourself. Mold your perfect body for yourself. Leave me and these children alone. Goodbye, Champion."

Delie strutted down the red dust road. Wow. What a woman.

However, she only got a few more steps before her weak ankles started acting up again. He stepped forward. "Delie, you know your feet hurt. Let me carry you."

"I can carry myself, thank you."

Champion's eyes followed her, longing to touch her again as she strutted down the road. He was pained and proud of her at the same time, but sorry there was a wall between them too high for him to climb.

CHAPTER THREE

She did not need him.

She had lived without him for seven years. And she would continue without him.

Champion Bates was not necessary to her life. She would make it home, every step, by herself, even if there was blood in her strippy shoes by the time she got there. Fortunately though, she made it to the outside gate. It was safe to take off her shoes. No blood. Praise God.

Delie eased her hands down her leg and carefully tugged at the edge of her shoe. Wobbling, she put her foot down onto the red dirt and sighed with relief when her foot met the dirt. She wiggled her toes around. Stabs of pain shot through her as she brought up the other leg to take her shoe off, but she knew she had an audience. Champ was watching her. A good time to give him a glimpse of what he had left behind. She eased a slow hand down her left leg and tugged at the gray shoe to pull it off. Seemed like he wanted to run to her, to make sure she kept her balance, but she held an arm out toward him, telling him not to touch her. She put the other foot down in the dirt and wiggled those toes. Sweet relief.

Despite her gesture, Champion came and stood next to her. He had his arms spread out like a shield, holding his pasteboard suitcase as additional protection. Inappropriate Delie strikes again. "Should you be doing that out here, Delie?"

Delie picked up the knives known as shoes from the dirt. No point in getting them dirty, even if they did hurt. "I don't see what business of it is yours. I told you to get lost on the main road."

Ha. Clearly, Champion's regard for her legs had not changed much. They were her best feature, and she made sure to take her time in feeling her way down her leg. There. Let him see some of what he had been missing. He may have found comfort and solace in the arms of other women in the big cities, but here, she had pretty long legs and could use them to her advantage. For whatever it was. "I know. I just wanted to make sure you got home safely."

"Well, I did. Thank you." She gestured off into the woods. "Go on and cut through to go home. It's overgrown now, but I'll make sure no one shoots you."

"That's pretty kind of you."

"Think nothing of it." Delie stood on the cold, but welcoming hard ground of the front porch area of the Bledsoe farm. The pain in her feet throbbed on. At least it dulled…a little. She wiggled her toes back and forth, willing them back to life. The pain was reward for trying to be cute—even though cuteness was utterly necessary when confronting the big, bad, boogey man.

Champion still stood there, gripping his apple cap, watching her toes take on a red hue as she wiggled them in the dirt. Couldn't any of the boxers out there have managed to get to his face in all of those years? Surely someone out there could have beat some sense into him about his so-called profession.

She folded her arms and stared at him. "Well?"

"I-I thought I would meet some of the children."

"Are you the welfare office? Thanks, but no. They don't need to meet you. Any of them." Delie's heart beat faster at the prospect of Champ finding out her secret. She yanked off the fox wrap so her fear would not be obvious to him. She had gotten rid of any expectation this day would come. She hoped it would. Yet, after seven years, had given up any hope it would come.

"Well, I'll just be on my way then." He lifted up the pasteboard case again in a bit of a salute.

"You do that." Delie stood inside the front yard gate to let him pass into the woods.

She watched as Champ walk towards the woods. His walk was different, a little draggy and sad. Her blood surged at her victory and warmed her face. *Yes, I've won.*

She had to admit the victory felt hollow. Champ was gone. Maybe this time for good since she had not been very nice to him, in spite of her great legs.

Champ continued his draggy walk past the barn. At that precise moment, Em came out carrying a pail emptied of mash for the chickens. Oh no. Delie's pained, bare feet flew to close the barn door, so her older sister did not see Champ.

Too late. Em's voice sounded out across the farmyard in an excited, high-pitched squeal.

"Champion Bates! What're you doing here?"

"Oh, my lord, Emerald! Girl, come on here!" Champ embraced her sister, picking her off the ground and swinging her around, just as he used to.

Great.

Delie stood there like dead wood, ignoring the sharp stone biting into the sole of her foot. She watched as Champ and Em embraced and had a fine time grasping on to one another, saying the other one looked good and a bunch of other nonsense.

With her arms folded, Delie waited patiently while they completely ignored her. She lifted her foot to take the sharp stone away. She almost toppled over because the other pained foot did not want to take all of her weight. Those two did not care though. They just babbled on, ignoring her.

She cleared her throat several times, but they paid her no mind. "Em," Delie finally spoke. "Where are the children?"

"They eating their lunch inside. It's just so good to see you, Champ. Has he seen, N—?"

"Champion has other things to do, Em, than see the children. Any of them."

"Now you know that's not even true, Em. I asked to see the kids, but Delie was kind of down on the idea."

Now, Champ took a turn to clear his throat. Jerk.

"Delie?" Em's plain face turned to her sister. Gee whiz. If there was anything that got to her more than Neal's earnest eyes on her, it was her sister's hangdog expression.

Emerald did not understand. She was not a very complicated person at all. For many years, the family thought there was something wrong with her, but she just preferred home and family. No adventure for her. So they made sure she knew home sorts of things, sewing and how to give perms the Madame Walker way, and they kept her at home where she was most comfortable. "Why? You ashamed of the children."

No. Because he had something else to do seven years ago other than stay and marry me. But she couldn't say that. Not in front of Em. "He's hungry and wants to go eat at his mama's." Delie didn't mean for her voice to sound so petulant, but there it was. The truth. Petulant and all.

"We got food right here, Champion, honest. I made the lunch. It's good." Em's face cleared.

"As long as Delie didn't make lunch. Sounds good to me."

They went into the house right past her as they elbowed one another like long lost buddies. Great. She better follow quick to keep careful track of what Em said and what she didn't say. Quite a tightrope act trying to stay in control of it all. And she needed to get one thing straight. "It has been a while since you have been here, Champion Bates. I have been known to cook from time to time."

"That doesn't mean it's any good." Em guffawed and Champ put an arm around her shoulders, laughing too.

Ha. Ha. Delie followed them into the house where all of the children sat at the table, eating beans with spoons and breaking up some cornbread. "Mama Dee, you okay? Why your feet bare?" Bonnie asked.

"Hey, little darling." It was good someone was glad to see her around here. "Mama's feet just hurting from walking too much on the road."

"We need a car." Neal stood and gestured as he spoke. "That would have helped you out."

Delie stepped over to him and grabbed his hands so his gestures were less wide ranging and free, trying, trying to make Neal and his caramel-colored skin that matched Champion's and those little silky curls on his head less obvious. He could be just another one of the children. He was. She loved them all, and Neal no better than the rest. "That's Bonnie by you in the door. She's four. Sitting on the other side, there's Willie. He's ten. Roy is eight and Flo is eight too. This is Neal." She left out his age on purpose.

"Well, well, Delie May. You been busy since I been gone." A shy smile crept across his lips. "Hey there, all."

The children laughed and warmed to him, almost instantly. Had it been nearly a year since Daddy died? The entrance of a male presence into the house was like a beam of light on a dark, dark day. Why couldn't Delie see the children needed a male so much? Delie bit her lips so she wouldn't cry. She had always assumed she and Emerald were enough.

"Someone had to do something when you decided to board an early train, Champ." Delie frowned.

"They all yours?"

Em was on the verge of opening her mouth and Delie got in front of it. "Of course. I'm their Mama now."

"Our mamas left us to the school house and didn't come back no more." Flo's sad eyes were focused on Champ.

"Wow, that's something now isn't it?'

"It is good cause Miss Dee took us in," Willie echoed out.

"God gave me extra presents to love and care for you all." Delie put an arm around Neal and helped him sit back down at the table. "And I am going to do it, no matter what the state says."

"We love you, Mama." Flo came to Delie and hugged her.

"It must be wonderful to have such a following. You always were the popular one, Delie." Champ's kept his voice low and quiet.

"All I ever wanted was a following of one." Delie focused on Champ's soulful black eyes, the eyes that had always entrapped her and caused her to give up everything, her whole world and her whole life. Those ones. "And I couldn't even maintain that."

"You have it, Delie."

If it weren't for the children holding on to her, she would have folded at his words. Delie shook off her doldrums. Sad times she could not afford. She had to be strong for these children.

"Thanks, Champ. Just can't use it now. There was time about seven years ago, though, when I was in need."

He took his brown apple cap in his hand and twisted it around and around, clearly nervous. "I know. I know."

The room was quiet. A wave of shame engulfed her because she did not mean to bring these things up in front of Em. Any kind of confrontation made Em nervous. She determined to change the subject. "We're all fine, right? Let's say it everyone."

"We're fine." The children echoed and Em, too. Just saying the words had helped them though many a hard time before. But now, now was just a hair different. Champ was standing there. He was the one to have been her savior. And here he was, coming to help, seven years too late.

"See?" Delie spread her hands and made sure a child was in each one. "We're fine. You can go on home now, Champ."

"What about lunch?" Em moved toward the kitchen in the back. "We got meat in the beans."

Delie could see Champ was tempted, but his cap needed more twisting. "No thanks, Em. I'll just leave you to it. It was good to meet all of you. Em, Delie."

"Champ?"

"What is it?"

Cotton was in her mouth, but she was able to speak it anyway. She had to. "Neal is six. He will be seven. In March."

Her words confused him at first. Maybe too much boxing had altered his way of thinking. It was entirely possible. "What?"

Now, Champ would know some pain. The kind she had been dealing with for a long, long time. Too long. "I just wanted to let you know how old all of the children were. Including mine."

He staggered back, just a step. Turning around, he walked back out of the front room to the door. The apple cap slipped from his hands as he ran off through the woods to the Bates property.

Yes. Run off. It had all happened just as her dreams told her it would. It was good she had learned to endure all by herself. Champ would never, ever be there for her. Embracing the young sweet bodies of the children was the healing balm she needed. Holding onto them was the way she kept the tears from streaming down her face.

The old secret pathway had disappeared.

Thick, lush green stuff had consumed the path in these seven years and made it harder for him to make it to his mother's place. He'd have to bring out a machete to get through next time. Best watch out for snakes up in here too. At one time, this path had been beat back to the red Georgia dust, but no more. It was all covered. By instinct, he knew the way. The way was their path. The secret cut-through he and Delie used to travel between the two properties. But the complete cover of green carpeted the pathway as if it had never existed.

In such a short time? How could it be gone?

The effort of clearing the path made his face moist.

His mind was reeling. Delie, his little sunny, funny Delie had a baby. Without him. How could she have kept it from him after all they had been to one another? Had his mother known?

The clearing to his mother's land appeared before him. Unlike the Bledsoe property, the Bates farm looked exactly the same. The farm was the same as when his mother had given him money to go off to the train just a little early. How had Mama done so well for herself and not helped the Bledsoes? He staggered up the small wooden steps and knocked on the door. "Mama?"

"Champion? Is that you? I been waiting for you since you sent that telegram saying you was coming." Effie Bates opened her door and enveloped Champion in a big wide hug. She wore a simple housedress. There was no additional girth on her frame. She had managed to keep everything the same since he left.

He put down the suitcase, but kept it by the door. He didn't want her getting any ideas. "Place looking good."

"Have to keep it up, been trying to sell it. No buyers around here though. Hard times."

"Yeah, Delie told me. She been trying to sell too."

The look of joy and ecstasy at seeing her only child instantly diminished. "What you know about that girl?"

"I saw her in town. I went there first." Champion fixed his unrelenting gaze on his mother.

She seemed nervous for some reason. Talking about Delie had always made her nervous though.

"Did you eat lunch, honey? I can fix you something. Got some cold tongue."

"I can eat whatever you got. Her place is a mess, seems like to me."

"They can't keep it up." The look of disgust on Effie's face was crystal clear. "Got all of those children over in there. First, this one needing something, and then that one. Can't afford no hired help—neither one of them knows what to do, so that place has gone down."

"Delie say one of them kids is hers."

"What she say that for?"

"Cause she tells the truth, Mama." Champion ignored Effie, who patted a seat at the checkered cloth covered pinewood table.

She stopped patting. "It's been too long."

"Way too long, Mama. Is this part of the reason why you been telling me to stay away from Winslow?"

Effie reached into her icebox and uncovered a pan of biscuits. "No, son. I just knew this town was too small to hold you. Always wanted more for you. Sacrificed to make sure of it."

"One of them kids is hers, Mama."

"Ain't saying he's yours. She was always a fast girl. That's why I told you to take the early train and never mind about tying yourself with a wife. You were too young at seventeen. She was too fast. A bad, bad combination." She set the pan down on the table and retrieved a pitcher of buttermilk. "Sit and eat now."

"We was young, but we loved one another." Champion sat down and pulled the biscuits to him, determined not to eat too many. "Where's the tongue?"

Effie pulled a pan out with the jellied cow's tongue on it and put it in front of him. Poor eats, but they would do until he could get him some steaks. He cut one of his mother's cold biscuits and sliced off the tongue making a little sandwich.

"Love come and goes, son. I wanted you to find a place in the world."

Champ chewed on the tongue sandwich while thinking of his so-called great life as a lonely vagabond, ham and egg fighter. Boxer. "Making a place is one thing. I needed someone by me. It has been mighty lonely. Didn't realize until I saw her today."

The plaits around Effie's head seem to expand at Champ's words. He always teased her about when her Indian blood came out on her, the red undertone showing her anger. "Well, now you got a fight. This is your chance to make it. Can't stop now because of Delie Bledsoe."

No. He couldn't could he? This was his way to prove to her all of the missed years had not been in vain. He had fought in all of the little out of the way places just to prove it to her. So she could know he had talent.

But something had changed. Things were different. The image of Neal rose in his mind. His curly hair. The tone of his skin, especially the red tone of his skin, all of those things were hauntingly familiar. "I keep going. Maybe cause of Delie and that boy of hers."

Effie stood. He had made her angry. That used to frighten him when he was young. Not anymore. "That boy ain't none of yours. She was away at school for years and years, Champ. No telling where she got that boy from. Her parents ain't said before they died."

"Did you ask them, Mama?"

"What do I look like getting into folks' business? Lona and I fell out over the Sunday school years ago, you know that. It's mine now. I sees to it."

"That boy wasn't born here?"

"No, he was not. Brought him in from someplace, John and Lona did. Ain't no one even knew he was Delie's until she came back from college about three years ago. He's a puny thing. No way he's a Bates. Bates men are strong like trees."

Champ made another sandwich and ate it. He paused to lick some tongue jelly off of his fingers. "He got Bates hair."

Effie stood by his chair and grabbed his shoulders. "That's Negro hair, Champion. There ain't no need for you to make up things that don't be. He ain't none of yours. In slavery times, they would come and get the Bates men first to do the fighting in front of the masters. That is what you come from. Does that little boy look like he can do any fighting?"

No, Neal did not. But that didn't change anything. "I was just pointing it out."

"I'm pointing it out to you. Leave it alone. Leave her alone. There ain't nothing for you there. You said you needed someone to fry your steaks for you while you train. I can do that, son. Delie can't even cook." Effie bustled away. "Got some leftover pudding here."

Despite himself, Champ managed a half smile. No, Delie couldn't cook. There would be no steak frying where she was involved.

But he had to know. He had to find out what she was talking about. He took up a napkin and wiped his mouth. "I need to rest."

"You do that, Champ. I can go up to the general store for the steak. It will make you nice and strong for this chance."

Champ took up the pasteboard suitcase and went into his room. Effie had left it unchanged. He sat down on the bed. The room seemed small and cloying as he stretched out on his old bed. No box spring supported the bed. Instead, ropes were pulled across the thin mattress to hold it up. Still, it felt better to him than a lot of beds he had been in lately.

Could he eat steak while Delie, Em and those young ones ate beans? A flap in this throat folded over. No way. God had given him this money for a purpose. He could still train and help her at the same time.

Taking off his glasses, he put them on the roughly hewn pine night table and rubbed at his blurry vision. Delie could say what she wanted, but he was going over there first thing in the morning to help her in some way. So what if he made a nuisance of himself? She would switch around and try to boss him off, but he had faced more formidable opponents in the past.

He lay down on the bed and drifted off to sleep, thinking about Neal's too-long curls and how much they looked like his when he couldn't afford a haircut.

CHAPTER FOUR

Delie did not have one of those dreams again in the night. God had protected her mind from an invasion of Champion Bates in her sleep. She woke up the next morning, feeling rested. What could they have for breakfast? Oatmeal. Same thing again, cheap and filling, no milk since they had no cow. No sugar since there was no money for that. Delie tried not to think about oatmeal the way she had it when she was the young girl of the house and her parents were the ones taking care of things, oatmeal thick with cream, brown sugar and raisins. Why couldn't there be oatmeal that way?

Champ hated oatmeal. A twinge twisted in her heart. Why did she have to remember he was not too far away at his mama's house? The realization, and his mama, made her cringe. But she couldn't lie abed thinking about it. Time to get up.

A knocking noise out in the barn made her freeze. What was that? It couldn't be one of the children. They knew better than to go out to that barn. She picked up her old silk wrapper, threw it over her pajama-clad body and sped outside to the barn, picking up a basket along the way.

Well, there was her father's shotgun, but she never learned how to use it. A basket was as good a protection as she had.

Champion.

He was in her barn, carrying out the old tool case of John Bledsoe's. "Morning, Delie." That smile. "You going to gather some collards with that basket or attack me with it?"

She paid no attention to his smart comments or the tingly feeling she had in the pit of her stomach with them. "What are you doing in my barn?"

"Fixing up them broken fence posts over in there. No wonder no one wants to buy this farm. You have to fix it up. Make it look good. Broken fence posts don't look like anyone wants anything to do with it."

Delie pulled the silken wrapper closer together on her body. "The nerve of you. No one asked you to come over in here and mess in my daddy's tools to fix up anything."

She didn't like the way he was smiling at her.

"Got that right. Just trying to do what John would have wanted." Champ got quiet and took off his apple cap, which he had retrieved from when he dropped it. "He was a good man."

"A good man who wouldn't want you in his tools."

"That's something, Delie. Your Daddy was quite the forgiving man."

"Maybe that's the same thing as a sucker. All day long."

"God don't see it that way."

"God? How many churches have you stepped foot in while you been tramping around trying to be a famous fighter?" Ugly words. She didn't like the way they sounded coming out.

Champ had done her a bad turn, but she didn't have to take that on herself.

"God is everywhere, Delie May. I try to see to it that I have a talk with Him often enough. Brought you a box of groceries. On the side porch. Excuse me." The still quiet of his response contrasted sharply with her shrill comeback in the early morning air. Something about their exchange made her ashamed. More of the yard stones stabbed her in her bare feet. In the February chill, her already stubby toes were slowly freezing and transforming into short stubs of ice.

Fine. He won this round. She turned from him fixing on the abandoned fence posts. All five of the children stood on the porch, looking at her. She went into Mama mode. "What are you all standing there for? Neal, you know not to be out in the cold. Get inside. Willie, go bring that box of food off the side porch."

She wanted to take her old silk wrapper and wrap it around all of their bodies, but she settled for spreading her arms and getting the four of them inside. Emerald went back into kitchen and lit up the old cook stove. Willie came into the kitchen from the side porch and the children plowed into the box and investigated its contents. "Bacon! Coffee!"

"They's more oatmeal." Willie said with disappointment.

"Oatmeal is what will help you grow and keep you healthy and strong." Delie patted the growing boy on his shoulder. "So, I'll have to buy you long pants instead of short. Like a man."

Willie took up the canister of oatmeal with a sigh and handed it to Emerald who began to fill a pot with the sink pump. "But, some bacon?" he asked.

"Okay. Just for today, in case Mr. Champion wants to join us."

"Yeah!"

The children babbled to one another of their good fortune, the overlap of the stranger at their house and this box of good food at the same time. Em went through the box more thoughtfully than the children did. "There's some flour in the box and syrup. How 'bout pancakes instead, sis?" Emerald put forward to her. "The children would love a sweet."

"Biscuits would stretch that flour further." Delie folded her arms. Emerald's quiet countenance was eternally patient, waiting on her approval. When had she gotten to be such a grouch? "Fine. Just for today. I'll help."

"Ok, but I'll make the batter."

"Maybe I could learn to cook better if people would just let me learn." Delie grumbled.

"Maybe." Emerald confirmed. "Or you're just trying to stay in here while Champ is out there."

"Maybe." Delie pulled the wrap even tighter around her body. It had gotten colder all of a sudden.

"He seems so sorry, Delie."

"Emerald. We cannot be bought with a few groceries and him coming to fix fence posts."

"You should tell him about Neal."

"I did. Why do you think he's out there? He wouldn't care a fig for me if he knew that Neal was someone else's. He never tried to get in contact with me after he left or come back to see about me."

"Something must have happened. You gotta talk to him about it. He's being so nice after all that." Emerald's capabilities did not preclude her from stirring up smooth pancake batter, Delie marveled. So much for being simple minded. Emerald swiftly chopped off a bit of the bacon to grease the cast iron skillet. She started frying up the cakes.

"He's just lonely." Delie peered out to see him fixing the fence posts in the back. He waved at her, but it was not an excited wave. Champ's wave this time was more subdued and respectful. She kind of missed the excited one.

"He does seem lonely. Maybe he knows what he did was wrong." Hisses rose in the kitchen as bacon and pancakes hit the hot skillets. Delie rubbed the flesh off of her arms. She hated the way her stomach rumbled at the smell of the frying bacon.

"I'm not taking up with a fighting man."

"Delie, that's what he always been. That's in his blood."

Delie turned her back to the window so she did not have to watch Champion working with his arms bulging out like that. His arms were not natural. Works of a vain man were not of God. She took up a fork and started trying to turn the pancakes with a shaking hand.

Emerald stayed her shaking hand. "Sis, pancakes tear if you turns them with a fork."

"Okay, then what?"

Emerald slid a knife under the four cakes in the pan so their golden sides were belly up. Her mouth watered. "You're amazing, Em."

"Mama taught me all she knew."

Their eyes met in a moment of kinship at the thought of their mother who died two years ago. Delie was the first one to look away. "She taught me nothing."

"You was the baby." Emerald slid the cakes onto a hot platter and got the pan ready for some more. There weren't enough to feed the children yet and they didn't want any fighting, so they would just wait until another pan's worth was done. "She wanted you to go on and do other things. You the only one of us who got to go to a high school place. Not through the mail like Ruby and Mags. And college."

She pressed down the bacon in the other pan with her fork, ignoring the hot spitting bacon grease popping on her bare forearms. She cursed the wrapper for not having long enough sleeves anymore. She would have to get Em to add some on. "I know. I still don't know why everyone always acted as if I couldn't do anything and had to be taken care of."

Emerald regarded Delie as she poured more batter in circles with an expert hand. "You needed protection. All women do."

She started lifting the limp bacon onto a platter and Emerald turned over the next batch of cakes. "Everyone has a job to do. That's why I took on the kids. I have to do my share."

"I would have never thought to leave Winslow." Now, Em turned to look out of the window.

"Me neither." Delie tried to ignore Emerald's quaking lips. This farm was her sister's world. How would she get her to go? "We can go to where all the children can get an education and can choose what they want to do. Our other sisters have done well up north. We should give it a try. Go where people want us."

"I guess." Emerald pressed the bacon to crispiness and put the straight pieces on the pancake platter. How did she do that? She put the other four cakes on the platter and handed it to Delie. "They need to eat. What about Champ?"

"He can get his at the end, I guess." She took up the platter and went into the large front room where the hungry children awaited.

Willie and Flo ducked into the kitchen to get the milk and syrup. She made them all say their prayers. Then, the children dug in. Delie had to make sure they minded the syrup enough, Neal especially, who would have taken it over for himself. He loved sweets.

But he had to learn how to share. He was so stick thin, extra syrup wouldn't have hurt him. She urged him to take an extra piece of the bacon, but barely ate her solitary pancake, even as Emerald brought in another platter of four pancakes to the cheers of the children.

A sharp knock at the door made them all fall silent.

Champ walked in with his plaid shirt on, rolling down his sleeves and buttoning up the shirt over his solid, muscular body. A lump formed in her throat watching him, and it wasn't just the syrupless pancake she was trying to choke down. "I'll wash up in the back." He gestured to the kitchen door, working his way to the kitchen.

"Children, say thank you to Mr. Champ for the breakfast."

A chorus of thank yous followed Champ through the front room to the kitchen. Neal's eyes followed him, in neglect of his breakfast.

"Eat." Delie pointed to his plate.

"Mama, we heard you talking out there. Is he a boxing man?"

Delie cut her pancake with a fork. "Yes." She did not elaborate. She knew Neal worshipped boxers only one rung down the ladder from the recently deceased Pretty Boy Floyd and John Dillinger. And because of their deaths, the boxers had moved up.

"I didn't know Negroes boxed."

"Negroes do a lot of things." Delie lifted the fork toward her mouth, and then abruptly turned it to Neal's instead. He opened his pink lips and she fed him the pancake. There. Now, he could chew.

"Delie, why you feeding that boy a pancake with no syrup?" Champ's male voice boomed throughout the house as he pulled up next to her with an extra chair. "Let him have all the syrup he wants."

"If he had all the syrup he wanted, the others wouldn't get any."

"I can get more."

"Where you get all this money, Champ?"

"Is it legal?" Neal's eyes shone. Delie could tell he was excited about the prospect of a criminal in their midst.

"Course. I'm in training. I got some extra funds. Thought you all would like some breakfast."

"We do, sir. Thank you, kindly," Willie said. Those were the kind of manners she liked. Delie beamed at him.

"You are welcome, Willie. There's more fence posting to be done out there. Care to help out after breakfast?"

Willie gazed up at her, eyes begging. The children were supposed to have lessons after breakfast, but things were changing. She nodded her head, giving silent approval. She chose not to give Champ any more approval with her voice.

"Is it true, sir?" Neal asked. "You a boxing man?"

"Yes, indeed."

At the worshipful look on Neal's face, her heart ached in her chest. There was such open love on Neal's features. Delie wished for her son that love could be given without restraint. Without her blocking the way. But she knew what it was like to be abandoned by Champion. That would not ever happen to Neal. She would protect him from the pain that loving Champion had brought to her.

Neal's loving eyes, as well as the rest of the children, touched him. "There's some work to be done around here. I'ma show you all a few things if we get to work here after this good breakfast your aunt made." Emerald beamed as Champion dug into the last of his pancakes. "It was her, cause your mama can't cook."

The children tittered.

She frowned. "For your information, I fried the bacon. And there are lessons to be done after breakfast."

"We can do lessons any old time," Neal protested. "It isn't like a boxing man comes every day."

"You like boxing?" Champion almost dropped his fork. The thin boy's eyes were shining with excitement. Like a Bates. The heritage of his family shone in the boy's eyes. Bates were fighters—they were the ones who had been selectively bred to fight for the master's entertainment. Was Neal a Bates too?

"I follow it some. Ever since Pretty Boy Floyd got killed last year, I follow the boxers."

"You do?" Champion looked over at Delie. She averted her eyes, before focusing them on him.

"Yes, Neal has always had a fascination with the criminal." Delie put down her fork and pressed her lips together, looking for all the world like her mother.

"Hmm. Hmm." Champ chewed the last of his bacon and looked at the children. "My ma, she called me Champion. That's my real name. Champion Jack Bates. We have had fighters in my family since the slavery times. We were the fighters on the old Suther plantation, back in Alabama."

"Wow." Neal spoke in a whisper, and a pleased feeling washed through Champ's limbs. He liked this boy's regard, more than just about anything.

"I'll tell you all about the boxer I was named after. My ma and dad, they called me Champion, but wanted me to be just like Jack Johnson, the famous Black boxer."

A frown, one that matched Delie's perfectly, came over Neal's small features. How could she have kept this from him? He had missed six years, long years of watching this smart boy grow and develop. He wanted to be angry with her for that, to hate her for that, but he had to know more, much more. "They ain't no Negro boxers, Mr. Champion, besides you. You must be wrong."

"Aren't any," Delie said.

"Aren't." Neal parroted. "In all my research, I haven't seen any. That's why I like seeing you, sir."

"Well, you ain't," Champ avoided Delie's correction swiftly, "haven't looked hard enough. He was the heavyweight champion back in '08. Mr. Jack Johnson. And, he was the kind of man who didn't take anything from any body."

"A Negro man, for sure?" Willie seemed stunned.

"He was blacker than all of us put together. And he beat everyone he came up against, had a perfect record. Just until the end, when he was an old, old man and shouldn't have been fighting no more."

"And managed to break the law and misbehave all over the place. A criminal." Delie gathered up the plates from the children before they started licking the syrup from them. They rarely got anything sweet these days, and they would lick their plates if she didn't stop them somehow.

"And a boxing champion." Champ put forward to them to see their little faces shine with the impressive accomplishment.

"What is your record, Mr. Champ, sir?"

"I have a record of 60-2. Them two was when I was young and still learning. I am getting ready for a fight now and came home to train. Got to have a woman to fry up some beefsteak for me so I can eat meat while I train. Got to get built up for this fight. It's going to be a white man."

"Before God, ain't no Negro man ever fought no white man." Willie breathed.

"Not since Jack Johnson. They put a stop to it. But I'm getting it done with this fight. Happening real soon. Got to build up for my training camp next month."

"We can help you, Mr. Champ." Neal's little voice was eager. "We can help you train, sir."

"Thank you kindly there, young man." He ruffled the boy's curls. They were as silky as a girl's. The boy's hair needed scissors, if Delie would let him. As he removed his hand, he regarded the boy even closer. If what Delie was saying was true, Neal was his son. He could take scissors to his own boy's head. And he would. She would just have to deal with it.

"You'll have to ask Aunt Em to fry the beefsteak, sir. Mama can't do it too well." Neal piped up and Champ laughed at that assessment.

"You think we can have some when you have it, sir?" Willie's eyes were bright with joy at the thought of eating beefsteak. The boy had not finished his breakfast five minutes ago, but he was hungry. Willie had that awful feeling in his belly, he could tell. He had lived with that greediness as a constant friend when he was a growing boy. The difference between him and this boy here was because of Jay Evans. With Jay's intervention, he had plenty to eat. This young boy did not.

His blood surged to his fists. Why was Delie letting these children starve down here when Jay and Nettie had plenty up north? *God, please let me be calm.* Champ had the feeling there was more to things than he knew, and he had no right coming in busting things up in Delie's life. Was he stirring up trouble with her because he was angry with her?

Champ nodded. "I'll be proud to share with everyone. We'll make sure of it."

"What's a beefsteak?" The littlest girl, Bonnie, Champ remembered, asked the question in such an innocent way, he could not blame her. Probably her entire young life, if she were four or five, had been a time of economic need. She wouldn't know. Champ put a hand to her rough braids and smoothed them down.

"You'll find out soon enough, little one. You'll enjoy eating one, and it'll help to build you up."

Emerald sat down at the table across from him and smiled. "This is great, Champ. Thank you for bringing us food and everything."

"You are right welcome, Miss Emerald Alonza." Clearly, Delie was not pleased at the way he played up to her sister. He couldn't be rude to Em. He and Emerald always got along.

Except for Nettie, he barely knew the other sisters. They were gone when he had come into Delie's life as a friend and playmate. Emerald was always the one who Delie had to take care of, because of the way she was. And because Delie had to take care of her, he did too, in a sense.

"If you're done, please take the children out while I clean up. And, when you all come back in from whatever he's going to do, you'll have lessons."

The children were none too pleased, he could tell. "It's best to do what Delie say. She can get real mad if you don't. She was always a bossy little thing when she was a girl."

"You knew Mama Dee when she was little? Like me?"

Champ stood and helped little Bonnie to her feet. "I was a bit older than you when I met her, but yes, I knew her."

"Did she have bad dreams back then too?"

The question, so out of the blue and so clearly asked by the child, took him aback. His gaze met Delie's. She seemed uncomfortable, as did everyone else in the room.

"Get them on out of here." Delie's voice became gruff.

What had Bonnie meant?

"Come on, you all. We going to finish the fence posts and then I'll show you a few boxing moves."

"Honest?" Neal's awe was crystal clear.

"Sure, easy stuff."

"What about girls?" Flo asked pointing to her and Bonnie. "Can we learn too?"

Champ went to the little girl and knelt down to face her on her level. "Let me tell you something. Remember how I told you I knew your Mama as a little girl?"

Flo's braids moved slightly as she nodded. Champ tugged a bit on one as he continued. "If she'd have been the one in the ring instead of me, she would have won them two I lost. Come on." He took the little girl by the hand. The touch of her soft palm moved him.

What had he missed by leaving Winslow? What had he gained? He hoped he wasn't too late to find out.

CHAPTER FIVE

"Delie, ain't nothing for you to take these kids and leave here. You still got your Daddy's old Tin Lizzie. I can swap that for some kind of bus and I'll take you all up to Pittsburgh."

Champion waited until all of the children, all of them, even Neal who clearly didn't want to, had gone to bed and confronted Delie.

He did not want Neal to figure into his plans to help Delie see the light. From the look of the boy, Neal would do whatever he said. No, this had to be her own decision. She was just so stubborn. He should have known she, the baby of the family, would turn out this way with her spoiled behavior as a little girl. Her willfulness had evolved into a powerful woman's will. She had to decide for herself, had to see reason.

He didn't realize how tall of an order that would be.

"Who do you think you are coming in here telling me what to do?"

"I'm your friend who is trying to help." Champ wiped his hands on his pant legs. This woman could drive him to distraction.

Emerald's eyes filled with water as they fought. Their sharp words scared her. He stepped over to her and put a caring arm on Em's shoulder. "Em, you probably should get on to bed yourself, honey."

"Don't tell her what to do either." That Delie. She knew better than that. What would he do with this woman? He remembered how she quivered in his arms in town. He ought to kiss her. She would get in line then.

"Champ, you right. It has been a long day." Emerald stood up and stretched. "I be in the bedroom if you need me, Delie. Night, Champ. Will you be back tomorrow?"

"Course, honey. If you all need me."

The thin line that formed on Delie's luscious, kissable lips was all the evidence he needed. In Delie's view, he had gone too far. Okay by him. He had been in training for a long time. He was ready to take her on.

They both looked toward Em as she entered the main bedroom and shut the door behind her. Back in the days when he had been paying court to Delie, her parents' bedroom didn't have a door. Better to keep the door open so they could hear whatever was going on with their daughters in that front room. A smile tugged his lips at the memory. The Bledsoes had done a good job protecting their youngest daughter. Except for their one night…

"What are you smiling about?" Delie demanded. "I don't know what kind of devilment, or whatever, you done picked up on your travels, but don't bring it up in here. This is God's house, Champion Bates."

"I was brought up at First Water, same as you, Delie."

"Yeah, but you got way away from it." Delie slapped a small determined palm to the table and stood up. "I don't appreciate you coming up in here trying to take over my life. You have no right. I been doing fine all by myself. I've been taking care of things by myself."

Champ bowed his head and regarded the chipped cup that was before him, one of Miss Lona's teacups. Was this one of the less chipped ones? What would Miss Lona say to see her teacup now? She had been so proud of keeping things nice. Miss Lona was a woman who was about showing the best of Negro folk, and she did it. What had happened to her legacy?

"Lookee here, I just come from up north where Nettie practically opened a drawer and gave me cash money."

His revelation took some of the starch out of Delie's backbone. She sunk into her chair. "I knew they was doing well."

"Why ain't they helping you?"

"I didn't ask them to help. That's all Jay's blood money. It ain't none of hers."

"She was handling it and he was trusting her with it."

"Nettie?" Delie seemed stunned. "Well, I guess she really is in love with that man. I just couldn't imagine that."

"They seem very happy together." Champ recalled the firm way Jay let his wife know what he had wanted without compromising her any. That was love.

Another reason why he had left Delie. He didn't want her just following him around like a whipped puppy dog. She would have lost her spirit, and it would have been all his fault for taking it from her.

He didn't want to take it from her now, but he had to help her to make it up to her somehow. "Take what Hank offered and go on up to your sisters. I'll do the driving. Then all you all be together again, just like John and Lona would have liked."

Now she'd soften up a bit. Instead, the expression on her face grew stormy. Her pretty freckles stood out. Well, he was wrong about that.

"You have a lot of nerve coming in here telling me what my parents would have wanted." Delie insisted. He knew he had gotten to her.

"I hadn't asked for them to take all of us in, yet."

"I can take you into town in the morning. Make a call, send a telegram, whatever you want."

"I don't want to walk into town again."

"The old Tin Lizzie is still out there. I'll come back tomorrow and see what I can do to get her going again and we can go to the junkyard in Calhoun and see what they got for a bus."

Delie jutted out her chin as she regarded him. "You ain't nothing but a farm boy, Champion Bates. What do you know about cars, buses and such?"

"I know more than you, letting such a fine piece of machinery rust out. Make Neal think he got to walk everywhere. "

"Daddy finally learned how to drive it." She looked away. "When he died last year, it just seemed pointless to get it going again. He wouldn't let us learn how."

"Then you should learn. If you knew how to drive it, you wouldn't have had to walk to town in too small shoes that hurt your feet. You could have just ridden in the car and looked cute."

She turned back to Champ and shooed with her hand. "Get on up out of here." He got to her. Heh.

"It's dark. I can get to my mama's in that thick growth. But tonight, I'ma stay out in the barn and get a head start on things in the morning." He wouldn't be able to sleep in Effie's soft quilted bed knowing they needed him here. All he knew was living rough. He could stay in a barn for a night. Even though the last time he stayed in the Bledsoe barn, he had been in Delie's arms as they planned a future together. One he had destroyed.

Her face softened, muting her dark brown freckles. She remembered. The look on her face told him she remembered that one night in the barn too.

"No one didn't ask you to be staying up in here either."

"I know, but I'll be fine with a quilt and a lantern. Then I can get a head start on the car." Champ pulled his glasses out of his shirt pocket and put them on.

"Since when you start wearing spectacles? School was not your strong suit."

"Since you a big-time teacher, Delie May, means you know schooling is not the only reason why some folk need spectacles. It's getting dark. I want to work by lantern light. I need some extra help to see."

Delie waved a hand. "You supposed to be in training. You need a good night's sleep like everyone else. Go on out to that barn."

She ducked into the main bedroom and came out with some quilts. "Here, suit yourself in the Georgia cold. I hope you freeze."

He took the quilts into his arms. Their arms rubbed against each other as they exchanged the quilts. The shock as their skin touched told him that nothing, nothing had changed in the way their bodies gravitated toward one another. Had the quilts heated up at their touch? *Help me, Heavenly Father.* He'd better plead to God for control or he could lose his mind with this woman. Or worse. "You don't want me to freeze, Delie May."

"Yes, I do. Go on ahead. Freeze."

In the ring, it's best to wait when the opponent has his guard down. There's a moment of doubt that Champ knew to take advantage of. He knew how to outthink his opponents, that's why he won.

But he couldn't wait this time. He had to know. Was her skin the same softness as that last night? He reached out to squeeze her hand. It wasn't the same. It was different. Something in her hand, in her touch was more reassuring, more comforting somehow. But there was also strength in her hand. He had to stop his jaw from dropping in surprise. Delie had grown up.

"Good night, Delie."

She said nothing to him. She jerked her firm small hand away from him, out of his touch and went into the bedroom and shut the door. Champ suspected, as he left out of the back door and headed to the barn, she would open the bedroom door again to keep an ear out for the children. The squeak of the hinges sounded in the night.

A warm feeling of pride in her went through him. She was a good mother and a good friend. What would it take for her to be a good friend of his again? A week. That would do it, a week out of his fight regimen to figure out how to get Delie to be friendly to him again. Now that she was back in his life again, he wouldn't let her go next time.

He didn't like what he was without her. He had grown up too.

Before she drifted off to sleep, Delie realized why she had come back to Winslow from Atlanta.

She wanted the chance to tell off Champion Bates in real life—to get back at him.

And the realization brought her eyebrows together in the middle of her forehead.

Was this why she had stayed in Winslow? To see if, in all of the dreams where she was screaming at the top of her lungs and waking up exhausted, he had heard her? In all of those times, prayers and dreams, she was yelling at him to come back to her. Now that he had, she was being all kinds of mean and rude to him for leaving her in the first place. Was that why she had stayed? To have the chance to make Champion feel miserable for leaving her in the first place, for making her feel small, mean and alone in the world?

Delie knew God did not like her to be so small. And the realization of its power hit her like a brick wall. She believed she did not deserve any better. She was willing to mire her life in poky old Winslow just to tell Champion Bates off. God had made her for more. Even if she was an unmarried woman with five children, she couldn't keep them here just for the sake of getting back at him. Even if it meant letting Champ help, she had to leave from there.

It would be hard to get Emerald to go, but it would be better for all of them in the end. She would send the telegram or make the call in the morning so her sisters would know they were leaving Winslow. All of them. For the last time. There would be no more Bledsoe presence in that small town anymore, after thirty some years of being there. It made her sad, but it was all, all of it, for the best. And most important, God wanted her to make her heart large, so she was prepared to sit still, listen and obey His word.

She would let Champion get them to Pittsburgh. Then he could go back to his life and she would make a new one for herself.

It was another night in a long, long time since she had gotten a solid night's sleep, throughout the whole night. No kids. No dreams of yelling at Champion for leaving her by herself in the world. Just sweet, refreshing sleep.

Until the coughing and sputtering of the Tin Lizzie woke her straight up out of her deep sleep. She sat straight up in bed. It was light outside. That was wrong. She had overslept and a gangster had come to take her Daddy's car. She shook the fog of sleep from her head.

Do not swear, Cordelia May. You are a Christian woman. A mightily provoked one, though. Out of habit, her gaze whipped around to Emerald's bed. It was empty. What was going on? She shrugged into her silky-feeling wrapper, frayed from years of use, stuffed her feet into her holey slippers and went out into the big front room. No children there either, just a table full of dirty breakfast dishes.

What was going on? Was this her life? No swearing. She wheeled around to the front of the courting porch to see Champ in the passenger's seat of the old Tin Lizzy, with Emerald at the wheel of the car—squealing in a very un-Bledsoe-like way. All of the other children, except for Bonnie who stood on the porch sucking her thumb, were stuffed in the back seat. They were squealing as well.

"What is going on out here?"

They ignored her.

They were having too much fun. Way too much.

"Excuse me," Delie called out, pulling the wrapper closer around her.

Emerald squealed with delight as she shifted back and forth in the car. Champ was next to her, laughing his head off.

"Emerald Alonza. Get out from behind that wheel. Women should not be driving cars." Delie stepped cautiously off the front porch. She didn't want to get too close given the wild way Emerald was driving.

Emerald pulled the car up next to her sister. Her broad face was in a full grin mode. Champ patted her on the shoulder. Why oh why did her heart pang whenever Champ showed someone else approval? Especially Em? Why should she still care?

"I'm driving, Delie."

"I can see that. A fine thing too. Don't you remember what Daddy said?" She turned to Champ. "We didn't need you to come up in here and corrupt my sister and the children."

"We was just taking a drive while you were sleeping, Delie May. No harm done." Champ stared at her as if she were the crazy one.

A fist inside her stomach closed up, ready to lash out. How dare he criticize her for getting a good night's sleep? No thanks to him. *Please, God, keep me calm and near the cross.* Delie breathed out and calm came to her. God had heard her prayer. Of course, He did. "All of the breakfast dishes are on the table, Em. That is not like you."

Em's brown eyes were alight. "I know. But I couldn't believe it when Champ said he would let me drive the car."

"You did real well, Em. Real well." Champ clapped a hand on Em's shoulder.

"Thanks, Champ." Em opened the door and got out. Champ slid over into the driver's seat. He turned off the ignition. There was blissful silence, then the children started up with loud groans and complaining noises.

"All of you. Out of the car. Help Em clean up. Leaving the breakfast dishes like that. What's the matter with you all? Get dressed and cleaned up. All of you out here in your bedclothes. Shame on you. Get on inside."

The children obeyed, but Neal was the last to get out. He dragged his feet the slowest. He waved his long eyelashes up at Delie. Another pang came into her heart at how much he looked like Champ. "We was just having fun, Mama."

"Fun time is over. Let's go."

Delie's air rang with authority. Neal knew not to mess with her. He went on up the stairs and Bonnie brought up the rear with a self-righteous tilt to her head, as if to say, *I'm the youngest and knew better than all of you.* Delie's lips twitched. Oh, how familiar Bonnie's posture was to her, the baby girl of her own family.

Champ's powerful strong arm bent on the edge of the door, encased in a rolled-up plaid shirt. He fairly burst with muscles and good health. A grin sliced his gorgeous face as he watched her—only dressed in her wrapper—again. "Ain't you the thing, Delie May? Getting folk to jump when you say and you in your bedclothes yourself."

"I had to see what was going on out here while you were making all of that loud noise."

"You was getting in that deep sleep. Still snore?"

Delie tightened the wrapper more firmly about her body. "I do not snore."

"You do." Champ said in that maddening way. "Always did. Better go on and change out of your bedclothes so we can get these errands done today."

"Ain't you the thing, Champion Bates? Coming around telling me what to do when you are the one who made sure to run off away from responsibility. The nerve of you." Delie hissed and went up the pathway, aware of the stones cutting into her feet again.

More pangs resonated in her heart at how mean she was being to him. Then it occurred to her that she had had a sound night's sleep. All of the sleep she missed worrying, yelling and being angry with Champ had finally caught up to her. She swallowed. Hard. She would have to try much harder to follow in the way God would want her to go.

Champ sat there in the car. He had to stay his hands from gripping at his midsection. Had he been on the receiving end of an illegal punch? It didn't matter. He had faced dozens of opponents in the ring and none of them could hit harder than Delie when she had a point to make. *Dear, God, help Delie with her pain and hurt. Show her that I am here to help. Show her that I am here to care until...* He took the spectacles out of his pocket again and put them on. Increasingly, he needed them in the light of day to avoid any oncoming headaches.

Would another fight make it worse?

He refused to believe it. He couldn't believe it. A wave of shame swept over him as he reflected that he had not done what Nettie said and gone to the doctor—their brother-in-law. Champion rubbed at his temple. He could still help Delie do as she needed to do to clear out of this hick town and get to the doctor before he would need more money for training next month. He would just put off going for another little bit, that's all. He didn't want to have to hear those words again.

He came out of the car, intending to go inside to help. Neal stood on the porch.

"Hey, there. I thought you was helping your aunt."

"I was. They are all getting it done. Sides, that's women's work."

Champ came up next to the boy and ran his hand over his hair. Bates curls. He could do something about that. "Y'all got some scissors around here?"

"In the kitchen."

"You know how to get them and carry them here safe, do you?"

"I do, sir."

"Go on ahead, then. Bring a towel. You need a haircut."

Champ situated himself on the porch swing and rubbed at his temples again. It would calm down now that he was in the shade out of the bright sun. He just had to be patient. Though he had to admit, patience was only a strong suit of his in the ring.

Neal was suddenly next to him with the requested tools. So was Willie. Might as well take care of him too. He stood. "Both of you all sit on this swing and be still. We got to make you gentlemen look nice for church tomorrow."

He took the towel and wrapped it around Neal and used his pocket comb to ruffle the curls of Neal's hair. The scissors were not as sharp as they needed to be, but they were doing the job of cropping close to Neal's head, so that he looked kept. Less pretty, even though Neal was, admittedly, a beautiful child. How could he not be with Delie as his mother?

Champ focused hard on his task to swallow the lump in his throat at all he'd missed, all Delie had to put up with without him. No wonder she was mad at him back there. No doubt he deserved it.

"Mr. Champion?" Neal piped up in a small voice.

"What is it, young man?"

He didn't know how to address him. He couldn't say son. It would bring all of his wrongs up front and he couldn't handle that now. Not with everything else. How much had Delie told him? Was she serious yesterday? All of that was still unknown. Young man would do for now. "Are you sick? You keep rubbing at your head. Aunt Em has tea for that to help you."

Champ smiled to himself as he clipped. The silken black curls fell on the towel. "Does she now? I'll need to get that from her. I'm just fine, young man. Fine enough to cut your hair so you'll look nice for church in the morning."

"It makes my head feel better already. My head gets hot sometimes with all that hair."

"No worries, Neal. You looking much better, just like a young man."

"Not like a girl." Willie shifted a bit and turned to see if Champ would laugh. He didn't. Willie became somber again. "Sorry."

"It's okay, Willie. Mr. Champion is here to take care of us. I been praying and he has come."

"You been praying?"

"Yes, sir. Every since Grandpappy died, I prayed to God to bring my mama a man to help her take care of us. She trying so hard. She needed help, and I been praying."

Was it possible he was here because of a child's prayers? Maybe his son's prayers? Did God care that much for them that he was summoned here for a reason? If that were so, he had to do what he needed to be able to provide. It was for them he had to fight this fight with the contender. Just one more.

Some would wonder why he would not go all the way, but anyone might decide to step aside if it meant winning a purse that big. There would be a lot he could do for them all, including Delie, if he could win this purse. She might love him again. She might forgive him again. If he could give her her heart's desire.

"What's going on out here?"

Delie's sharp tone almost made him drop the scissors on the porch. He gripped them closer, not wanting to hurt the boy's tender flesh. He was about to even up the jet-black stubble on Neal's head.

"We're getting haircuts to look like gentlemen for church, Mama. Isn't that great?" Neal reached up and touched the black stubble on top of his round little skull. Champ immediately snatched the scissors away from the top of his head so Neal wouldn't prick his finger.

Delie wore a plain brown dress this time, one that fit just right, but still showed signs of wear. He didn't know much about fashion, but her dress was a few years out of date and threadbare at the collar and cuffs that crept half the way up her forearms. He would buy her whatever she wanted when he won the fight. He would fix it when he won the fight.

"I didn't say anything to you about giving haircuts? What right do you have to do that?"

Something in her firm tone made him want to take the scissors and hand them over to her. Instead, he gripped them firm in his fist. He would not back down to Delie. If this was his son, he had every right to cut his hair, as much right as she had not to.

He opened his mouth to respond when fat tears started to form in Delie's. He watched her, stunned and open-mouthed, as she stepped toward the towel where the black curls had fallen. She knelt down, picked them up fingering the silky black curls. Her hot tears crisscrossing her dark brown freckles in white trails down her sweet cinnamon-colored face.

Delie's tears. This was the reason he had left without telling her anything. He could face and defeat men bigger than him, but he was nothing but a coward in front of those tears. And he had caused them. Again. He couldn't get anything right. Ever.

Please, God, help me to get it right, just one more time.

CHAPTER SIX

He had messed up so bad cutting Neal's hair, she couldn't even be glad he got the car running again. Opening the door for her, she sat down in the front seat next to him, not looking one way or the other. In silence, they went to get gas and drove to the junkyard to see if there was a car or bus big enough to trade this Lizzie for.

None of this registered with her. The rigid set of Delie's back ran parallel with the seat in the car. If he offered himself up to her, just to take one in the gullet, would she hit him? Better to apologize to her, now. "Delie, I didn't know. I'm sorry."

She turned her large jewel eyes toward him. All of the Bledsoe sisters had those eyes, but Delie's eyes, like glittery diamonds turned grown, moved him the most. Maybe he could buy her some, once he won the fight, to prove his love for her and how he had never, ever forgotten about her. Now, though, those eyes were large and shiny with moisture, all because of his stupid mistake. "Neal's curls were precious to me and you cut them all off. They're fodder for the pigs."

"Delie, pigs will eat about anything, but not hair."

"Whatever. They're lost to me now. It's all your fault."

On the ropes…again. "I didn't know." He repeated. He sounded like those fighters that had been in the ring one too many times. Maybe he had been too. "I'm sorry."

"Maybe if you had come around more, you would have known."

And there it was. The silence between them that popped up. The emptiness. The unanswered question. *Is Neal mine?* Instead he said. "I stayed away too long. You were away a long time too."

She rested her hand on her chin. "I had to be. I was at college. And before."

Before what? Something beat a striking drum in his heart, like the sound of a gong or the bell in the ring before the fighters came out of their corners. The connection was deep and abiding, provoking his thoughts.

Before what? Math was not his strong suit, but he could count. Could Neal be his? Delie would have had to have the baby somewhere, not in Winslow, and then go on to school. That was five years. That about matched the time frame that she had come back to Winslow two years ago. Who had raised Neal up? Who had been his Mama and his Daddy? Had Delie done it all by herself? Or was it Lona and John? If Lona had died two years ago, that would have been the time that Delie would have had to come back home to help with the house, and then poor John died only a year ago. What a timeline. What a life.

Best he could do was fight this last fight and give her most of the money to try make up for his losses. Since she hated him so, he supposed he would come on back down here to Winslow and live on his mother's farm until he died or something.

Champ bristled. To him, that did not sound like much of a life. He wanted a family. A pretty little girl like Bonnie. A wisecracking kid like Willie. A thoughtful quiet boy like Roy. A mischievous boy like Neal, following him around. A questioning child like Flo. Yes, he wanted this family, but in order to have it, Delie had to forgive him. Would she? He took a deep breath and plunged in. "Is Neal mine?"

"What do you think, Champion?"

There was no special animosity in her question, but who knew with Delie? She could be impulsive, the very thing that drove him wild and delighted him all at once. "He's a lot like a Bates." Punch drunk again. Slow, slow, slow.

Delie's pretty green printed scarf played in the wind as the Lizzie chugged along. "What does that mean?"

They were circling each other. He'd better be careful before he got jumped. "You know, the Bates line."

"I don't know anything about your people. Why should I?"

"Delie, about my family's heritage. Us being boxers on the plantation. How we was selected to fight for the pleasure of the masters. One of my grandfathers got to go to Europe to fight. Don't you remember?"

She turned those jewel eyes on him. "I don't know why I should know anything about your family. I'm college educated, so I can't possibly retain all of those little things for all of the big things I have to know. Please pull over to the bank so I can pick up the money from Hank first. Then the junkyard."

She'd have been a good shadow boxer. She gave a pretty little dance around his question about Neal. A slow steam built up inside of him. Well, he was here now, wasn't he? Didn't he need to know about his blood?

This was a draw this time. Not a win. He pulled over as she directed. Not waiting for him to come around, she opened her own door. "Thank you."

Champ turned off the car, fully aware they were illegally parked in front of the bank. "I can come in with you."

He addressed the wind, since Delie had swung into the bank by herself, moving as poetry could only be read. There were some words written by a young poet that he liked to read when he was by himself. A Mr. Langston Hughes, who spoke about the beauty of the brown-eyed, brown-skinned girl. He could say the poem to Delie. She might like to hear that.

And then he remembered.

He used to write poetry. Bad poetry to read to her, way long time ago, back when they were young, free and in love.

Was there nothing he could do to remind her of that past life?

Looking both ways, he stepped out of the street onto the wooden curb. He could protect her now, even when she didn't want it. With purpose, he followed her into the bank.

"Hank, you said if I left town with the kids, you would give me $200.00."

"That was the time before, sugar," Hank drawled, taking in Delie's legs with his lecherous gaze, yet again. Sometimes she regretted they were her best asset. They sure didn't seem to be helping her today. "This time, it's $100."

"That won't be enough."

"These are hard times, honey. You gotta take it when you can or at least when you can get it. Less, there's some other way you want to make up that other $100. I can talk to the board and see what can be done."

She would not miss this feeling. Always leaving the bank feeling as if she had to take a full bath in the galvanized tin tub. God's love had made her clean enough and this man, this Hank, always tried to make her feel dirty. She drew in a breath, about to proselytize or at least ask about Mary Anna, which sometimes served to deter him when she sensed Champ next to her.

No, she smelled his spicy scent. Now, he was touching her. Her brain threatened to lighten and fly clean out of the top of her head. But his iron-hard arm slipped around her waist and pure emotion rushed to the surface of her skin, causing prickles to form there. She didn't ask him to do that. She wanted to be angry. She prayed. *God, let me be angry.* Who in the world prayed to stay angry? She did. Anger kept her upright all these years. Lordy, how much she wanted to lean into his iron hold, but she could not. She would not. "Any problem here, Delie?"

"Well, Champ Bates." Hank stood and offered his hand. Champ did not take it. He stood with his arm firmly about Delie's waist. Hank sat back down and Delie took a small measure of satisfaction in Hank's foolish response. "I heard you came back into town. You all back together again?"

Delie opened her mouth but the words did not come to her lips fast enough because the prickles had wrapped themselves about her throat and cut off her air. She could not speak. Champ jumped in, "You could say that. You made her an offer and she come to take you up on it, I hear."

"Well, that's true. What she say?"

"That you going to give her money to take those babies on out of here, so that the state money can go directly to Winslow."

"Well, now, Champ. That's kind of harsh the way you talk."

"That's what you said to her? Or something else? Or you cutting the money to her?"

"I haven't said any of that. Let's sit down here and talk this through."

Yes. Let's sit down. Delie wanted to sit, because her knees were about to give way and she didn't want either one of these men to see that happen. Once again, words failed her.

But Champ knew. She knew that he knew. His arm was iron-hard, but the skin that covered it was like a down pillow, and he wrapped it about her even more firmly. "We don't want to take up too much of your time, Hank. We'll just take that cash money into Delie's hand. Got lots to do before we leave on Monday."

"Isn't that something?" Hank marveled. "Why there's been Bledsoes here forever. What will Winslow be like without them?"

Delie didn't know. She didn't care. "We really are in a hurry. How's Mary?"

Hank's face went red as he opened a nearby drawer with a key. "She's doing all right. Baby will come before long."

"Give her my best, won't you?"

"Too bad you can't stop by to see her before you leave."

"Yes, it is too bad." They watched with their breath catching as Hank counted out $200. It had been years since she had seen so much cash money at one time. Hank offered it to her with a trembling hand. Her own hand trembled as she took it and put it away in the gray purse.

"Thank you, Hank." Champ intoned with his voice as smooth as the warm honey Lona used to prepare for her cathead biscuits. "We'll be leaving now."

"It was always Champ and Delie when we was growing up. One word: champandelie. Now you all are back together. Life is something, isn't it?"

"Isn't it? Good Day." Champ steered her out of Hank's office and through the bank, holding her all the way. He held onto her arm as he walked her to the car and opened the door. He leaned forward and held her forearm just a tad more firmly.

And stopped her from falling into the front seat. A dizzy feeling came into her brain as he squeezed her waist and spoke to her, his warm sweet breath in her ear, smelling faintly of licorice, growling with sweet longing, so reminiscent of her dream. "There hasn't been a day, not one single day when I didn't dream of you, Delie. Dream of us. Wanted you to be next to me again. Not one single day in almost seven years."

That did it. God answered her prayer with a shot of anger that gave her the strength to break from that iron. She sat down on the front seat and closed the door so he had to step back to avoid getting hit. "Yes, I know," she turned and faced him. "I spent that same time, more than two thousand five hundred days cursing you, hating you, Champ, for leaving me like you did. Like a coward. You're always talking about Bates' strength. What about cowardice? Well, I'll tell you, I'm not raising Neal to be coward. I got my money. I can get on ahead."

"Don't be a fool." Champ went around to the front of the car. She tried not to look at the muscles bulging through his coat as he cranked the Tin Lizzy to get it started again. If he was the least bit affected as she was, he sure had a funny way of showing it. "I said what I was going to do."

"And when you are done, you can go back to whatever woman's arms you came from, Champion. I don't need you." The red tips of his ears were a dead giveaway. He was embarrassed. He had been around even though he purported to think of her all of that time. He had not been chaste and did not stand firm in the Lord. Even though she suspected what kind of rough life he had lived without her, she was hurt.

She avoided his eyes. She was so very weary of him hurting her.

"Ain't never been anyone else's name written in my heart, Cordelia May. Never."

"Drive the car, Champ." The tears rolling down her face threatened to freeze in the February wind as he drove away, and she couldn't stop them. She hated that she knew how serious he was when he used her full name that way. When they went to full names, they were serious. But, she didn't want that knowledge any more.

Let that woman, whoever she was, have it so she could get on with her lonely life raising needy children. It was the right recompense for the too easy way her life had gone as a child. She would atone and stay by herself. God's plan for her was clear and she would obey Him.

Delie was too quiet. He had gone too far. They were right back where they started when they left the house. By time they reached the junkyard, Delie was still mad at his move. Why couldn't she have thanked him?

Good thing he had gone in the bank when he did. Hank eying her up in all the wrong ways and her upset. She needed him, no matter what she thought. He had spent so much time out in the world, building himself up, fighting to come back here and make it better for her.

And no thank you from her. Not a word as he drove the Lizzie in silence to the next county where the old junkyard used to be. Thank God it was still there. "Old Lou!" he called out for the owner. Or the man he hoped was still the owner.

He opened the door for her to get out of the car and carefully closed it behind her. Her straight carriage had not just come from how he messed up with Neal. Watching her mince across the junk in the junkyard, he didn't want to think of how much struggle and pain had been a part of Delie's life without him. So much struggle, so much unhappiness since he had left. Her life sounded awful, no wonder she hated him so. She would never forgive him.

"Who's out there?" A creepy old voice rose out of a shack like structure in the middle of the yard. It was the dealing place.

"Me, Champ Bates. Paul Winslow's old chauffer."

Delie stopped in her tracks at his words. "Why you have to go and bring him up for?"

"Connections, baby. Watch and learn."

"Champ Bates, you're so arrogant."

A little man stood up out of the shack and came to where they stood. His beard was like cotton on his dark brown face. His overalls were holey and patched. Old Lou was still old. He hadn't changed. Champ came forward and shook his hand eagerly. "Been years, Old Lou."

Old Lou shook Champ's hand, but he was staring at Delie. "Who is this?"

"This here Delie Bledsoe. Live over in the next county. She looking to get on up North. We come to see what we can trade this here Lizzie for to help." Champ kept his voice light and friendly.

The whole negotiation process was always tense and difficult, but he could manage, so long as he stayed on his toes.

"She a beautiful woman. Yes, Lord."

Well, he didn't see that one coming. Her freckles stood out against the blush filling her pretty face.

Old Lou had to be a hundred years old. He was Old Lou when he was a youngster coming here in Paul Winslow's car to get parts to fix the cars in the family garage. Still, the remark knocked him off kilter a bit. But, he couldn't let this geezer get the best of him. "That's why I come back for her, Lou."

Now Old Lou looked at him. "You left this beautiful woman?"

"Yes." Delie's voice punched out as she tucked her gray purse under her arm. Woman choose the wrong times to get talkative. "Been back here by myself for years."

"But I'm back now, Lou."

Old Lou started waving his arms in the air turned around and headed back for the shack. "Can't afford to deal with no fools. Not in these here hard times, when even the white man is having it hard. No fools. Take that Lizzie and get on down the road."

"We looking to trade the Lizzie for something big, Lou. Gotta get this fine lady and all her family up North." Champ put all the need in his voice to make the man see.

"Shouldn't have left her out here all alone in the first place, man. What was you thinking?" Old Lou entered the door of the little shack and turned himself around, about to sit on his seat in the dealing place. A sure sign that meant the deal was over.

Out of sheer desperation, Champ waved Delie forward. "Say something to him." He whispered.

Nothing. No words.

"I see you got a fine old bus taking up room over there."

Delie whirled her head to where Champ pointed. "That old rusty thing?"

Old Lou came out the shack. "Now listen here, girlie. That's an old Greyhound. Year 'bout 1924. They don't build them like that no more."

"I guess they don't since it was 1924."

Old Lou laughed and slapped a palm on an overall pants leg. "Lord, girl, you're right. Pretty and smart. What you got to offer me?"

The old geezer was fixing his eyes on Delie's legs. Mercy. Champ breathed out. Hard. Now he could see how it was. Delie would have to carry the deal. He was just a bystander. "Tell him you got cash money."

"I still don't see why we want that rusty bus."

"Because," Champ offered up in a very loud stage whisper that he hoped the half-deaf Old Lou would not hear, "we have to get a bunch of people a far distance."

"All right." Delie said to him. She turned to Lou and fixed him with one of her sweet smiles. Couldn't Champ have one? Just one? Apparently not.

"We have cash money."

"Cash money?" Old Lou heard that sure enough. From the light on his old face, the man was on the verge of singing "Happy Days are Here Again," and running around the junkyard. He doubted this man had seen cash money in years. "You come by it proper, pretty girl?"

Now Old Lou got some attitude. Heh. "I was raised Christian, sir. I would thank you to remember that."

"No offense, pretty girl. I just got to ask. Old colored man got cash money these days, people be asking where he getting it from, so I figure I got a right to ask a young pretty girl the same."

Old Lou had sidled himself up right next to Delie. Champ could not stop himself from rolling his eyes. "What you talking about, honey?"

Champ made a gesture. Delie paid him absolutely no attention. "Fifty bucks."

Old Lou laughed again and slapped his knees. "Bless you, honey. We all got to start somewhere. You talking the Lizzie too?"

Delie looked taken aback. Why the shock? What did she think they were here for? "I guess so, sir."

"Well, honey, if you talking the Lizzie too, I take it off your hands in exchange for the bus for another, 'bout, one hundred and twenty dollars."

"How do you know I have that much money?"

"Lord, pretty girls always come with the right equipment."

Okay. That's it. "Eighty dollars and the Lizzie." Champ threw in with a protective glance toward Delie's legs.

The old geezer didn't see or hear Champ. "Back in the slavery days, you could buy a man for a couple a hundred. Work him like an old mule, too. Nobody say nothing. Pretty girl like you, always go for higher. Close near up a thousand dollars. Somebody look at them freckles and think about having them next to they cheek. Women are mighty valuable, even today. Ain't nobody with any sense thinking about leaving a good woman behind."

Champ adjusted his glasses and kept his line of sight on the rusty 1924 Greyhound bus. What was Old Lou going off and talking about slavery for?

Delie stepped forward and put a hand on his arm. "Would one hundred and the Lizzie do?" She gulped hard in her throat as the man grasped her fingers and laid a slobbery kiss on the back of her hand.

Had Delie just upped the offer when the man had not even made them another offer yet? Mercy. Why had he even brought her here?

"We thinking the same, pretty girl. We got us a deal. And I tell you what. For all of the trouble this one here put you through, and about to put you through, I fills it with gasoline."

Well, well. They got something anyway. Champ's mind was still reeling. He'da got Old Lou down to ninety dollars and no gas, but it came out just the same.

"Thank you, sir." Delie let her hand continued to be slobbered over and he waved her over to sign papers of ownership.

"I'll go on over and take a look at her." Champ spoke aloud, but the two of them were in their own world as Delie accepted the man's invitation to go into the little dealing shack to exchange money and sign the papers.

Champ stomped over to the bus in his old shoes and took off his jacket. It would take all of his doing to get this old bus going and he didn't want to get dirty. Besides, if she didn't want to speak to him, he could play that game as well. Except, he couldn't. He reached and stretched for a way to talk to her as he drove the old bus off of the lot with Delie sitting on one of the benches with the less amount of danger on it by way of a rusty spring.

She was still upset, but he couldn't hazard a guess as to why. All he saw was the long, shiny tear tracing its way though a maze of dark brown freckles.

"No one wanted that old car, Delie. It was twenty years old."

"It was my Daddy's car."

Champ's mother had raised him not to swear, and he didn't, but he came mighty close to being provoked. Some of the bus seats had broken springs and things on it. Once they were back to the house, he would show the children how to help fix it. The bus was roomy enough for all of them to get to Pittsburgh. Even if it needed some fixing, he was handy that way. He could do what needed to be done.

It was a mighty tall order to get her to believe in him.

A good bit of the hurt impacting him wore away when he swung the bus into the Bledsoe's front yard. The kids and Em were all gathered on the front porch cheering their arrival.

At least someone approved of him. When he stopped the bus and opened the door, the kids rushed the opening of the door and yelled in. "Calm down. Step back now." He stood from the driver's pit and held a hand out to Delie. "Come on, Delie."

Gallantly, he kept his hand out. He would outlast her. Practice for upper body strength. So what if her arms were folded? He had training. He could keep his arm up.

He hadn't trained well enough. Shooting pains traveled up his arms and stung him in his shoulder.

Please, God. Help her to know I am here. The time ticking by was a battle of wills, despite the children clustering around the door, begging Delie to come out. When he opened his heart to God and let His light shine through, Delie stood, worked her hips around the stairwell. And, miracle of miracles, took his hand.

The children cheered as they came off of the bus together, hand in hand. Once they reached the ground, she broke from his hold, grasping each one of the children by the cheeks, head or hands and let them on the bus.

Champ's heart was glad when he saw the children playing on the seats, but he remembered how some of them needed some repair. He turned to Em, "You gonna have to bring out your sewing basket."

"What in the world would you want with that?" Delie folded her arms with a skeptical look in her face.

"Some of those seats need repair. I don't want any of the kids getting hurt."

"I'll be back with my sewing basket, Champ. I'll help you out." Em volunteered and went into the house.

Delie's arms came unfolded. "It's amazing how everyone just does what you want them to do."

"Not everyone. Not Old Lou." He regarded her with a curious glance.

"I won't be so easily manipulated. I have a college education."

"Yes, you keep telling me."

"You might have gone to the college right across the street, Champ. We had plans."

Pain pierced his heart once more. "I remember."

"But no. You were a Bates. Had to gone on to boxing."

"It was fighting what brought these kids some meat to eat. What about your college got them something sides beans?"

He regretted the words as soon as they came out of his mouth.

She had a surprising strength as she took a hand and pushed him aside, getting back on the bus. Definitely his equal in every way.

Champ just stood there, dumfounded by his callousness. Em came next to him. "Here's the basket, Champ. Delie still mad?"

"She'll always be mad at me." He took the basket in his hand. The strange appearance of its gingham cloth ruffles and prettiness had no impact on him.

Em patted his shoulder. "It'll take some time. But she loves you. Always has."

"She sure ain't acting like it now."

"She been dreaming of you coming back a long time now. She can't even sleep in the night cause of her dreaming. I ask her, Delie, why are you awake? Go back to sleep." Em shook her head. He watched Em work her way through telling him the story. Em's open heart was revealing more than she knew. "She always say I have the same dream. I yell and yell at Champ, mad at him for leaving me when he did."

He was about two feet tall thinking about what he had said to her at the bank.

"And I tell her, every night before she go to bed to pray to God to protect her in the night. Sometimes it work. Sometimes not. Delie always dreaming you come home." Em's brown face was lit up like a brown sun. "And then you did! Isn't God amazing?"

He helped Em gather herself up to get back on the bus. He could attest to God's amazing hand. But God also made more complexity than Em even caught on with her simple way of looking at things. Something told him to come back. God. He might lose his sight in the process, but that was less important than making things right with Delie again. Now, how would he do it? Would it be enough for her to love him again?

His life beyond the fight stretched out long and lonely at the notion of living without her in his world. He had to convince her somehow. He just had to.

CHAPTER SEVEN

He would pay for staying away from his mother's for another night.

But he had to make sure Delie, Em and the young ones were safe.

So at night, he stayed over in the barn again. And when the echo of his mother's footsteps thunked on the cold red earth, he knew it was her come to see where he was. He had more work to do on the bus before church began, but he could feel his mother's footsteps through his skin. Sure enough, as he worked on the chassis, his mother's feet marched right past him up onto the Bledsoe's porch. He scrambled to get out from under the bus. Pulling up his suspenders as he ran, he went over to her. "Mama, what you doing here?"

"Wondering where my son had gotten off too." Effie Bates's voice boomed out on a Sunday morning, on purpose, Champion knew. She didn't care who was sleeping. If she was up, everyone ought to be up.

Delie worked to take care of those kids, and worse, those sleepless nights he had caused. She needed her rest and so did they. He took his mother by the elbow and guided her off of the porch back down to the bus, trying to be quiet. "I'm here. What do you want?"

"Well," Effie fanned herself as Champ guided her over to the bus and helped her on so she could speak freely in her loud voice. He sat in the driver's seat, as she ensconced herself on the front seat, looking every inch the queen. "At least you ain't in the house with her."

"No, Mama. Delie's a Christian woman. I wasn't trying to compromise her." Champ said, even as he remembered, with shame, the one time he did, right in the barn where he slept at night.

"If you say so. You supposed to be training, and you over here with her not doing your training but working up under some old bus. Are you getting ready as you should?"

Champ didn't want to admit it, but he was distracted. Very. "I'm doing some conditioning work. I said to Delie I'ma take her and the kids up to Pittsburgh, and then I'll be back for training."

"For how long?" Effie stopped her self-imposed fanning. "I mean, you best not blow this chance. Not on her."

"Mama, it'll take a week tops to take her on up there. Then, I'll be back down to train until the end of March."

His answer seemed to satisfy her. It didn't make him feel satisfied, though. He had an initial plan, but all of these other things came up and distracted him. Getting involved with Delie again meant he had to think bigger than himself, beyond himself. There was the way he spent the training money on making sure the children got better food, for instance. He was supposed to be eating beefsteak, but it would be dry and tough in his mouth if he had to think about those kids not having any.

"Fine. I'm on my way to First Water for Sunday school. I see she and her children ain't even awake yet. What kind of way is that to be? God demands that He be worshipped and they sleep."

"She's tired. She needs to rest."

"You best not be knowing anything about her resting habits."

"I told you I didn't."

"Good. Keep it that way. I'll see you at the church. And back here in a week."

"Will there be a picnic today?"

"You know there is, every third Sunday in the month at First Water. This one will be special because you are here."

"Yes, ma'am." Champ helped her down off the bus. "I'll be seeing you there soon."

Champ watched as his mother pranced down the road to First Water. Another wave of guilt entered his limbs. He could have offered her a ride. He should have. But, if he started up the bus, he might have awakened Delie or one of the children, and he wanted her to sleep.

He laid himself out in the red dirt and began to shuffle back under the bus when he caught sight of Delie standing in the door. Too late. He waved at her and got back to work. They would send out one of the kids to tell him when breakfast was ready. He wanted to be sure to remain on task, so everything in his life would be at peace as he resumed training.

Delie watched Effie Bates sashay her wide behind down the road. The two of them had been at loggerheads for years. It was only very recently, as a woman who had a son herself that she could even begin to understand Champ's mother. When she did, Delie did something she started to do when she was eighteen and straining to give birth to Champ's child. She prayed for her. *Dear God, please bless Mrs. Bates as she continues to love her son and help him in his quest. Help me not to blow up at her in church today. Or after. Amen.*

Delie went back into the house to see Em setting the table in the kerosene-lit room which was in some disarray because they were still packing stuff. "We don't have no picnic basket to take with us."

"It will be alright, Em. We're the ones getting treated today. It's our last Sunday at First Water." Saying the words seemed extraordinary. Even though Delie had left the church before, she had always come back. This time, it would be permanent. They were the last of the Bledsoes. Effie Bates had won control of the church. Lona was not resting easy in her grave, but Delie could not think about that.

Em's chin quivered in the semi-lit room. "I'm going to miss the old place."

"I know, honey. But we got to think of what is better for the children. They can't stay down here in a place with no school and no hope but to work in the mill and be all stooped over when they are young."

Em swallowed. "I know. That's what keeps me going. Let me get the bacon on."

Delie watched after her as Em went back into the kitchen. Getting her to come on the journey would not be easy. She had to make Em feel as if she were needed desperately so she would not have time to reflect on the pain of leaving her home. Flo came out into the big room, scraping her feet along the boards of the floor. "I'm hungry."

"We'll be eating soon. Go on and get dressed."

Delie ducked into the small bedroom and got dressed herself in her gray suit. The gray suit was her best and she wanted to look special for this last time at the family church.

Once they moved up north, maybe she would have the chance to find a job. A job could mean more for her, more for the children. More for Neal. She had her teaching certificate. There was such hope in her heart, except, what about Champion?

He would probably go back to wherever he came from after he went to Pittsburgh with them. *Dear, God, please send Champ back to wherever he came from before he came back here. I'll be fine without him.* Honest.

Resolved, she sang a hymn suitable for Sunday morning.

She sang until Champ pulled the bus forward. It was running smooth and sure. No clunky halting sounds like yesterday. Delie turned around as some of the children ran out to the bus.

"Hey, this is great!" Willie crowed as he ran into the yard half dressed.

"We can go anywhere on this bus!" Neal's eyes shone with joy. Whenever he was happy, Delie's heart expanded in her chest and she was so full she would burst from happiness. And now there was jealousy. Champ came along and made a new look appear on Neal's sweet features by being here, just by being a man.

"Come on. Let's get on. And be careful to pick a seat without an open spring in it. We gonna work on those when we get home." Emerald ran out too and helped the children onto the bus.

Delie went out into the yard and waved her arms. "Get off the bus!"

"Why, Mama?" Neal leaned out a window and gave her a sweet smile.

"You all aren't finished getting dressed and we gotta eat breakfast before church. Don't you all remember?"

Some of the children, including Neal, groaned. A small hand slipped into hers and grabbed at her cold fingers. Bonnie. Her trusty comrade.

The children shuffled off and went into the house. Even Em looked disappointed. "We weren't going to be gone long, Delie."

"Honey, you don't want the bacon to burn. Come on now." Delie patted her sister's shoulder.

"No. No wasting food."

"That's right. Go on now." Emerald went inside with the children.

Champ was the last one off of the bus. He was still half dressed himself, wearing an undershirt and suspenders. The back of the undershirt was streaked with red dust. "Always interrupting the party."

"Someone has to be grown up here. You are filthy dirty."

"I'll take my shirt off. I gotta wash up anyway. Can one of you ladies wash it and hang it up for later?"

And before she could stop him, Champ had peeled off the undershirt and handed it to her, wearing only his suspenders on the top part of his body.

Delie averted her eyes. Looking at him would be like looking at the sun—she could go blind in all kinds of ways, and that wasn't happening. "I guess Em has some hot water heating up with the coffee. You can go and put on another shirt. If she hangs this one out, it will be dry by the time we get back from church. Don't want you to catch cold before we start out tomorrow."

"No, ma'am. I'll go wash up by the water pump." Champ wandered off to the back of the house.

Don't look. Don't look. Well, there was no harm in looking now. He was walking away. Even in his back, every single muscle was chiseled and outlined in smooth, glistening butterscotch skin, bracketed by the black of the suspenders.

Delie's mouth went dry.

Next week she would be back in the bosom of her family, safe from harm. She could hardly wait.

A half hour later, Champ shouted out "All aboard!" and closed the bus door. Even Em looked excited as he pulled the bus out onto the dirt road that ran in front of the Bledsoe house. She would be leaving the place where she had grown up within twenty-four hours. How would it be for them in a new city, a new place?

They pulled up to First Water in a lot of commotion. People marveled at the bus. But there was only one face Delie saw—the scowling, disapproving visage of Effie Bates. "My, what a whole lot of foolishness on a Sunday morning. Causing a lot of disruption to the Lord's day!"

Champ helped each one of them off the bus and gestured to her. His hand gripped hers with strength and purpose as she came down the steps with little mincing steps, careful to keep the gray skirt down and untorn.

"Please, Mama. We're here to praise God this morning."

Effie smiled all over herself as she fixed her arm in the crook of Champ's arm. Delie's hand was back in the cold when Champ let go of hers. Which was the whole problem in counting on him. He would always let go. Better to rely upon herself and what she could do. Champ was completely oblivious to her as he basked in the glow and admiration of the women in the church. *No, I'll not be jealous.*

A little hand gripped at her tight skirt. Neal. This was what it was about. She took his soft hand in hers and they went into the church together.

First Water had been the bedrock of the Bledsoe's family faith for longer than she was alive. How could it be the same somewhere else? Her sisters' letters were full of discussions about the churches up in Pittsburgh, even Nettie's own small congregation, but it wasn't the same as old First

Water. Delie was surprised to feel tears welling at the corner of her eyes. Things would change. Her life, their lives would not be the same.

The pastor spoke in the midst of the service. "Sister Cordelia, the church wants to wish you all well as you join the family up north. We collected a special love offering as you journey on to get up north to see about letting these children of our community find opportunity for themselves. I just want you to let them know sometime about where they come from. Don't hesitate to let them come back home sometimes, amen."

"Amen." Delie echoed, making a silent promise to herself and to them.

The love offering was fifty dollars. Delie's heart was touched. These mill workers and farmers came up with so much help in these hard times of trouble.

While the children frolicked and played at the picnic after church, Delie kept her distance from Champion as he fixed a plate for his mother and carried it to her. Em whispered to her as they cut pie. "Why are you so mad at Champ, Dee?"

"I'm not mad at him." Delie told Em as they dished up generous squares of dried peach pie on small plates in the church hall.

"He loves you."

Em's point of view in the world made everything so stripped away, so easy. Far from it. "That's nice, honey. Why you so concerned about love?"

"Everybody is. It won't ever happen for me, but what about you?"

"Me, lovely? I'm taking care of you and the children. That's what God wants of me now."

"We got to take care of ourselves one day." Em's beautiful face emptied. "When we get up to Pittsburgh, I can stay with Ruby, and the kids can stay with Net and Jay. Then you be free to be Champ's wife."

"Wife?" Delie laughed as her heart hurt. "I am not trying to be anybody's wife, Em. I got to take care of these kids. They are my responsibility."

"I love them too." Em's face became a stormy mask. Her sister was so transparent. Delie always knew when she hurt Em. And she had. She put the pie server down and embraced her sister from the side. Em's head went down on her shoulder. She would not have damaged Em's sensitive heart for anything. She knew all too well what it was like to be hurt. Like an exploding pain in her chest—these things hurt almost as much as seeing Champ fawning over his mother and Effie preening over her prodigal son returned home.

But it would be Delie he was leaving with in the morning. It was enough. For now.

The next day, Delie prepared to leave the place where she had grown up. More than prepared. It had slightly appalled her she had to return to it when she finished with Spelman College. Her life, the life she had designed away from Champ was all mapped out after graduation. But, her mama died.

Lona and John never got to know that all of their daughters had been able to move on and out into the world. Delie puzzled over this as she loaded some suitcases into the compartment on the side of the ramshackle bus. "That's the very thing they prepared us for."

"Who?" Champ sidled up next to her with more suitcases. Why was he honing in on her own self-spoken thoughts? He frustrated her to no end.

"My parents."

"Oh, yeah. Sure enough."

"What do you mean, wise guy?"

"It means they always wanted better for you all. That's what everyone round here think. Oh, the Bledsoe girls. You want to get a Bledsoe girl. You got you one of them Bledsoe girls."

"Oh really?"

What would he say now? Delie put a hand on her hip and stuck it out. She wanted to see him squirm and she was not disappointed. "Of course. You all prime stuff."

Delie paid no attention as a mass of wiggling squirming young humanity passed her by and excitedly got onto the bus. She was happy she didn't have to worry one of the children would sit down on an old seat and get injured by a spring. Several of the churchwomen had come by after church with special needles and thread and sewed enough patches and cushioning on top to make sure they were all comfortable. Delie nearly cried at their thoughtfulness. "Then why did old Winslow do so much to hurt us?"

"Meaning Mr. Paul?"

Delie tilted her head. "Yeah. Him."

Before Mr. Paul died, Champ had been his last chauffer. And Delie guessed the glories of his job played a large part of what had driven him away from Winslow. He had complained about being a chauffer to no end. "He knew what you all was. Count on it. He was the one who said it."

"Really?"

"He did. Claimed you had the makings of a fine wife. Pretty too."

For some reason, this embarrassed her, but she would never let Champ see her discomfort. "Of course. It's why he spent so much time torturing my sisters to move them on from here."

Champ worked his hat in his hands. "You got it all wrong. You all leaving took, and is going to take, the heart out of this town." He put the hat on his head. "I got to come back here after I take the kids up. I ain't looking forward to what it will be down here."

"I'm sure." She surveyed the empty front yard of the Bledsoe house one last time. "But you chose it. Let's go."

"Where's Em?" Champ asked. He ran up the short steps of the bus and came back down fast. "She's not there."

She called out, "Em? Lovely? Where are you, girl?"

Nothing was in the house—they had made certain. Delie and Champ ran around all the outbuildings. She ran out back to the orchard and saw her sister there, clinging to a peach tree with tears running down her beautiful brown face. "I ain't going. Don't make me go."

"Come on, Em. We going to adventure now."

Em sniffed. "That's easy for you to say. You been to the college. I been nowhere. I ain't never wanted to."

The air around her changed and once again, Champ stood next to her. She didn't have to incline her head or look around. She knew he was there.

"Hey, Em. Come on. We going to get on the road."

"You go on without me."

"How we going to do that? You're our precious Emerald. Come on."

Champ moved from Delie's side closer to Em and put an arm around her shoulder. His expression was tender and full of caring and love. He never looked at her with such affection. "I can't leave here. Mama and Daddy said not to."

"Aw. Things changed after they died, Sweets. They're in the ground now. They know you got to get your own chance at things. That's what they always wanted for you and your sisters."

Em's head drooped onto Champ's shoulder. "I scared."

"It's okay to be scared. Come on. We be scared together." Champ slipped a hand into the fold of his strong arm and eased Em away from the peach tree. "I got you, Em."

Promises, promises. It almost made Delie sick. Or jealous. "Come on, Em." Delie said the words, although they were completely unnecessary. Champ had her.

With pride and a high step, Champ escorted Emerald right onto the bus. He made Neal move to another seat behind Delie and sat Em right behind him. He had made Em comfortable with such ease. She hadn't known what would happen, but he did. He slipped into the driver's seat and looked at her. "Ready?"

"Yes, I am."

Champ closed the bus door and pulled the old rickety bus out, making sure to look both ways until he drove in the direction of the rising sun. He pulled off onto the road away from Winslow. For good. A sea of relief washed over her. After years of staying here, it was high time she got on with her life.

With Champion Bates at the wheel. Not the way she planned it, but this bus ride was just the first step.

CHAPTER EIGHT

"Winslow's gone now. You sit right up front with Champ, Dee. I can sit on back with the children." Em offered.

Champ could see Delie's jaw grow tight, a sure sign she was jealous of her sister for taking his attention. He chuckled inside. Delie still cared. She might not have wanted to, but she still cared for him. The thought warmed him in the cold February bus where he had to drive on mostly unformed and unpaved roads to get to Atlanta. In Atlanta, they could have lunch, take a bathroom break and continue on. He hoped to make North Carolina by nightfall to stay in a place he knew was safe.

"Where we going to stay tonight?" Neal had asked him. He had tried to move in the seat behind Champ, but Em evicted him so Delie could sit there. Though, she had not yet moved over.

"Well, buddy. I know of a place or two. We want to try to get to North Carolina by nighttime. We got lots of driving to do."

"So leave him alone." Delie chimed in.

"That ain't what I meant, Cordelia May. Not at all." Champ shook his head to clear his vision and show he did not agree with what she said.

"I just wanted you to have peace and quiet. It is probably very jarring for you when you aren't used to being around children."

"These are good kids. Wouldn't hurt a flea."

Small giggles came forward and warmed him.

"Let's see how he feels after being trapped on a bus with you all. He may change his mind."

"Sometimes going on all over makes a man realize how small he is in the world. Having a child? Well, that can make a man feel pretty large instead. A good thing."

Champ's words made the children ramp up and get excited. Neal kept asking over and over, "Where you been at Champ? How you fight? Who did you fight? What kind of punching?"

Champ laughed at Neal's excited questions. Neal may have been small, but he saw things, knew things. He got his insight from his mother. If Champ was his father, what had Neal gotten from him? Was it true when his mother said she saw nothing of the Bates in him? Nothing at all? The silky feel of Neal's hair in his hands before he cut it kept nibbling away at the edges of his heart like a mouse on cheese. A small quiet discontent. But, it was there all the time. Every day.

The children were laughing, but Delie did not. If it would make things right with Delie, he would cut off his right arm to make it up to her. But it wouldn't. All he could do would be to use his powerful right hook to fight and get what she needed to take care of these kids. Delie deserved it. Neal deserved it. All of the kids did too.

The other sad part was his selfishness had cost him Delie's love. He could never get it back. "I been all over," he began in a slow storytelling style, thinking as he was driving, mulling over his words to avoid offending. "I even been to England."

Delie shifted toward the cold window. Away from him. Oh the things they had shared when they were young and foolish enough to think they could make a difference in the world. She longed to see things. He had promised to take her and he had backed out on his promise. No wonder she hated him.

"Where's that?" Neal's little voice piped up.

"It is across a big water," Em said. Champ knew there was a smile in her voice. "You got to get on a boat to get there. It takes days."

"Ten, as a matter of fact. I had to go. It's where boxing all got started. I had some one who wanted me to know the Marquess of Queensberry rules. They are the real rules in boxing."

"Wow." Willie sat back in his seat.

"It was like a little school I got to go to. I learned a lot."

"There's some learning appropriate for children and some that isn't." Delie's voice cut into his warm reminiscence like a bucket of cold water thrown on a sleeping body. "I would thank you to know the difference."

"I'll keep that in mind, Cordelia May. Thank you." Champ navigated the bumpy road. "Anyway, over in Europe, you can fight anybody. Color don't matter over there. I did pretty well for myself. They have nice big purses over there. Good times."

"Why didn't you stay on over there then, if you had it so good in Europe? Lots to keep you well-schooled over there, no doubt."

"Well, maybe, Delie, but it wasn't home. As bad as things are here, I wanted to get home to make a difference over here. I fought over there and fought all kinds of men, all colors. I want to show we can do the same in the United States."

"And hurt people in the process."

The merry atmosphere changed on the bus. The chirping happy voices of the children were now silent and quiet. And Champ was responsible. His heart had been filled with joy and now it was as if Delie had dropped his heart from the top of that Big Ben clock he had seen in London. "You know I wouldn't have it, Delie. Believe it."

"Whatever you say, Champion. You're the one driving the bus."

No matter how she meant it, Champ took this as a cue to laugh. So he did. If he laughed, the children might not react so much at Delie's upset. And they did.

"I sure am. I'm going to take you all the way to Pittsburgh, in comfort and style."

"We appreciate it, Champ." Em's voice was quiet. She had not laughed with the children. Even from her perspective, Em understood Delie was upset, and Champ didn't want her to feel defensive for her younger sister.

"I know, HB. I know."

"Who is HB?" Neal wrinkled his brow and Champ smiled at how easily his little face twisted into all kinds of interesting shapes and expressions. If blindness was God's plan for him, he could experience joy in his heart at seeing the beautiful face of Neal, who might be his son. And the face of Delie, one more time. Even when her beautiful face bore a scowl and the pretty freckles stood out on her medium brown skin in sharp disapproval— most of the time.

"HB is Aunt Em. When we were children, I courted your mother and I used to call your Aunt, Honey Bun. HB."

The rear view mirror reflected Neal's contorted caramel features again. Confusion. "Children don't court. Adults do," Neal said.

"We were young people. Before we were grown up." Delie told Neal loudly over the hum of the bus. The admonition was for Champ as well, he knew.

"Yes, we used to have lots of fun." Em chimed in. "Champ would drive us all around in the car. All the time."

"Your Aunt Em, she was our chaperone. We all went to picnics together, plays at the church, movies down in Calhoun, anywhere. We had some fun times."

"What's a chaperone?" Bonnie piped up. She had not said anything all this time. Champ got the feeling she was the most guarded of the children against him. Children could feel so much. And he understood Bonnie's feelings were for Delie all the way. Still, he was amused by her little voice, delicate brown skin and cute black braids. A girl child, what a delicate thing she was. Yet, it was clear if Champ saw fit to hurt Delie, Bonnie would fight him like a bear cub.

"Someone who comes along on the trips to make sure there is no trouble with the courting couple."

"What trouble?" Bonnie asked.

Delie cleared her throat. "Aunt Em just went with us in case a tire went out or something and someone had to go back for the tire inflator."

"Oh. Okay." Bonnie said. The tone of her voice let Champ know she was satisfied. Delie had been right—some things were not meant for children to know about and hear. Troubling territory.

But Willie, as one of the older children had not been fooled. Willie snickered at Delie's answer. Had Delie talked to the boy about being a man? Well, she couldn't. She wasn't a man. He was. Better talk to Willie alone sometime, to help her out. He could contribute there, before he had to leave them. The thought of leaving the little group made his palms sweat in the cold. He gripped the wheel harder.

"Was there a certain place you were planning to go in at Atlanta?" Delie changed the subject with grace and beauty. What a woman.

"I was going to Black town, Sweet Auburn. You know it."

"I went to school there. I wanted to show the children."

"That's right. Spelman. You want to go there instead?"

"If possible. There are places to eat there and the buildings have bathrooms. I just wanted to see it one more time."

What would it be like to see her school? He wouldn't pass up the opportunity to get to see the place Delie had been after he left. "No problem. Tell me where to go."

Now she was forced to move to the seat behind him. As she leaned forward, he could smell the scent of her hair. Her scent had not changed. She washed it with lilac water, she told him once, long ago. Her smell of lilacs haunted him all the way across the ocean and back. Delie. Now he was fortunate enough to be this close to her again.

"We aren't far." She gave him the directions in a loud, bossy tone, but Champ wasn't fooled. Her voice meant she was nervous. If he placed a hand on her heart, her heart would be beating very, very fast. Of course, if he touched her there, he would be touching something else as well. The thought of touching her there made him clench the wheel harder. He dismissed the thought instantly. He had better focus on driving this bus safely, for all of their sakes.

Champ pulled the bus through the gates of Spelman College and Delie's heart beat fast. She would always be indebted to her college home because here, she had found a way to learn and grow without Champ. Here, she was free. It had been a strange existence, though, pretending to be a coed at the all female college. When Champ pulled up next to the green, she got off first. Even though it was February, the grounds were still green. Always. Green was the way she would remember Spelman, even though as she stayed here, her heart was broken.

The children got off and started running around on the green. Bonnie stood solemnly next to her but stepped forward as if she would step through a decorated arch a few feet from them.

"No, no." Delie held her back and stood next to her. "When you come back, in the class of '53, you can go through. On Graduation Day."

"That's an awful long time away."

"It's a tradition. And when you come to a place like this, you got to respect tradition. Let's go to the restroom and then to the café for lunch. We can get something hot to eat." Delie took Bonnie's hand and turned away from the arch.

Champ was next to her and pointed to the arch with a thumb. "No one can go through that arch until they graduate?"

"Yes."

"I remember when Delie went through. Mama was so proud. Daddy too." Em's face was full of pride when she first spoke. It took another second for a sad cast to emerge. Champ took her hand and tucked it into his arm.

"A special day, I know."

"Yes, it was. Wish you could have been there. You would've been proud too."

"If he had been there, I wouldn't have been there, Em." Delie wanted to take back the mean words as soon as she said them. The anger would confuse Em. "Never mind."

"You got a degree. That's something special." Em's features made a puzzle.

"Of course it is, honey. I know."

"The first one in the family. Ruby went to nursing school, but it isn't a college degree, Delie."

"You're right. Here's the café. Everyone should go into the bathroom and wash their hands and faces. Can you take the boys, Champ? There's a restroom for boys over in Barnwell."

"Of course. Let's go, guys." Delie's heart twisted to see Neal put his hand in Champ's and walk off. Did Neal love Champ already? More than her? It might not be a surprise if he did. She had not been there for the first few years of his life. Why should she expect he would love her? He had the hardest time of all of them when Mama and Daddy died. Neal knew them and loved them as his parents. Champ turned around and looked at her. "We'll see you at the café."

Delie stepped to the entrance of the cafeteria and sniffed. "Swiss steak, it seems like." A small dark-brown skinned lady walked by holding a big pot, which threatened to dwarf her. "There's Miss Gert. She runs the café."

"Is it you, Delie? My lord, girl, good to be seeing you!" Miss Gert nearly dropped her pot.

"I got a little brood here. Wonder if we can trouble you for some lunch. We can pay."

"That's fine, honey. Such lovely children. Who they belong to?"

"Me."

Delie could see Miss Gert was confused to figure out how she would have had this many children after graduation, but she did not like to bring up how she had gotten the children. Any of them. "We're moving up to Pittsburgh and I wanted to stop on the way to see my dear alma mater."

"That's all right, child. And well you should. Who is he?"

Champ must have come back with the boys. At a women's college, whenever a man appeared on campus, there was a stir. Sometimes Morehouse men came to the café for lunch, but they didn't look anything like Champ. No one did. "A friend from back home. He's driving us up to Pittsburgh."

"Does he need some Swiss steak too, honey? We got plenty."

"Yes, ma'am. All of us. Eight. I can pay."

"I would refuse your money, but times is tight right about now. Have a seat here, sir. You want a plate of Swiss steak? Potatoes? Greens?"

"Thank you, ma'am. I appreciate everything you want to give out." No woman could resist Champ's easy charms. When Miss Gert returned with a plate heaped high, including dinner rolls, Champ practically rolled up his sleeves and dug in. Many of the other cafeteria ladies called themselves helping Miss Gert, but really they came to see a man eat. And he sure did. He ate as if his life depended on it.

"He's a handsome one. You sparking with him?" Miss Gert asked her to the side, fortunately.

"No, ma'am." Delie tried to be light about it, but she couldn't, she just couldn't. And Miss Gert knew.

"Hmmm. Woman got this many children from somewhere needs a man."

"That's what a lot of people say. I'm doing fine on my own."

"You are? You think that's what you came to this here school for? To be on your own? Yous supposed to be an ornament in a man's life. Why do you think we keep having all of those dances for with Morehouse?"

Delie remembered the Morehouse men. She had never thought much of them, because they were like children. So many people during her college experience seemed very young to her, after what she had been through and then having to leave her baby at home to be raised by her parents while she was at school. "That never worked out for me, as much as I love this school." Delie's gaze rested on Neal. He was eating more than he usually did, trying to mimic Champ no doubt.

"We all need somebody, Delie. You was one of the smartest ones back in the class of '32, I remember. But you such a pretty one, I knew you would find the right one to help you with the tough times."

Delie patted her arm. "Thanks, Miss Gert. Maybe not pretty enough."

It had been a long time since Delie had been under the scrutiny of an older woman's experience and expectations. Mama had been gone almost two years now. What would she have said to Champ's return? Doubtless, she would have approved of Champ back in her life. After her own hard times when a terrible group attack left Lona pregnant with her oldest sister, Lona had still married her sweetheart and had four more daughters with him.

Almost as if Lona were speaking, Miss Gert said, "Forgiveness can be a big, big thing, child.

Bitterness can eat you up inside. Remember. Go on now and eat up your Swiss steak."

Delie sat down at the table with the children and ate her steak, potatoes and greens. Everything was delicious, but it all stuck in her throat watching how everyone was making a fuss over Champ, bringing him more food and at last, some slices of sugar cream pie.

Champ's hazel eyes twinkled at the cafeteria women and the coeds when they came in and gave him interested gazes. But in between times, Champ's eyes and the unsettling gaze he always had were on Delie. "What you looking at?" Delie put a forkful of potatoes between her lips.

"Just making sure you eating. You too skinny."

This made the children laugh. "Mama, you skinny." Neal said, right on cue.

"I eat enough to keep myself going. Lots of times, I got to eat a little less so my children can have a little more. Maybe that's why I'm so skinny."

Even the children understood Delie wasn't trying to be funny. They quieted, even as the cafeteria filled with noisy coeds. Champ gazed at her with a strange look. "You've done well for yourself in a hard time. I'm mighty proud of you, Delie."

Wow. How nice. She supposed she could take pride and spread it with butter and eat it. She didn't want to snipe at him anymore, so she just shrugged her shoulders.

"Thanks for showing me the college part of you. Helps me to know you a bit better."

"You been to college, Champ?" Willie asked.

"The college of life." Champ smiled as he used his napkin to wipe his lips. The gesture mesmerized her and she didn't like it.

"Where's the pie?" Delie asked to break the trance. Flo handed her a slice on a plate. She put the tip of her fork deep into the wedge and ate the rich smoothness quickly, marveling at what Miss Gert was able to do with limited supplies at the college. She had never minded eating at Spelman, but there was always something else on her mind. It didn't matter what she ate, Delie just stayed thin with the appropriately placed roundness on her frame.

"It always did take you longer to eat up your food."

"I like to savor things. "

"Yes, indeed." Champ's eyes were all on her now. His glasses did not break the intensity of his stare, but Delie wished they did.

"Lot's of these coeds think you are collegiate with them glasses on. You can go and speak to any one of them." Delie ate another triangle of her pie slice. "I'm just eating pie."

"I'm fine right where I sit, Cordelia May. If I'm not, you be the first one to know."

"Don't want to trouble you any."

"As I said, I'm where I want to be. I'ma take these children back out on the lawn and we can work up a little football game to burn off some of this good food. Who wants in?"

Without fail, every single child did. On their way out the café, Champ made sure to stop and praise Miss Gert effusively and all the cafeteria ladies returned the gesture. Only Em stayed with her.

Of course, as Delie ate the crust on her pie, she was faced with stacks and stacks of dishes to get back to the dishwasher in the kitchen. Typical, Champ had left her with a mess to clean up. Her life long job seemed to be cleaning up other people's messes. Certainly in the college, it was her job to lug dishes back to the kitchen and wash them to help pay for her tuition and board. "Gotta take these dishes back to the dishwasher, Em. Wanna help?"

Em always would help doing a domestic chore. Her sister was such a love. "This is what I used to have to do to earn my keep around here."

"Really, Dee?"

"Yeah. That's why I never mind washing the dishes. It's the cooking part that was always hard for me."

"You're good at washing dishes."

"Come on. Let's go." Delie scraped and piled them up like an expert. What sad-eyed scholarship student had taken her place back next to the wash bin? She didn't want to take money from the children, but she would take a dollar and slip it into the girl's apron pocket. She could, and should, use the little extra to buy something for herself. Something of her very own.

CHAPTER NINE

He was not hungry. Not in the permanent kind of way. Not in the gnawing way he used to be hungry.

He had years of being a ham and egg boxer, chasing a dream, and the realization he was not hungry startled him. The bus was cold, but the company of the children and their laughter was a balm to his wounded heart.

Delie had been on the campus as a lonely girl, because of him. She had gone to school, for years right next to Morehouse, a college full of well-educated, professional men. Better men than him who could have married her and taken Neal to raise and would have loved her.

Something in his heart raged. *No.*

She rejected them before but she sure could have them now. What was to stop her from finding some man up there in Pittsburgh and getting married?

Something in his stomach rolled around. *Stop thinking of it or you will lose all the good Swiss steak you just ate.*

It made him feel better to drive straight into South Carolina, cross the line and see the little sign. At least progress was being made.

"You being quiet, Champ. What you thinking about?" Neal's voice piped up.

Some other man marrying your mother and taking you, the children, and her away and there isn't anything I can do but pray. So Champ prayed. The prayer was probably too fast and he promised to make it up to God, but he was driving a rickety bus full of kids, Delie and her sister with his shaky vision. Champ wouldn't risk them. God was taking care of them. "We got to find a place to stay tonight."

"How we going to do that?"

"I know a place in North Carolina, but we got to get there. Probably stop there tonight."

"A hotel?" Delie asked. At her question, he understood Delie was not widely traveled. She had only been back and forth between Atlanta, Winslow and to Pittsburgh once or twice. She had never been out of Georgia much, despite her best efforts at trying. Well, here she was now.

"There's a lot of places won't take folk like us, Delie May. There's a lady I know, she can take us in."

"A lady?" Neal squeaked and Champ's heart nearly sank as Delie's heart-shaped face came into his rear view mirror view.

"Humph. A lady." She folded her arms. Still mad. Well, at least she cared. All he wanted at this point was for her to care about him.

"You must think I lived a pretty wild life away from you in these years."

Delie was surprised he confronted this head on in this way. Good. She needed plenty of surprising. He had some other ideas. "I don't know what to think. You just didn't need me or Winslow much. Must have been someone else."

"I been living hand to mouth over these years. Got even harder when times got hard. A man got to learn how to take care of himself before he takes on a wife."

"Don't know how a man could find comfort in the world being by himself. Makes no sense to me."

"It does to me." Champ insisted.

"We're different people."

"I guess so."

Always had to have the last word. So spirited. So different. He would hold his peace for now. He would have more to say later and surprise her.

"Getting low on gas."

"Well, find someplace then."

Champ shook his head. "Not that easy."

Delie threw up her hands and turned toward some of the children, chastising them for being so noisy. "I don't see why not."

No, she wouldn't, having lived in her little cocoon of the world. "I'm just saying to you. When we stop, don't flash out all of the money. Get together all you got in the smallest amounts to pay. 'Bout twenty dollars. We can get some gas and hope it will last us beyond Raleigh a bit."

Delie started digging in her gray purse. "I don't know why it has to be all secretive."

Champ winced as the bus bumped over the county roads toward a little town called Gaffney in South Carolina. He was hoping to get over the border into North Carolina, at least, because you never knew what could happen in South Carolina.

At least this gas station was just off of the bumpy road, Mobiloil. Champ stopped the bus and there was quiet. "Good thing there's a field over there. Everyone will go at this stop. Everyone, even you Willie."

Willie didn't roll his eyes, but Champ could tell the boy was completely humiliated at Delie pulling some bathroom paper out of a bag. "Let's go," she told the kids. They all started climbing off the bus and lining up next to the big tires.

"Let me have the money afore you go." Champ was the last one off of the bus. He did not like the look of the gas station. No one came out. They were studying them. Studying to see if they were trouble.

Delie took the money and shoved all of the small bills and coins into his hands. Champ kept it there in his hands and kept his hands visible.

"Well, Champ. Why don't you put the money away?"

Champ pursed his lips in the age-old sign for Delie to hush. "They watchin."

"Who?"

"Whoever owns this here gas station. Don't go to the bathroom yet."

A small whimper came from Bonnie, but it couldn't be helped. Better a dirty child who could easily be cleaned than they all be full of buckshot.

Champ stepped forward and held out the money in both of his hands. "Good Day." He spoke loud. The small gas station only had two pumps and a sparkling white building where the end of a gun loomed. *Please, God. Help these ones to have a heart. I ain't come this far to have Delie or any of the children be hurt. Or himself.* He walked in a straight line toward the gun end.

"Who Champ talking to?" Roy blurted out.

"Shh." Delie gathered the children close to her, like the good mother she was. Champ did not dare take his eyes off of the gun end, though.

"Needs us some gas to get on to Raleigh. Don't want to stay. Gotta get these kids on to a new home up North. Got cash money to pay."

Good thing he had been training or his arms might have started hurting him. Walking toward the gun, he held out the money. "You can even count it first, if you need to, sir."

A short white man with wispy hair in pants and a plaid shirt came out wielding his shotgun. "Don't want no trouble."

"Not looking for any, sir. Just want to buy some gas so we be on our way."

"Put the money on the table in there." The man directed him. "I'm counting it first."

Champ really didn't want to do that, but he had no choice with the shotgun on him. He put the money on top of a rickety looking wooden desk. A thin woman with a set mouth holding an older baby stared at him with wide eyes. The older baby had on nothing but a diaper in February. Even with this poor hello, his heart ached at the sight. "How do, ma'am." These people would be glad to get this cash money.

The little man came in and put the gun next to him, counting the crumpled up paper, coins and pennies. "Going up North, you say?"

"Yes sir. A little orphanage. Wondering if the children could use the facilities."

The man was about to open his mouth, and what would he say? But the woman in the housedress spoke first. "Got woods out back."

"They'll be fine with that. Thank you. Okay to start filling up, sir?"

The man's hand didn't go to his gun. "Go on ahead. Use the first one there."

"Thank you kindly."

Champ backed away to the pumps. No way was he turning his back on that gun. "Take them on into the woods back there."

A protest formed on Delie's lips, but as Delie and Em rounded up the children, the gun glimmered in the fading daylight. Quickly, they went in the direction Champ pointed in. Delie did not look happy, the sight of the woman in the ragged housedress holding the half-dressed child in the window of the gas station stopped her. The small container of bathroom paper went behind her small purse. He was glad she had the good sense to see how much better they had it than these poor ones. The gas glugged and chugged into the bus. The noxious scent rose into the air as he prayed. *Help these ones, Lord. They in a mighty need.*

One by one, the children came from the wooded area with their needs satisfied and climbed back up on the bus. They were more quiet than usual and Champ was pleased they could understand the situation they were in. He purposely took the pump out of the hole sooner than he was supposed to. There was gas enough to get them to

Raleigh where they could fill up in the Black neighborhood at their stop for the night.

"Thank you kindly, sir." Champ waved to the morose family, and as quick as he could, got up into the driver's seat of the bus, got it started and continued down the bumpy country road.

No one said anything for a long time, but as Champ took the wheel, Delie's small hand rested on his shoulder and squeezed him. For a second. The warmth of her hand spread through him and he couldn't tell it was February at all. More like a summer's day.

Night travel was out of the question for him. He didn't see as well in the fading daylight and darkness. The winter made for a very early evening, so when he crossed the border into North Carolina, he drove straight through the center of the state to Raleigh with no stops and made it, thankfully.

The tobacco city had been a good place for boxing at one time, and there was a nice community that supported him. He would never forget, and he knew they would be glad to see him. He turned onto a city street and pulled into a parking lot next to a church. "Wait here, you all."

He hopped off of the bus and went to a simple built wooden manse next to the church, knocking on the door. A young man he didn't know answered the door. "Yes?"

"I'm looking for Miss Irene. She the wife of the pastor here."

"Ah, I'm sorry to report Pastor Jenkins died last year and Miss Irene moved. I'm the Pastor now, Pastor Brown."

Champ shook his hand. "I am mighty sorry to hear it. Very sorry, indeed. Pastor Jenkins was a good man. Do you know where she moved?"

"She's just down the street. In a little apartment."

"If you give me the address, I'll be on my way."

Pastor Brown looked over his shoulder. "That your bus?"

"Sure enough. I'm taking some children up North and we need a place to stay tonight."

"Oh. They moving, huh?"

"From Georgia. This our first night. Miss Irene took care of me a few years back when I was in a bad way. Thought I could get her to help."

Pastor Brown smiled. "Yes, she's like that. But I'll be glad to open the church to you. If the children can make up beds with blankets and pillows."

"We got ours. Great."

Pastor Brown reached behind the door and grabbed for a hat and coat. "I'll open the church to you first, then I can get Sister Irene. I know the children must be cold and hungry."

"They are. Thank you for your help."

Pastor Brown walked out to the bus with him. He opened the small church with a key.

Champ stepped up on the bus and addressed the noisy children. "Bring y'alls blankets and pillows. We stay here tonight. On the pews."

"Is there anything to eat?" Neal asked.

"We'll see. Let's get into the church first and get warm. It's mighty cold."

Delie's large eyes fixed themselves on him.

"What's the matter?" Champ asked. "This is the best we can do tonight."

"It's just what Mama and Daddy used to do. Take in travelers because they were not welcome anywhere else in Winslow."

Champ remembered. "Yes, Miss Irene did too."

"Is she young and pretty?"

"What?" Champ started at Delie's question as an embarrassed feeling caused his blood to rise. "Girl, come on and get these children off the bus."

The children got off of the bus clinging to thick quilts and a pillow. Champ helped Em off, who was clinging to her own bedding. Delie got off without saying anything to him. She came face to face with a middle-aged woman with a round stomach and a handsome young man who had be Pastor Brown.

"Champ Bates, you scamp. What you doing back in my town?" Miss Irene boomed out.

Champ embraced her in a hug. "I told you I would be back one day. I couldn't stay away."

"It is good to see you, boy. Who is this beautiful creature?"

"This is Delie, ma'am."

"This here is Cordelia May?" Miss Irene enveloped Delie in a hug and Champ shook his head, smiling. Miss Irene loved everybody.

"Hello," Delie said from a muffled shoulder.

"This here is Pastor Brown."

"He the new Pastor here. My man died last year."

"I was so sorry to hear," Champ squeezed her shoulder.

"Thank you. All he want to know, Champ, is did you get the fight? My man died wanting to know."

"I got it." Champ's blood surged inside as Miss Irene squeezed him one more time. Always good to feel support and love. He hoped Delie would show him some. And soon. "I know I caught you unawares, but if you ain't got any chicken, we'll take whatever you got."

"We making some sandwiches now. Get you a nice hot breakfast in the morning."

"Well, I tell you more when we got some food in us."

Miss Irene clasped her hands together. "Good. I be waiting to hear. Champ's a great fighter. He's a warrior for the Lord. Come on, honey."

Miss Irene drew Delie away and Champ shut the bus door. What would Delie have to say about this North Carolina friend of his?

"I told him to go on back and get you. I said to Champ, you ain't never going to be happy less you go back to her and explain. That's the way God was leading him. And helping him to build up his purse and talents to be ready for the big fight."

Never, in all of her imaginings of the fun Champ was having out in the world, did Delie imagine the short, squat maroon-colored woman who was before her. Miss Irene grasped onto Delie with warm, moist hands and kept squeezing her arm.

Irene stopped walking with Delie and reached up and put her hands on her shoulders. In the bosom of her family, Delie was considered short, but this woman was much shorter than her. Miss Irene was reaching up. "You just the one too. I can see it. You gone help him be ready."

"Me?" Delie wasn't confused. She just sounded puzzled. Her mind was blown away at the thought of Champ going to church and spending time in Raleigh with this type of woman.

"You, daughter. He is the one who going to lead the way for our people. He's John the Baptist."

Delie blinked. "Champ? John the Baptist?"

"I know you come from good Christians. You know who the Baptist was?"

"Yes, ma'am. I just never thought of Champ that way."

"And why not?" Now, Miss Irene seemed insulted.

"He's Champ. I know he got a good boxing arm but I never…"

"Good? Oh no, honey, he ready for the big fight. Fighting a white man? So they can see what we are as a people. That we are people. First time I saw Champ Bates in the ring, I knew him for what he was. He going to be something. I'm hoping you ready for it all."

"Yes, ma'am."

Irene opened the door to the church sanctuary with a confident arm and let Delie go. The little church was quite fancy inside, much better looking than First Water. Folks stayed inside First Water all of the time. One time, Mags and Asa sought shelter there when the lynch mob was after them. But, Delie couldn't imagine staying here. This church even had red velvet stuffed cushions. Delie started to protest when Miss Irene exclaimed. "Looka here! These lambs of Jesus want feeding, don't you?"

"Yes, ma'am." Willie intoned and Miss Irene went right over and squeezed him on the arm. Hard. Delie could tell from his closed eyes. But, she had raised him right. He didn't say anything.

"Oh, praise Him, there ain't nothing I love more than a hungry boy child. Reach up into this here basket, children, and help yourself. Get them cups out and pass them around and have some milk. Help you all to grow up big and strong."

Delie had gone to Bonnie and lifted her onto her lap, but Bonnie went gratefully from her hold to Miss Irene's magic basket.

"Thank you so much. I don't know what to say." Delie showed her manners as well as Willie did.

Miss Irene's eyes, reddened with age, but still alive with spark and brightness lit upon hers. "Say you going to support Champion. He need you. He going to need all of you. I'm so happy to see these children here." Miss Irene squeezed Neal next. Neal looked happy to be squeezed hard, even though there wasn't much meat on his little arm.

"I would have thought a bunch of children would have just been in his way." Delie said in a light tone, even though she was talking about some serious stuff.

"Oh no, lamb. Ain't no better thing than a gift from God to make a man fight. And Champ's fight isn't just for him. It's for us all."

Miss Irene's words were, frankly, spooking her. Champ was her childhood buddy. He had a special gift. And he had chose to privilege it over her. End of story.

"Yes, ma'am." The lessons John and Lona put into their baby girl, reinforced by four older sisters, ran too deep to be denied.

Miss Irene shook her head and held out a cookie to Neal. He took a big bite and chewed on it, wiping wet crumbs from his mouth with the back of his hand. "I seen Champ, first time in the ring. My man, he was a boxer too. Afore he was a preacher. Made me know boxing real, real well. When they get desperate, I'll judge."

"They let women judge a fight?" Delie marveled. Neal slid away from Miss Irene with his cookie and brought a wrapped sandwich to Delie with a china cup of milk. Delie unwrapped the paper from the sandwich and bit into it. A nice, thick ham sandwich. She had not had ham for a long, long time. The sandwich was delicious, spread with a spicy mustard.

"I said they had to be desperate, didn't I?" Miss Irene gave another sandwich to Em, who smiled and thanked her. "But they knew, still do round these parts. I'm of God. I wasn't going to lie about anything. I would count them points as they need to be counted. I got an eye. And I tell you, Champ is the best natural fighter I ever seen."

"Why thank you, Miss lady." Champ came next to Miss Irene and squeezed her. She squeezed him back.

"Never mind. Last thing you need is flattery clouding up your head. Did you eat? Been having beefsteak? You ain't been building up, have you? Grab a sandwich on out the basket." Miss Irene looked heavenward. "Lord, I have a mighty work to do on this here scamp. Help me to do it."

Champ reached in and palmed a sandwich. Delie watched the whole thing disappear into his body in a terrible fast way. He palmed another. "No milk." Miss Irene's tone was stern. "I got some peptic water for you to drink."

"May I have some?" Neal asked. How would he know what peptic water was? That boy just wanted to mime Champ. Clearly if Champ was having some, that was good enough for him.

"It's time for you to go to bed, Neal." Delie jumped in. "Please thank Miss Irene for the good food."

Miss Irene looked from Neal to Delie. "Is he yours?"

"They all are, ma'am." Delie always took exception to the question.

"You know what I am talking about, girl."

"Yes ma'am. Yes, he is." Delie was instantly contrite. This woman meant no harm.

"Look just like his mama. How old are you baby?"

"Six." Neal took another swig of milk.

"Hmph." Miss Irene said. Nothing more. Miss Irene's single utterance condemned her. In one single word, Delie was as exposed as if she were in her teddy. Outdoors. In February. Every hair on her body stood up and tingled.

Miss Irene could do math. She knew.

"I'll be seven next month."

"Okay, Neal. Miss Irene is busy now."

"I ain't busy. And he look just like you, too," Miss Irene said to Champ.

Champ choked on his second sandwich. Delie slid her glance away from watching him work on his ham sandwich. "What you say?"

"I'm saying this precious lamb look just like his mama. He a pretty boy child with those long lashes, bless him." Miss Irene squeezed Neal again. He was into the swing of things this time and squeezed back on Miss Irene's plentiful arm meat. "Got others, girl?"

"I got the rest from my school."

"Yes, I see. Sometimes God gives us an unexpected gift. Bet you never thought you be a mama, did you?"

How did she know? "You right. My sister helps me a lot though."

"I can see it. She's a wonder too. God gives us some things and not others, but your sister, she going to have her own life. She a pretty lady too."

"Thank you, ma'am." Em wiped her lips.

"I've been charged with her care, ma'am." Delie explained, trying to see if the insightful Miss Irene understood about Em. She didn't like to speak about her sister's limitations in front of her though.

With a wave of her hand, Miss Irene poo pooed the notion. "Your sister is a grown up lady. Older than you, right? Champ told me you was the baby."

Hardly. "Yes, ma'am."

"Then she got her own life to live. She might find it in Pittsburgh. A good time to go to find opportunity."

Delie began to feel a little defensive. "My sisters will help us when we get there, but Em will end up living with one of us."

"So you say, but not you. You got work to do."

"Yes, taking care of these children."

"And Champ. He going to need you."

Exposed, all nerves and heart on her sleeve. Who was this stranger who could see into her heart and her needs? "He didn't need me before when he left town."

"It don't change what he needs now."

"Delie, that wasn't true."

Suddenly, she wanted some fresh air. "Wasn't it? So why did you leave then?"

Champ stared down at the half-eaten sandwich in his hand. He quietly wrapped it back up in paper. "I had to go. I had to see what I could for myself."

"Without me?"

"If I had a brought you, youda been part of all of the pain and discomfort I had to get somewhere. Sleeping in train cars, traveling all the time on the road, even with other hobos, fighting here and there to make money. I knew I was going to have to do those things. I didn't want you around."

"And all I wanted was you. The whole time."

"Me too. You think I didn't?"

"No. You never sent anything, not a telegram, not a Christmas present nothing." Delie pressed him.

She would not cry.

She would not cry. As much as she thought it away, the sharp pain behind her eyes still came and settled in for the long haul.

"I had nothing, baby. Nothing." Champ spread his arms. "And, I sent you"

"Well, that's nice to know now. Excuse me." Delie wrapped herself into her gray fox coat and stepped out into the cold February air.

Yes, here come the waterworks.. It was better to be out here, crying. She didn't want the children to see her being weak.

Champ came behind her, stood there, and touched her. *Why, God?* She shrugged her shoulders away from him. But his hold, oh God, his hold on her was firm and sure.

"Please don't touch me." She wanted the words to come out strong and they didn't.

"Delie, I'm sorry. Please forgive me."

"No." The freeze in her heart was still there, still strong. As she said the small word, it was big and the bigness of the small word spread strength throughout her body. It reinforced her, even as her voice quivered.

"I never stopped loving you."

"I don't want to hear this. Please. All you have to do is drive this bus, and I didn't even ask you to do that."

"I wanted to. I want to help you."

"All I want is to get to my family. The people who really love me. Even when I was low and desperate and alone and pregnant with a baby I didn't want. You're not my family. So, I don't want you to say those words to me any more."

"Baby, please, just listen."

"I said no. No more. If you say that to me again, I just won't speak to you any more on this trip. Better yet. You can stay here in Raleigh where they love you so much and I'll drive the bus."

"You don't know how to drive no bus."

"I'll learn if I have to. Just so you don't say it to me."

The silence between them was eternal.

He took his large warm hands off of her shoulders, and the cold night air wrapped around her like a blanket. "For God so loved the world He gave His only begotten Son."

"He did. And I'm giving mine the chance to make sure he grows up healthy and strong. We don't need you, Champ. We'll be fine."

The sound of his footsteps walking away from her was a blessed, sweet relief. She sagged. She didn't want to be strong in front of him anymore and to act as if she didn't care. Because she did. She cared very, very much. Too much.

Be strong for the children. She had nothing else for Champ, no matter what strange Miss Irene said. She knew her mind and heart. *Believe in yourself.* Not in some bible-quoting boxer who ran out when things got tough and inconvenient. *I feel better now.*

She waited for a good warm feeling to hold her up and give her more strength.

It didn't come.

Caring had come into her heart and made her weak and vulnerable again.

CHAPTER TEN

The silence in the church cast an eerie glow about the room as they all tried to sleep, but the tension between Champ and Delie caused unrest among them.

In the strange stillness of the church, Bonnie barked. Or was that a cough? Champ turned over half asleep. Before he could even fully register what happened, Delie was up off of her pew like a shot out of a cannon. In the medium darkness, Delie wore a thin nightgown over some overall pants. Her nightgown needed to be thicker in this cold. He would make sure to get her a nice flannel one, when he won the fight.

"She's a little warm." Delie fretted. Champ stood instantly and pulled his overcoat on over his clothes. "What are you doing?"

"I'ma go for a doctor."

"Sit back down and get your rest. You need to rest to be able to drive the bus in the morning. Children get colds sometimes."

"I'm doing what I said." Champ sat back down as she said, because his knees went weak at thinking the child needed medical care. "The something I can do is get a doctor. This is Raleigh's best Black neighborhood. There are doctors. Bonnie doesn't have to suffer like in Winslow."

The light shifted in Delie's pretty face and Champ's rushed breath matched a sharp pain as an Irene-like grip surrounded his heart. Poor Delie. She had been living in the shadow of fear all of this time. "All right."

The release on him when he was able to get out of the church, away in the thin morning air, like the first punch, was a relief. He was the reason for Bonnie's cough. The bus was not warm enough for the children and he needed to do something about it. It was a problem that could worsen as they went further north. He determined to ask Irene about it in the morning at breakfast. He didn't want to take up too much of the time and boarding space at Living Well Christian Church, but clearly, one of the children was in need.

As he remembered, a doctor's sign hung outside of a small yellow clapboard house just two blocks away. He knocked on the door. Almost instantly, a graying gentleman turned on a light inside and came with him back to the church. When he returned, the lights were up and Delie embraced the small girl as her head lay on Delie's shoulder. What a caring mother. He always wondered why, when they were growing up, she had professed to never want to take on the role. He would have to ask her sometime, when she would talk to him again.

"Thank you." Delie said to him as she stood next to the pew where Bonnie now lay.

After the examination, the doctor packed up and turned toward them. "The church is warm, but if she's been on a cold bus all day, she may have caught a chill. Better to stay a day if you can to ward it off in the other children than to move on."

"Of course," The words came rapidly to his lips. Anything for Bonnie. And Delie.

"We don't want to hold you up from your training." Delie's response spoke to the concerns of her heart, he could tell.

"Dee, it's done. We can stay another day. Miss Irene will be glad to have us."

And he was right. When Miss Irene came to the church basement and cooked up big pots of coffee, with juice, eggs and side pork with hot biscuits, she was very happy. The shadow appeared on Miss Irene's red-boned features when she scolded him. "We can get these children something to do down here in the Sunday school room, but you need to be training. Got a steak?"

"No, ma'am."

"I'll bring it and Delie can fry it for you."

Em hooted and Champ smiled in companionship at Em's outburst.

"What'd I say?" Miss Irene looked around in confusion.

"I'm not the best cook, ma'am." Delie volunteered.

"Nonsense. Who else is going to fry Champ's steaks for his training? You done lost valuable time already. No sir. Your lovely sister can take care of the babies and this morning, I'ma show you how to prepare a steak for Champion. You got to learn."

Clearly, Delie looked as if the last thing she wanted to do was fix Champion's steaks.

"I can do it, Dee, if you want." Em offered up. Her sister's sweet countenance showed how willing she was to sacrifice for Delie.

"No, Em. I need to learn. I'll do it this time."

"Good. I want my steak to have a sweet taste." Champ tossed off. If looks could kill, he would have been slain and buried right here in North Carolina. Not a state he had thought to spend his end moments.

"She'll do a great job. I'm gonna help her." Miss Irene insisted.

"Thank you, ma'am. I need all the help I can get when it comes to cooking."

"And Champ, I don't want you hanging around here this morning. Go on down to the gym. They gonna help you out. Come on back for a lunch you won't forget."

"It's the God's honest truth." Champ said with a heavy tone and Neal and Flo giggled. His stomach reeled a bit at Bonnie's sad face as she poked at her eggs. He vowed to get her something special while he was out.

Delie never minded shopping— too much. Miss Irene had grabbed her by the arm as they made their way down to a mercantile run by a Negro man. Raleigh was a wonder, an entire Negro community doing well for themselves. She had not seen such a sight since college, where such a sight was not unknown in Atlanta's West End neighborhood. When they reached the mercantile, the store was nearly empty. Fortunately, a cow had just been butchered and the grocer cut up several steaks.

Delie held out a hand. "We don't need so many."

Miss Irene stayed her hand by squeezing it. "Don't be foolish, child. The children'll need some building up too. Maybe that's why the baby was sick. Babies can't live on beans."

Embarrassment came to Delie's cheeks in the form of a slight warm redness. How did Miss Irene know what the children had been eating? Or not? Miss Irene squeezed her arm as the steaks were butchered with the thudding sound of the cleaver hitting the chopping block. It rang on throughout the store. "I know what it is like to feed babies. It's good of you to take them on."

"They had been abandoned once in their lives. I couldn't do it again. God had it in my heart to take them, even though I never thought I could."

"Is Neal Champion's boy?"

At Miss Irene's question, the air went whooshing out of Delie's lungs. "Well, ma'am. Goodness."

"Anyone with a set of good eyes can look at Neal and see he's a Bates. Champ ain't claimed him yet, has he?"

"Claimed him?"

"Put his name on him. Is Neal a Bates?"

"No. No. He's Neal Bledsoe. John Neal Bledsoe. We called him by his middle name to make him different from my Daddy. When he was living."

"Well, I don't know what Champ is waiting for." All of a sudden, the affable Miss Irene was all ruffled up. Even the butcher man was startled. "I'ma have a word with him. You ain't said nothing to him have you?"

She couldn't help it. Tears welled up in her eyes, "No ma'am. When Champ left, I didn't even know I was going to have a baby. The one time we were together. The night before he left—before we was supposed to leave on the train. Only once…" Delie broke from Miss Irene's grip, remembering the sweetness of the one time. Her only time to have been with a man and Neal came from it.

"Why ain't you told him yet, honey?" Miss Irene's regard was deadly quiet now. Delie nearly preferred her to be all ruffled up.

"He left me, Miss Irene. I was there. I was the one had to have a sick baby by myself."

"Is this sweet baby sick?"

"It's one of the reasons we moving. He's got a weak heart. There would be better care for Neal up there. Better education. Just some better."

"Why don't Champ know about his boy being sick?"

"You never met Effie Bates before. She has convinced Champ Neal couldn't be his. There's a whole thing about Bates men and how strong they are. So, Champ doesn't look at Neal and claim him. To me, Neal looks just like Champ did when we first started running around Winslow together as children."

"I don't care 'bout his mama. You're his woman. Neal is his child. You got to stand up for this family you done made."

"And unmade. Miss Irene, if Champ wanted us, wanted me, would he have left me to wait at the train station, all night long, not knowing he had already left? He wanted his boxing talent you keep talking about more."

"And he's fighting. He came back and he's fighting for his family now. It's a different thing."

Delie patted Miss Irene's moist hand. "I don't know about that."

"He love you? Did he say it?"

Delie nodded. She really preferred not to think about their confrontation last night, because then she had to make the next move. And she was not up to it.

"And you love him?"

Was that why her pain was so fresh? She loved Champ? Yes. Yes. She knew she did. It was funny. It had been a long time since she had one of those screaming dreams when she was yelling at him. She had all the opportunity now to yell at him and be bitter. "I have to keep on for my children. I can't worry about him."

"And you can get a Daddy for them. There ain't any better than Champ. Look, honey, he was young. He made a mistake. What about forgiveness? God tells us we got to forgive."

"But not forget, Ma'am. I'll never be left behind in a train station again. Not knowing. I can't do it to myself again. And survive."

Miss Irene accepted the wrapped packages of steaks and went to pay for them. Delie, wiping at her eyes, tried to stop her from paying for it, but Miss Irene had already shoved some well-thumbed coins and wrinkled paper money at the cashier. "We going back and make him a good lunch. And I'm going to pray on this. We gone lift this up to God."

"Welcome to my life, ma'am. I've been lifting this up for years."

"Maybe that's why Champ came back, honey. Don't leave him twisting out there for long. He need you."

"Maybe." Delie said and picked up the steaks from the counter. One corner of the brown paper showed a little seepage of fresh red blood.

A bleeding center. A complete reflection of where she was just now.

Champ smelled a hot searing smell of beef as he entered the church's basement from the side door. *Whew, praise God.* There wasn't anything like pure seared meat. The Swiss steak at the school was wonderful, but it was all covered in gravy and broken down. Just the pure basics of beef were a wonder. And a thrill.

"Champion. Get on in here."

Champion followed Miss Irene's voice and Delie was in there with a long pronged fork, turning over the steak meat.

"I can't eat all of that!" Champ protested at the unexpected, but stirring sight of Delie frying up his steaks. She did care.

"Some is for the babies, Champion. Some is for you. You better eat it too. How did the four and twenties go?"

"Just fine."

"I'ma leave here after lunch and ask after you down to the gym. You better be telling me the truth, boy."

"I am, ma'am."

"Delie doing a fine job here of frying up these steaks."

"How in the world did it happen?" Champ tried to lean on the doorjamb, just to see the tension go from Delie's face. It didn't work though. She didn't smile at his poor attempt at humor. And he couldn't blame her. Not one little bit.

"She cooking with love and care and attention. It's amazing what a woman can do with a little care in her cooking." Miss Irene intoned a bit of wisdom, just as if she were quoting the Bible.

Delie was beautiful and stirred him, as always. The heat from the stove made little beads of sweat rise on Delie's skin. Strands of her jet-black hair escaped her bun and wired all around her beautiful face, shaped like a perfect heart.

"I can do things too, Champ." Delie blew the hair out of her face in a certain way which made her pursed lips look very attractive and dangerously kissable.

"I never said you couldn't, Dee. No, No." Champ held up his hands and started to walk away. Never let it be said Miss Irene could not do a miracle.

"You go on and get the children for lunch. They need a hot lunch to warm them up."

"And please check on Bonnie," Delie shouted after him.

He didn't feel chastised. He had a purpose and a stride to his step. There were some rooms in the back where there was a lot of shouting going on. Sure enough, the children were in there being generally unruly. "What's going on in here?"

Em gave a weak smile at him. Champ put a hand on her shoulder. "Discipline not your strong suit, Em?"

"They just having a good time."

"And what about little precious over here?" All of the chairs in the crowded, but warm Sunday school room were small. Champ did not want to smash any of them by settling his muscular bulk on one. They were, however, the perfect size for small Bonnie. She sat on one sucking her thumb. Champ went over and picked her up. She was not as warm as she was in the night. *Thank you, God. Please see to the health and welfare of these children.*

"How you feeling, baby girl?"

"I want to go home, Champ." Bonnie fretted and laid her small braided head on his shoulder. There was an ache in his chest at her plaintive words.

"You all help Miss Emerald clean up in here and go on to lunch. Delie done made us a good hot lunch."

The children were instantly silent. "Don't rush cleaning up, you all." Neal whispered to Willie and Flo. They all snickered as they took their good old time cleaning up pencils, crayons, and papers.

"Listen up, we going to eat every bite. Folks are having hard times and we are glad to get a good hot meal. No wasting the church's money and time, hear?" Champ spoke in a stern voice, but gave Neal a wink.

Neal nodded his head. The other children did likewise. He was clearly the ringleader and Champ had a thrill of pride shoot through him.

Bates men were always leaders in things. Maybe Neal was his after all. But, as soon as the thought occurred to him, there was pain.

Pain at what he had missed in this boy's life. He smoothed down Bonnie's braids with his free hand. "You all clean up this room and your plates good enough and you can come down to the gym after lunch and watch me train."

Neal's hazel eyes brightened up at the prospect and they worked a little more efficiently at cleaning up.

"You get the other ones, Em. I'ma see what I can get this little precious here."

He cradled Bonnie in his arms as he went into the large dining room where Delie was setting the table for lunch. She stopped what she was doing and came over to them. Champ sat in an adult-sized chair and Bonnie settled into his chest. "She still feel warm."

"But she getting better." Delie's voice lightened. Her tone made him happy and his palms were dry again. "You need to eat some of this here lunch to build you up, Miss Bonnie."

"I just want to lay here on Champ. He's soft."

"I'm sure he's not wanting to hear that right about now." Delie snickered a little bit and Champ smiled up at her. The smile went away behind the clouds again, but he had gotten her to open up a bit. Praise God.

Miss Irene bustled in with the platter of steaks and peered at Bonnie. "How's that lamb doing?"

"She getting better." Champ couldn't restrain a chuckle at Bonnie's assertion of him as soft. Maybe he needed to be at the gym some more.

"Let her go, Champ. She'll be okay." Delie reached for her. Bonnie shrank back and snuggled more into Champ.

Champ's heart ripped in two at Delie's disappointed face and Bonnie's need to snuggle into him more. "Let her stay here a little longer, Dee."

"Your steak is going to get cold."

"If it do, I put it back in the skillet."

"You just don't want to eat it."

Champ reached out a free hand, grabbed at one of Delie's and pulled her to sit in the chair next to him. God, it had only been a few days, but seemed a long time since he had palmed her warm softness into his hand. Now, her hand carried more strength, more steel, more toughness, more of everything Delie was.

And when she sat down next to him, he laced his fingers through hers and didn't want to let her go. To his surprise, she didn't let go of his hand either. "I told you, Dee, I'm going to eat my steaks." He put a special emphasis on the s. "Bonnie wants to nap a little. I'll put her down on those soft cushions over here." He tilted his head to the stage area where there were some pillows stacked up.

"We all going to eat our steaks and then there be a special treat after lunch." Champ inclined his head to the children who were trudging in to the lunch table.

"Yes, Mama. We are." Neal said with too much enthusiasm.

Dee's pretty face glanced around for answers, but Champ put a finger to his lips and then to hers. He did not move. Neither did she. Delie's lips were always soft. Under his finger, they were softer than they used to be. The only thing preventing him from reaching down and tasting her were the children running around, watching their every move. Dee's lips moved under his finger, "She asleep now. Put her down."

Champ stood and carried Bonnie's little body in his arms to the little pseudo stage in the church corner basement and laid her down on the cushions. As he did, the love and goodness in this child surrounded him.

God, let me have the strength of a man to do what is right for this child, for all of these children. They deserved better. Standing up from putting Bonnie down, he realized Neal had been abandoned too. He had abandoned Neal. He had not known about him, but the end result was the same. He turned. Delie was still sitting there in the chair away from the table. What had he done to her? Could she ever forgive him? He had to start and be the one to forgive her. He reached out his hand again to her. "Lead me to the steaks, my lady."

She laced her long delicate fingers through his and stood. "You better eat it, Champ."

"I will, honey. Every bite." But the warmth of Delie's hand laced through his was nourishment in and of itself. He had to do more for her, enough for her to be convinced he meant what he had said.

Now, he understood. The hard work was not just going to be defeating the white fighter but repairing his family.

CHAPTER ELEVEN

The touch of Champ's hand on hers, something she used to take for granted, made emotion kept hidden so long explode inside of her chest. She was once again a child in Winslow watching the fireworks on Independence Day. How did he, how could he touch her in that way?

She had only touched children for so many years. Champ's touch, a man's touch now, was new to her and had not happened in so long.

Too long.

Oh, she was attractive. Any number of men who lived in Winslow would have taken her out to a juke joint, gave her some corn liquor and had a wild night.

But no.

She had held off. She had waited and sacrificed for this moment. The moment in the bank when Champ touched her and it was as if all the past had not happened. The heat and the intensity between them was the same. There was only one difference, though.

Now, she knew what it was like to get burned. Burns caused lasting damage, scars and pain. Burns still stung whenever you touched them. And she was different. She couldn't enjoy his touch without remembering the sting of the burn.

"This steak is delicious." Champ chewed thoughtfully. No other child had touched their steak until he had. "This ain't like no Tramp steak either. This is good."

Delie smiled at Champ's good memory. Growing up, they both liked Charlie Chaplin. They were always dragging Em to the picture show when they were trying to be alone. Em ate her steak and smiled too.

"It's mighty good, sister."

"Thank you. Children?"

They dug in as if they hadn't eaten in months, and they hadn't. Well, steak that is. "This is great, Mama." Neal chirped. As usual, all the other children chimed in behind Neal, the natural leader of the children. Delie looked over her shoulder on the stage cushions to see Bonnie sleeping peacefully, with a little trail of shiny drool on the side of her cheek. She looked adorable.

"Well, thank you. And thank you, Miss Irene, for showing me."

"I ain't had no problem with it. It's the first and last time I'ma make steak for Champion. Now, you got a woman who will make your steaks."

"Yes, ma'am." Champ said and bowed his head to the task of finishing. Now, he was embarrassed.

Well, she wasn't. He was thinking of Effie and she knew it.

"That's a nice notion," Delie cut into her own steak, which was fork tender and perfectly savory in her mouth. She chewed, swallowed and spoke. "But Champ is only taking us up to Pittsburgh this week. He's going back to Winslow to train."

"He what?" The tone in Miss Irene's voice of complete surprise and shock said she had not known. Ha Ha.

"He's going back to his mother. She'll be frying his steaks this time next week, most like." Delie continued eating her steak as if butter wouldn't melt in her mouth.

And it wouldn't.

"Champ, why're you going back to that one horse town? It ain't for you anymore. I've been telling you."

"My mama need me."

"She don't need you. If she in such need, tell her to move her behind up to where you be in the north. You ain't never going to make inroads as a fighter lessen you stay up there where all the action is." Miss Irene folded her hands over her big paunchy stomach and tsked. "A man who don't know his place in the world is a mighty sad thing."

"I'm knowing, Miss Irene." Champ did not look up as he ate his steak and speared another.

"I hope so. That baby feels better today. You need to get yourselves on the bus and get on out of the South as fast as you can."

"We leaving in the morning, Miss Irene. Don't worry."

"Good. Delie will take care of the baby. And you. Get your self on. If you can, take them babies to see Washington, D.C. They needs to know they have a place as Americans in this world."

Delie wanted to say something about going there. As a teacher, she knew what a learning moment it would be for the children, but she really didn't feel as if she could hold Champ up any longer. He just had to get back to Effie.

"It's an idea." Champ reached for a third steak on the platter and grinned at Delie.

She would not oblige him by grinning back. Maybe he did need to think about breaking away from Effie. Increasingly, she was coming to understand the way Effie had controlled the flow of information to her from Champ. His trust in his own mother was misplaced. When would Champ grow up and begin to realize the truth for himself?

"This is mighty, mighty tasty."

"Thank you." Delie sliced a bit of potato like the lady she was.

"I'm taking the kids down to the gym after we done eating here. You want to come?"

She looked over at Bonnie who was sleeping. "I don't know."

Miss Irene waved her hands. "I'll stay here with the sick lamb. Don't worry. Go on now."

"I can stay with her too, Delie. I had the kids this morning, you all take them this afternoon." Em said. She did not like the look on her sister's face. She never minded having the children. This sudden development in her independent sensibility reflected something new for Em. No, Delie did not like it at all.

"Fine. We'll take you on down there to train and we'll come right back."

"That's not what I was thinking. We can get the kids to run around a bit. Play. Have a gym class. It'll be fun for them." Champ stopped to wave his fork in the air before he continued.

"Yeah, that sounds like fun!" Neal shouted and the rest of them echoed him.

The notion of Neal in particular running around did not sit too well with her, but they should have some time off the bus to play and run around. "I guess."

"There was a time, Delie, when you liked to run around and play." Champ speared more of his steak. "I remember."

"It was a long time ago. When I was a little girl."

"Wasn't no little girl. You was a little boy."

"How could Mama have been a little boy?" Neal's face twisted into a mask of confusion.

"I didn't discover she was a girl until I had known her about five years or so. One day, all the dirt got knocked off of her and there she was." Champ put down his fork and knife and made gestures around his body to show Delie's developing shape.

The children laughed and laughed. Miss Irene cackled and Em laughed a little bit herself.

"Hush on up, you all. You'll wake the baby." Miss Irene put a finger to her lips, but she clearly got at kick at smiling at Champ. Her scamp. Ugh.

"Champ is right. Delie liked Georgia red clay back then, sure enough. Even more after she met Champ. They both ran around dirty. You couldn't hardly tell one from the other," Em echoed.

Neal regained his confused face. "Did Mama have long hair?"

"When she was little she did. Then, when she got a liking for the dirt, her hair didn't grow out for a long time. Delie was the baby and Mama got tired of trying to put pigtails on her. Ruby was gone. Mags was working in the mill, and Nettie was sick. I wasn't much older than her. I couldn't keep her in pigtails. Mama say, cut them off. She'll be wanting them back one day."

Delie remembered. And when she realized Champ was a boy and she was a girl, oh, it seemed her hair wouldn't grow fast enough, long enough.

"Yeah, it was short. For a time, I went around with a big bow on top of my head. That was how folks knew I was a girl."

"I wish I could have seen you then, Mama." Neal's hazel eyes sparkled.

"No, you don't, son. I wasn't nothing to look at."

"Oh, yes you was. You always were." Champ said. He meant to be joking, but Delie knew he meant something else. *Help me to be strong, God.*

"Go on and eat up all of those steaks if you can." Delie tried to appear nonchalant as she took a swig of milk, but it was hard, mighty hard to appear as if she didn't care.

Especially when she did.

He wanted Delie to come to the gym. His boxing had always been a sore spot between them. Did she still hate it like she used to when they were growing up?

Especially if he was thinking about a life with her.

A life with Delie?

The realization hit him as they walked to the gym with the four children ahead of them. Champ feared Neal would trip on the sidewalk or something, because Neal kept looking back over his shoulder at the two of them together. Was he being protective of his mother?

He knew well what that was like. He suspected his protectiveness might have been a reason Effie did not remarry after his father died when he was only a few months old. Clearly, though, from the smile on Neal's face, the boy was glad Champ escorted his mother down the streets of Negrotown in Raleigh. For him, in this moment, Neal's happiness meant Champ's happiness. The children laughed and skipped the three blocks to the gym. When they got there, he opened the door and viewed the gym with Delie's eyes.

The gym was none too clean inside, but there was a cleared area where there were bleachers placed for observations by trainers and others. "Have a seat, Delie. I'ma get these kids busy so I can get on to work."

He set the older boys to jump roping and had Flo help him with the medicine ball. "What about me, Champ?" Neal begged.

"Neal, come on over here and sit with me and watch. You shouldn't run around too much anyway." Delie waved at him.

What for? If Neal was a Bates, he could take it. "Hey, Neal. Come on and hold my feet during the sit-ups. You count. Show me how high you can go with your numbers."

Delie seemed to be satisfied with his activity even though there was still a fearsome look on her face. Why was she so protective of Neal?

Her protectiveness reminded him of his mother. Was Effie the same kind of protective? No. Champ's situation was different. He had no father. But Neal had…no father either. And that drove him hard to do many sit-ups. Neal's counting started falling apart around the 215 mark. "No, Neal, 216 next. Put down the medicine ball, Miss Flo, and come over and help us."

The shy girl did so gladly. Champ noticed her little maternal flourishes, even though Neal seemed a little resentful at the girl's help. "What's wrong, Neal?"

"I don't want her help. She's a girl."

"Hey, hey." Champ stopped the sit-ups. "We all need help sometimes. Your mama always helped me with my schoolwork when we was growing up. I don't think I would have got my diploma if it wasn't for her."

"Really?"

"Yes. She's mighty smart. She helps you all the time, doesn't she? And she's a girl."

"Yeah. Even though she was different when she was little."

Champ patted his head again and marveled at how fast his hair was growing back already. "It was just an expression. She was very much a tomboy. She liked to do boy things. She was my best friend."

"Are you best friends now?" Neal's wide eyes looked just like his mother's. Effie's eyes. He had never realized it until this moment. He had to know, even if Delie didn't speak to him anymore. Even if it wiped away all the progress he had made with her.

"I hope so. I would love to be her best friend."

When Champ looked over at the bleachers after doing all of those sit-ups, there were several other boxers gazing up at Delie who seemed as if they would like to be her friend too.

Okay, that was the last straw.

He needed to confront her about what was between them. It was just a matter of finding a way and the right time to do it.

When they were growing up, whenever Champ boxed in Winslow, it was always outside. He would be stripped to the waist and working so hard at whatever was thrown at him. The fights back in Winslow were all about making Champ suffer, but he never did.

Delie remembered the battle royals. The organizers would just pair all kinds of fighters up with Champ, just to see who he could take on. He was fighting grown men when he was eleven years old and beating them too, that's how good he was. White men came from counties around, even from Alabama and Mississippi to see Champ fight. At the end of the fights, they would rain silver money on him. Delie remembered, with warmth in her face, how he would scramble around to collect every single glint of silver laying in the grass and take the money to a satisfied Effie Bates while Mr. Paul Winslow and the other white men dealt with paper money in the corner.

The directions Champ and the others got were to make it look good. But Champ made every fight look easy. He had a devastating hook and eventually, Delie understood how well he used it. He was smarter than the other fighters.

Champ always made wisecracks about his lack of intelligence whenever she and he worked together on their school lessons. He never prized his education enough. He could have finished high school if he wanted to, but he had that train to catch. It was always his decision, but it made her mad how often he underestimated himself.

Now, watching him fight after so many years, the thin shirt he had on was soaked with perspiration, but the wet shirt clung in a desperate kind of way to every single firm muscle that ridged his toasted tan stomach and chest. The outline of his chocolate colored nipples jutted through the sleeveless shirt and his bulging arms shone in the half lit gym.

Her tongue stuck to the roof of her mouth. She swallowed hard, trying to work up enough saliva to disconnect it. Not a boy's body, where he was like a stick. But a man's. Have mercy.

"And whose doll baby are you?" A deep male voice came from behind where she sat on the bleachers. A tall chocolatey colored man came sliding into the rickety bleachers and sat down. The heavy impact of him sitting there was made clear.

Actually, I'm no one's doll baby. The retort was on the tip of her lips, but Delie knew saying something like that was one of those inappropriate things she was prone to say. "I'm waiting for my boyfriend."

What just came out of her mouth? And why? Because it suited her purposes? Or because it was true? Was she Champ's girlfriend? What were they exactly? She was certainly not his doll baby. How easily the lie had come to her lips, she almost touched them in alarm.

"Of course, of course. A man can appreciate the view, can't he? You just bring a certain kind of light to this foul place, young lady."

"Well, thank you. The gym does have a rather potent odor, doesn't it?" Delie couldn't help but give a little giggle.

"It's all sweat. All men. And all terrible. I highly recommend someone as pretty as you stay out of it. Even to watch your boyfriend work out. Who is he?"

Delie pointed below. "That's him."

The man peered over her shoulder and shrank back just a tiny bit. "Oh yes. Champ. Yeah, he got something special. I sparred with him a bit this morning."

"Something special?"

"He say he getting a fight with a white man up North. So, I help him spar. One of us got to make a way through. Your boyfriend, he got a special talent. So I don't mind him beating up on me a bit to help him get ready."

"Well." Delie folded her hands in her lap. "Isn't that nice?" She wasn't sure what to say.

"Things can get mighty rough with someone like that. You ever change your mind, give Allan a call." The man named Allan extended his hand. Delie could see his long fingers extending toward her, which was all rather fearsome. She hesitated a moment and Neal's little voice sounded in her ear like a clarion call as he sat himself next to her.

"Are you all right, Mama?"

"I'm fine, sweetie. Just passing the time with Mr. Allan here."

"Hey there, little man. He's cute isn't he?" Allan shifted his hand to Neal, but Neal did not shake it. Allan's manner changed in a flash.

"Champ his daddy? I didn't realize he was that kind of boyfriend. Excuse me." Allan stood up and stretched over the bleachers to make his way toward Champ and the practice ring set up for sparring. Willie, Roy and Flo came over and sat by her, as Champ got ready for the sparring. As they did, Delie hid her gaze from Neal's intense one.

"Champ is getting ready to spar. Let's watch him." Delie tried to sound excited and happy.

"Did that man say Champ was my Daddy?"

"I guess so." Delie pulled Neal to her and put an arm around him. Oh God, she didn't want him to have to find out this way.

"Is that true?"

"I guess so." The words were out of Delie's mouth before she could even stop them.

Neal said nothing for a very long time. Her fear rolled around in the pit of her stomach like an aggie marble—the kind they used to play with as children.

Champ moved swiftly around the ring. Allan tried his best to throw punches at him, but just as Champ did in Georgia, he beat Allan up in a methodical and thorough way. The man didn't have the right stuff against Champ. Not many did. Either that, or Champ was extremely motivated today. Delie guessed he had seen her speaking to Allan. Poor Mr. Allan.

"If he my daddy, why wasn't he around?"

"I don't know. He left a long time ago, before you were even born. Before he even knew you were around. He wanted to be a great fighter. And he's beginning to reach his dream."

"More than he wanted a little boy?"

"I told you, he didn't know you were in my belly." Whew. Those little talks she had with Neal rather recently about how babies were born had come in handy.

"You didn't tell him?"

"I couldn't find him." Oh, there were the water works coming again. Delie blinked hard, willing them to go away. Fast. Faster. "I tried to."

"It seems really dumb. Don't any parents stay with their children?"

And Delie could see how he would think that from his perspective. She left when he was born to go to college. Flo, Bonnie, Roy and Willie's parents left them behind. And now he was finding out about Champ. Who had left him unknowingly. "Sometimes, when parents can't pay for a child, they might leave to find a way to support them. It happens."

"I wish parents would stay." His little features were so downcast it brought a pang to Delie's heart.

"I'm not leaving you. Never again."

"And what about Champ?"

"I don't know about him."

"Can you ask him?"

Delie put her arm around her son and pulled him to her. He made it seem so easy. "We'll see, Nealsie. We'll see."

CHAPTER TWELVE

"What are you so quiet about? You had a good session today. Allan helped you out in sparring, pretty well." Delie's pretty voice chirped as they walked the children back to the church in the evening.

Still, her question got on his nerves.

"Allan? It's Allan now? Since when you calling strange men by their first names?"

His question seemed to fluster her. Good.

"That was how he introduced himself to me. I don't know his last name."

"And you should have let someone introduce him to you."

"And who would do it? One of the children? I didn't know anyone else there. Good gracious, remind me never to ask you about why you are quiet."

Most of the children walked on ahead. Neal dragged his heels, and Champ wanted him to walk up this time.

Champ growled, "Go on with the others, now. You don't need to mind grown folks business."

If Neal didn't have a Bates sparkle, that boy was about to say something to him, maybe even sass him a little. Champ was sure of it, but Delie made a gesture with her hand, the delicate, firm hand he recently had the pleasure of holding. Would she let Allan hold it? The thought made the steak she cooked for him swirl in his belly.

Neal walked up and went along next to Willie.

"Is Neal mine?"

He watched her face closely to see if any kind of gesture would betray her. Instead, maddeningly, Delie was as cool as ever. Not even a freckle flinched.

"If you don't know the answer, then anything I say won't matter to you."

"What kind of thing is that to say to a man? I just want to know if the boy is mine or not."

Oops. Now, he got a reaction. Delie's cinnamon toasty skin didn't get red a lot, but it did just then. All the way to the tips of her pretty ears.

"So all of your pretty talk yesterday about loving me was just talk, wasn't it? 'Cause if you loved me, you would love the children. All of the children. And it wouldn't matter if Neal was yours or not. And you would trust whatever I said."

Champ had to admit she had a point there. "I just wanted to hear it from you."

They were within sight of the church and the children went in. Delie stopped her footsteps and faced him with folded arms. Her fighting stance. *Help me, God.*

"What you are saying to me is all of those years we grew up, side by side, you really didn't know me. For all that time."

Why were women so exasperating? "Look, I have prayed on this, and it was on my heart to say to you."

"The nerve. Don't bring God into this. If you're lead by God, He has spoken to your heart and you know the truth from the made up stuff. You know who is telling the truth."

"I just wanted to hear it from you."

Delie was silent. A long quiet moment went by and Champ despaired. It would have been better for her to say something. When she did, he wished she hadn't.

"Do you remember the time we were together?"

Now, it was his turn to be uncomfortable. Did he remember? He had been on a fool's errand ever since, trying to recapture the one time, the one night in the Bledsoe's barn with Delie sneaking out, suitcase in hand, ready to leave her parents and her sister behind. Everything about the moment, the twining of their limbs, the heat they shared, the salty sweat on their bodies, everything had been emblazoned on his memory ever since.

What a shame. What a waste to live one's life in anticipation of reclaiming one special moment. But, in that moment, he would declare, avow and swear he had seen the face of God and had known there was something larger and bigger than himself. A moment of his life and it frightened him beyond all measure. He would rather face Jay Evans or get back in the ring with anyone.

"A little."

Delie huffed. "A little? Is that the best you can come up with, Champ? Do you think I don't know you? I know you." Her sharp fingernail threatened to pierce the thin covering of his work out clothes. "I know it was magic for you too. And in the moment, the one moment we had together, we made magic. If you knew me, you would know I could never be with someone else."

"I've known you since you were nine."

Delie held up her hand and he reacted as she wanted him to, with silence. "Your professions of love mean nothing to me if you cannot love all of these children equally and without reservation. Taking us to Pittsburgh and taking your behind back to Georgia'll better serve you. I don't ever want to see you again."

And she walked away from him.

He couldn't get mad at her. He had angered her. He was a complete heel.

But there was the memory of Allan hovering over and around her. Some unnamed college man from Morehouse, surely one of them had tried to be with her. And whoever it was, his mother said Delie had dated after he left Winslow.

Delie was so beautiful, much more than she knew apparently. She might have found comfort at his leaving in someone else's arms. His mother told him so. He had to believe his mother, didn't he?

Resolute. Stubborn. And strong. She would go on despite him. Without him. And he was driving her straight into the arms of some other, better man. He meant nothing to her. But she was everything to him. How in the world had he gotten himself into this fix…over a woman?

Murder was not permitted in a church, Delie was pretty sure. If she tiptoed over to the bench where Champ slept like a sound log and held one of the church's stuffed cushions over his well-shaped lips, it would do nothing. Champ's arms were so strong and bulky; he would flick away the interruption to his breathing like blowing a fly out of buttermilk.

God would not mind if she undertook some other method to get Champ out of her life and her heart. *You know I have been tortured by this long enough, God. I have not had a good night's sleep in years because of this man. You want me to have my heart and mind free for You, so tell him to get lost.*

It wasn't right. God didn't bargain.

Ok then, help me so I can be free. I need all my time and energy for the children. For Neal. To help him to be strong and healthy. I don't have time for Champ.

You don't have to be alone.

The understanding came to her in a clear clarion call. Delie shook her head. *No, God. You don't understand. I've got Em.*

Miss Irene said Em could have her own life. How would it work? Maybe Em might find her own opportunities when she got to Pittsburgh. She had a gift for sewing and could do hair. She might want her own chance. Was it fair for Delie to hold her sister back because of responsibilities she took on herself?

You don't have to be alone.

I have been alone. All alone. And I'm just supposed to forget that?

You were never alone. God was always with you.

Now, there was the truth. Even during the long, painful delivery with Neal, lying in her sister's bed in her sister's beautiful house, she screamed out to God she would never go through the pain of loving someone again.

The birthing pangs, the terrible pain of it all, was a harsh reminder of the sin she had committed with Champ in the barn. She had taken a decision out of God's hands and made up her own mind and it had gotten her into trouble. The only thing to do was give it back to God, and she did. Delie laid back down on her pew, not wishing to wake anyone else in the silence. God was with her, and she would leave it all in His care. That's how it would be for the entire trip. Then he could go on with his life and so could she.

As they left, Miss Irene squeezed all of them in turn and pinched their cheeks. "I don't want to see you all in Raleigh never more."

"What are you talking about, Miss Irene?"

"You know what I am talking about, Champion Bates. You was mighty welcome here, but now you got to go. You got other fish to fry."

"What's all of this about frying fish? What about my best girl?"

Miss Irene gestured to him and whispered in his ear. She placed a gentle slap on Champ's cheek.

Delie stepped forward. "Thank you for all you done, ma'am."

"I know you come from a good Christian family. Pray. You need to pray about Champ. And, you know I be right here in Raleigh praying for you."

"Thank you."

"And send me a telegram of when the wedding will take place."

Delie laughed and bent over to kiss the woman's sweaty cheek. "Love to you, Miss Irene." And she got on the bus. Champ looked over his shoulder at her to get the signal to leave, but Delie wasn't saying a word to him. He made up his own mind without her as he shut the bus doors and pulled out of the church parking lot back onto the back bumpy roads of North Carolina.

She blocked the loud morning chirping of the children from her and fell asleep on her bus bench. Her staying awake all night in the church and having a conversation with God had gotten to her. She had to sleep. What she was not prepared for was the silence of the bus when it conked out on the side of the road.

Delie sat straight up. "What happened?"

"I don't know. I have to go up under the hood to see."

Delie had spoken to him—which she had not meant to do, but she was startled at the quiet. The children were unusually quiet too. They knew something was wrong. Bonnie was much better, but she snuggled next to Delie at the unaccustomed quiet of the bus. Champ came back on the bus with dirty hands. Delie handed him a towel, which he used to wipe thick black grease on. "Looks like the fan belt."

"Where are we?" Neal shouted out.

"We just made it into Virginia."

"Can't we go back to Miss Irene and the church?"

"No, we made it too far. I got to get to the next town and see if someone got a fan belt, maybe two to put together." Champ looked at her.

"Will you all be alright? I think the next town is about 10 miles off."

"That's far."

"I can make it in a few hours. Close the doors and don't open them for anyone." Champ grasped her hand with a semi-clean palm. Delie didn't mind.

Her heart beat a little faster at being left alone, in the cold with the children and no Champ.

"I'll be back as soon as I can."

Oh God. Is he abandoning me again? Why? What have I done now? Is it because of Neal?

"We'll be here when you get back." Delie put an emphasis on the last word.

"I'll be back, Dee. Don't worry." He seemed extra aggrieved at having to reassure her. But he had never been in her shoes. He didn't know what it was like to be left behind.

"Bring out all the extra blankets. We'll keep warm." Delie spoke with more certainty and confidence than what was inside of her. "We'll keep warm."

But there was no food. Miss Irene had given them a bag of doughnuts when they left Raleigh, but they were all gone. How would they wait for Champ, stay warm and keep from being hungry? In a matter of hours? She might have to defy him and go out and seek help. Champ had no idea of what it took to survive under trying circumstances.

He never had to.

It was enough to wait twenty minutes. But forty minutes was too much. Bonnie had started to cry and her baby girl tears made Delie want to cry. How could she have done this to these children? What kind of mother was she? She had to risk going out. It meant defying Champ's order, but these kids were hungry.

Only thing was, Virginia was not known as the friendliest place. But, maybe if she had money...

"There appears to be farms around here," Delie said peering out the bus window. "I'm going to go and see if I can buy some food from one of them."

Em's eyes widened. Delie could see the memory mirrored in her eyes of the time when the Klan had come and burned crosses on their lawns for Bledsoe defiance. They had been nine and fourteen. Even in Em's mindset, she knew what the stakes were. "Delie, be careful."

"I will, HB. Don't worry. I've got to try."

The only other person on the bus who had a remote idea of the chance she was taking in randomly approaching a stranger's house as a Negro woman was Willie. "Take care, Mama Dee. Please."

"I will. You be a big man. Stay with Em and help take care of the children." Willie seemed to like what she said, and she liked leaving him on a good note.

Fortunately, there wasn't much snow on the ground so Delie could make a quick path down the road to the farmhouse back in the other direction. It had a long pathway up the road. There might be anything, dogs, gunshots, but she had to try. She took a cautious step onto the dirt pathway up the road and went toward the small, plain farmhouse. *Please, God. Please, help these people be nice and help my family to get a meal. I am all these children have. Please help them.*

You are not alone.

The comforting belief echoed throughout her mind and firmed up her resolve, as she used her fist to knock on the door. Once she did, there was a rustling inside and Delie steeled herself for what was to come. She could feel her palms itch inside her gloves.

A middle-aged woman with skin the color of peaches and cream came to the door. She wore a simple housedress with cut off gloves and opened the door just a sliver. “Yes, may I help you, girl?”

Delie shrank. This was one of the reasons why she didn’t like to approach strangers or go outside of her own neighborhood. She was not a girl.

“Hello, ma’am. Our bus broke down back a ways and I wondered if I could get some food for my children. We can buy it off you.” Delie added hastily so the woman did not think they were beggars.

There were beggars a plenty now a days. “I have five children under ten and my sister and we all need to eat. If you could spare whatever you have, I would appreciate it.”

Delie waited. There was no telling what her reaction to her proposition would be. She would have to endure whatever insult would be hurled at her, even for asking this favor.

The woman's facial expression was a mass of confusion. "There was a boy, a tall buck he was, come to the door about an hour ago. You know him?"

Her description sounded like Champ, but she could not be sure. Champ was nobody's boy, nor was he a buck. "He sounds like our driver, ma'am."

"Yes. He was going back to Meriwether for a part. He asked for food for a bus of kids. I got soup here in a bucket and some sandwiches. I have cake too and a bucket of milk. I was about to bring it out."

He had thought of them. He was not going to abandon them. *Thank you, God.*

"Oh, ma'am. Thank you."

"I got a wagon here, I could bring it down if you want."

"I can help you with the wagon, ma'am, and we'll return your dishes. Thank you so much."

The woman shrugged her shoulders. "It's a Christian duty to help. It would be great to open a little sandwich stand out here. There ain't nothing for miles around. It must be hard having children in this cold."

The woman had made a kind of hobo stew, cobbled together chunks of carrots, potatoes and tomatoes with whatever she had on hand, no doubt. The wax paper squares were of ham sandwiched between thick slices of homemade bread. That was more ham to eat, but she would take whatever she could get. "The cake looks delicious, ma'am."

"It's an apple cake. It just came out the oven. I was going to wrap up some squares."

Delie gave a little laugh. "By the time you cut it out of the pan, my oldest son would have eaten half of it already. I'll bring the empty pan back to you too. Just put the pan on the wagon and a knife and we can cut it up."

They both wheeled the wagon carefully down the long driveway. The woman saw the bus. "Oh my. Where you folks headed?"

"Pittsburgh. My sisters live there."

"It's good to be back with family, isn't it?"

"Amen, ma'am."

"Is the buck a friend of yours?"

"You might say that." Delie gritted her teeth, ignoring the woman's usage. She was trying to be nice and Delie wanted to oblige her.

"If you don't mind me saying so, he must care a lot about you all to risk coming to our house. Don't ever know what you are going to get these days when you meet a stranger."

"True enough."

The women were quiet while pushing the little wagon toward the bus. Delie opened the door. "Here's food, little ones. Calm down. I'm back. Champ arranged a hot lunch with this nice lady here." She turned to the woman, who had embarked on the bus behind her. "I'm sorry, ma'am. I failed to ask your name."

"Angela."

"Miss Angela. She's an angel of God for us today, I would say."

Em rushed forward to help Delie hand up the buckets and dishes and things.

"Thank you, ma'am." Bonnie intoned politely. Delie could see Angela was charmed.

"Such a cute one."

"Thank you kindly, ma'am."

"And you've kept your figure nice having all these children."

Delie said nothing. Some things were meant to be shared, others weren't. "Thank you."

"I'll leave you to eat, then."

"And I'll return your dishes. Thank you kindly."

The satisfying sounds of the children eating warmed her heart as Delie turned to Angela and gave her five dollars.

Champ had thought of them first.

That was a heartwarming realization. Champ had thought about them before he went on down the road. She sat aside a sandwich and some cake for him so he could eat when he came back. He needed to keep up his strength. He was the one in training and he had thought about them.

A small tingle in her stomach seemed to pose the question of forgiveness. Was forgiveness even possible, despite all Champ had put her through?

She could not wait for the belt to be fixed so they could go somewhere where she did not have to be afraid to approach a stranger's door anymore. She still hated Champ beating up on people. But, because of it, it was Champ who made a life with dignity more and more a reality for them.

For that, she would be grateful to him for the rest of her life.

But gratitude didn't mean he deserved her heart. Did it?

CHAPTER THIRTEEN

The icy cold ground seeping through his boxing shoes was nothing new to him, but the time apart from Delie and the children was.

He did not like this unsettling feeling, and even though he had arranged lunch with the farmwoman, he wanted to get back to the bus as soon as possible. The walk was good training. He tried to jog in places to get some training in and keep warm. At his pace, it took him about an hour and a half to get to the town and some time to explain what he needed at the garage. Just as he knew, they would not have a fan belt for a bus, but fortunately, since he worked with cars in the jobs he had done between boxing matches, he knew how to cobble two belts together to make a proper sized belt for the bus.

The people in Meriwether looked at him askance when he paid for the fan belts with cash money, but he did. There was a diner down the road where he was able to order a hamburger with onions to eat. He had to take it with him, of course, and eat it on the way back. The burger kept his fingers warm. The kids sure would have liked a hamburger. At least he had seen to them getting a hot lunch. He hoped the farmwoman would do it.

Alternately, he jogged and ran to get back to the bus. The dark was beginning to fall and he wanted to get going again, on to D.C. where there was another place to stay he knew and trusted. His stomach twitched with dread at the thought of the children having to sleep on the bus. He could not fail them. He did not want the children to have to stay on the bus, in the cold, especially with Bonnie getting over a cold so recently.

As he turned the corner, the farmhouse where he had stopped emerged in the darkness. Delie was coming out of the house waving to the woman.

He stopped at the bottom of the hill and Delie fixed him with a saucy look.

"I thought I told you to stay on the bus."

"How was I going to return her dishes?"

"Once I fixed the bus, I could have driven back."

"And then lost time. No thanks."

Companionably, she put her arm through his.

She wasn't mad anymore. He nearly lurched forward in surprise. She so willingly touched him. To show he could handle it, and his emotions, he joked with her. "Lord, woman, your fingers are cold."

"And you?"

Delie giggled a bit and Champ waved back to the nice woman in the farmhouse. The woman was a bit old-fashioned, but it all could have been worse for them. Far worse. And it wasn't. *Thank you again, God.*

"Thank you for thinking of us, Champ." Delie's words echoed his thoughts so well.

"What make you think I wouldn't?"

"I'm just thanking you."

She might as well have said her thoughts. They were so loud. "I was just a boy back then."

"And I was a girl."

"Boys don't have as much sense as girls."

"Ha, ha. It's time you admitted it."

Champ made a gesture with his hands, relishing the feel of Delie's cold claws on his arm. "You went to school and you a teacher. I'm up here traveling around, punching on people. Who got more sense?"

"Champ. You could do whatever you wanted to. It was always up to you."

"Get on. I do what I got to do."

"You sure? So many people told you—fight. Ever think of trying something else?"

No, he hadn't. Not until that doctor told him about his eyes. He could keep what sight he had as long as he stopped fighting.

But the doctor might as well have told him to stop breathing. Fighting was a Bates thing. It was in their blood. Neal was a Bates. Wasn't he? And he didn't look like a fighter. What would Neal do if he didn't fight? What could he do? "I do what I got to do."

"You could try." Delie's voice was small in the cold, but it was there. What would it be like to have a woman like Delie, cheering him on, helping him along? Something special, he knew as much for sure. Could he give up boxing? For her? For himself?

"I don't know anything."

"You have this fan belt. You make this bus work, and that's a gift from God. And despite these tough times, that's something people need."

Could he help folks with their cars? He liked the sound of that. And he had always liked cars. Helping folks with their cars had been the very thing he had done to get along when the boxing matches were few and far between. "Let's see what I can do for this bus."

And he had to admit, it kind of warmed him when he and Delie walked up to the bus and the kids and Em were cheering. "All right now, you all."

"We saved some food for you, Champ. And some cake." Neal screamed as loud as he could.

Delie sat down next to him and put an arm around him. "I'm surprised you greedy little gremlins didn't eat it. Miss Angela offered us her outhouse for bathroom breaks. Let's go while Champ works on the bus."

Champ went back outside and lifted up the hood of the bus. Could he do it? The belt on this bus was not made for anyone long term, clearly.

He should have seen it in Georgia, rather than putting them through this. *Is it fair to regret what I didn't see coming? What I didn't know? Maybe it is best left in Your care.* And there in the Virginia cold where it was beginning to snow a little bit, he prayed for what he needed to be able to fix the bus well enough to get the children to their new home. He moved a few things around and took out the engine to install the fan belt. With a heave, he put the engine back in. As he did, Delie came up behind him holding Neal's hand.

"Your work looks mighty specialized to me, Champ."

"It's just something to do, Dee."

"I couldn't do it."

"Let's see if it works. You get on behind the wheel and start it up. Just don't run me down, no matter how much you want to."

"Ha, Ha." Delie stuck her tongue out at him. The small daintiness of her tongue struck him all of a sudden and made him feel light in his head.

"Get on with yourself, girl." Champ chuckled.

When he slammed down the hood, Delie's face appeared behind the wheel. Was that it? Could he have done it? Would what he did be enough? Champ gestured to her to turn the ignition. Delie did.

It didn't catch.

Please, please, God. It is getting cold out here and I can't ask the nice lady for the children to stay the night.

"One more time." Champ shouted and the words practically formed themselves into the frostiness.

Delie started the bus up.

A cough. A sputter. Followed by the familiar clunky purring of the ramshackle bus ready to head on down the road.

"Yeah! Champ can do anything!" Neal screamed again.

Champ broke out in a wide smile. He caught himself and paused to give God all the glory. *Thank you. Thank you. Stay by my side and help me to get these ones on to their home.* He jogged around to the side and Delie slid out of the driver's seat with her large brown eyes shining at him. "Good job."

She might as well have kissed him. He would have liked a kiss better. Maybe, now that he had fixed the bus…better not tempt fate so soon after she resolved that she never wanted to see him again after they reached their destination. "Let's head on down the road and surprise Em and Flo with a running bus."

With confidence and God surely with him, he turned the bus around to pick up the rest of the little family so they would not have to walk their way back in the cold.

It had not occurred to Delie that Champ did not believe he could do anything else until their shared moment walking back from Miss Angela's house in the cold.

Had he left her to do the only thing he believed he could? Delie tried not to look at Champ's broad back as he drove the bus with proficiency on to Washington, D.C. He had said there were places he knew of with beds where they could stop in Virginia and take part of the next day to see the Capitol building and the White House and a special sight he had promised to show them.

Delie prayed. *Give me strength, Lord. Give me kindness*. What was it like to be a seventeen-year-old boy with his girlfriend mooning over him, grasping at him, asking him for promises and certainty? A seventeen-year-old Negro boy who thought, because he had been told it all of his life, the only thing he was good for was to let other people beat up on him. Would she have stayed under those circumstances?

Of course, I uphold my responsibilities.

There had been moments of complete fear remembering how she might not have enough money to take care of the farm. The failure. The dread. And what was the first thing she had wanted to do? Get away from Winslow.

Was meeting all part of God's plan? God allowed her to understand Champ's feelings by putting her in a very similar circumstance.

She breathed out a little sigh. The realization hit her close in her mind's eyes. Delie looked down at Neal and remembered how she had brought him into the world, crying, screaming, begging, praying for Champ and the frowning faces of her older sisters looking down at her. They loved her, but they did not love the way she was being while having the baby.

"You got this way being a woman. Don't stop being a woman now." Ruby had groused at her.

And she understood.

Was she making things hard for Champ by bringing him into the company of her older sisters again? Probably. But he had seen Nettie. He had survived her. *What a relief.* However, Ruby and Mags had to be dealt with, and her heart sank all over again. She hoped they did not make him want to go away.

Even though he said he was going back to Winslow.

Champ brought them into the city center of Washington, D.C., just outside of Alexandria,

Virginia. "This here is an old town." He spoke over the children's chatter. His deep male voice made them listen to him. "A lot of history is here. We passed up where old George Washington lived, and now we seeing the places where he liked to meet with his friends."

"Where are we staying, Champ?"

"I know a boarding house. I can take the boys in a room with me. Delie and Em, you take the girls in a room with you. We be okay."

"I didn't mean to make you responsible for the children. You need your rest to drive the bus and not be badgered with a bunch of boys all night."

"We aren't badgering him. We aren't going to be a problem!" Neal shouted out.

Delie heard the near tears threatening Neal's voice.

"We going to do whatever your Mama says," Champ's voice was stern.

She appreciated the backup. Still, Delie grasped Neal's hand as Champ went around a corner.

"I just wanted you to get your rest so you would be able to drive tomorrow." She kept her tone light, wondering how he might feel.

"I'll be alright. And sometime late tomorrow, you be back with your sisters. All five of you together again."

"Yes, that is true." How thoughtful of him. It didn't even occur to her until he said it. With the exceptions of some rare occasions, like Nettie's wedding, and their parents' funerals, they hadn't been together as a group for a very, very long time.

"Then they'll all gang up on me and beat me up. And I'll get a rep as a sap and lose the fight."

"No, Champ. No. I won't let 'em." Neal formed his hands into tiny fists and began to pommel the seat in front of him. Delie grasped one of the tiny fists and kissed it.

"You've got to behave and go to sleep tonight. You understand?"

"I will, Mama."

Something tugged at Delie's heart. At some point, if Champ were taking responsibility for him, wasn't it for the best? And, he was willing to take on Willie and Roy too. Could he want them all? Was Champ grown up enough to want them all? What did she have to say about it?

Light dawned in her, but a cloud came with it. He had better never abandon her again. No more. Or her sisters would beat him up and he would not need to worry about fighting a white man, because the Bledsoe sisters would take care of him. Permanently.

The boardinghouse beds weren't the greatest, but they weren't pews. And the boardinghouse meal was mostly beans and vegetables with side meat, the fare they were used to eating. They might have done better, in a restaurant, with meat for Champ, but he insisted they all eat in the boarding house since it was part of their lodging. "It would be an insult. We can have a good lunch somewhere tomorrow."

Delie didn't care about an insult, if it meant they all got a hot meal, but she did worry about Champ getting what he needed to get built up for the fight. "Maybe eggs at breakfast in the morning?"

"I doubt it, probably just bacon biscuits. You still in the South, girl. But it's about to change. You'll see what I mean soon."

Intrigued by what he had said, she could not sleep. What was going on with Neal on the other side of the wall? But as soon as her head hit the pillow, she slept soundly and did not even mind it when Bonnie kicked her in the stomach and groin throughout the night.

Just as Champ predicted, the boarding house had Vienna sausage biscuits for breakfast. No eggs. He loaded up the bus for sightseeing. Delie had only been outside of Georgia on the train to Pittsburgh twice before, so this sightseeing was new to her. He drove the bus right past the White House. "Looka you all. That's where old FDR lives." Neal practically screamed into Delie's ear, he was so excited.

"And Eleanor Roosevelt," Delie reminded her son. "She's a great lady. Does a lot of things for our people. She works with Miss Mary Bethune to help get Negroes into better Negro colleges."

"Well, what about Negroes getting into white colleges?" Champ put in.

"I never gave it a moment's thought."

"Times is hard now. I think a whole lot of white colleges up there would want Black students if they knew they could pay some money. Even ones up there in Pittsburgh."

"Champ." Delie leaned forward. "I already have a college degree."

"Yea, Champ. We was at Mama's school. Remember the Swiss steak?"

Leave it to Neal to remember by the food they ate. Delie chuckled.

Champ said, "You can get more than one, right? Don't they have graduate degrees? Some teachers even get them to learn how to teach better. Some people go to school at night sometimes."

The idea of another degree hit her like a lighting bolt. She always enjoyed learning. When she walked through the archway, she had resigned herself to thinking it was the end of her education. She waved the idea away. "I got five children. I don't have enough time or money for extras."

"You going up to your sisters, they can help with the kids. I can help with the money."

The words, ones that she had been dreaming to hear for years, came across to her with firmness and surety. But the vision scared her.

"I'm too old."

Champ went around the corner. Magnificent monuments came into view, the tall and imposing Washington Monument on the right and the Lincoln Memorial, which was much closer on the left. Champ parked the bus. "Yeah, you are kinda old." He laughed as she hit him in the shoulder, a punch just like a butterfly wing to his iron-strong arm.

He boomed out. "Come on, we got to hurry if we want to see old Abe. Don't know if the park service likes this big old bus being here."

The children scrambled off of the bus in the cold. Champ got off first and handed Delie, Bonnie and Em down gently. Delie didn't know what to think as they approached the large, humble, terrifying white marble visage of Abraham Lincoln. So awe inspiring.

Champ put his hands in his jacket pockets and Delie stood next to him. “A great man.”

“He was.” Delie stood very near and slipped her hand into the crook of his arm. “Make sure to read the inscriptions, children. What does it say, Miss Flo?”

She paid half a mind of attention at Flo’s lisping away of the great words of Lincoln.

Champ whispered. “He paid a great price so’s you could go to graduate school, you know?”

“Stop it.” Delie squeezed his arm. Or tried to. His arm was rock solid.

“He did. You got to do what you got to do. So do I.”

“The white man who freed you wants you to fight another white man?”

Champ nodded, completely solemn. “Maybe.”

“I don’t believe it.”

“Give it a try.”

“We’re a great people, Mama.” Neal said and his voice echoed throughout the internal part of the monument. “Listen to me!”

“You all are being way too noisy. Come here.” Delie removed her hand from the crook of Champ’s warm arm and gathered the little group to her. “You all are capable of great things. We can do things because Abraham Lincoln made it all possible for us to be free and not be slaves. So when you don’t want to do any more schoolwork, and you want to give up, think of what you could be. How it could be. As slaves."

"I would not have ever been no slave," Willie insisted.

"You would have done whatever you needed to do," Champ chimed in on the lesson. "Do you think my grandfather and his father wanted to fight? They did it, so I could have choices."

The children might not have registered the change in his voice, but Delie sure did. It touched her. She put her hand back into the crook of his arm. Her heart surged at the way he welcomed her touch by sticking out his arm to her.

The small gesture made her think of the possibilities. Standing there in their little small group, more light came into her soul. New possibilities. New chances. This is what this move was for. So many had gone before them, including her sisters. Delie had not thought about why they went, but it was to take advantage of what this man had done to free the slaves. The belief she might have some small role to play in all of it struck her as wonderful, and just a little bit ridiculous.

"Thank you for bringing us here, Champ. To remind us."

"You're welcome, Delie." His eyes met hers and their connectedness jolted her. The way he looked at her made her insides melt like liquid. The firm pink outline of his full lips was ever so tempting. For some reason, his lips made her think of the kind of filling up and erasing of hunger as the steak had done at the church.

"Let's go. We don't want to cause trouble."

She took her cold hands out of the warmth of the crook of his arm and forced herself onward.

CHAPTER FOURTEEN

One of Champ's jokes was that he would turn the bus back around and go back to Georgia and the kids would laugh at him. But, as he drove closer to Pittsburgh, a sinking feeling within him grew sharper. At a stop, he bought the kids some soda pop, but he was careful not to drink one himself because the bubbles would make him explode. He had traveled all over, and he had been in Pittsburgh just the previous week. Why was he so nervous?

Those sisters. Her sisters. He had last remembered them as a boy. While he and Delie were growing up, it had only been Em around, and Nettie sometimes. He did not know the older ones. He still thought of the older sisters from a five-year-old vantage point. They loomed, tall and larger than life, especially Ruby. In Winslow, Ruby was legendary for her defiance of Paul Winslow.

The whites always used her as an example for what happened to Negroes when they got out of line. "We going to run you out like Ruby." They would say and snicker.

They were wrong.

People did not know how much Ruby was involved in turning things around in Winslow. Money Ruby made as a nurse went directly to fund lawyers and legal cases in Georgia and Turpentine County to stop the lynching. Because of her efforts, Champion could grow up as a young man and not be afraid to be lynched. The last lynching occurred in 1919 and even though it still went on in other places, it had stopped in that part of Georgia. A remarkable accomplishment. Champ hoped he would get the opportunity to tell her so, in a non-nervous way.

But Ruby would probably hate him for what he had done to Delie. As would the other sister—what was her name? Mags. He gripped the steering wheel harder.

"We're getting closer." Delie got excited as they crossed the border into Pennsylvania.

"About two hours. We could stop for lunch."

Delie hung her head. "We'll have to. The children are hungry."

"I know I am!" Neal shouted as they all laughed at his antics.

"Anywhere you know we can eat?" Delie started to look around furtively.

"Oh. We've crossed the Mason Dixon line. We're in the Promise Land, baby. We can go where we want to go."

"What are you talking about?" Delie's eyes blinked. "Where we want?"

"Yes. We don't have to worry. We can sit in the restaurant if we want. We don't have to eat out of greasy paper bags. We can eat as we wish, where we wish."

In the mirror, out of the corner of his eye, Delie had sat back in her chair. The smallest tears trickled down her face. "What you crying about, girl?"

"Now we can go anywhere, I don't know if I want to."

Champ understood. "We could find a Negro neighborhood, but it wouldn't be for another hour. They have a place where busses stop to have something to eat. It's the Post House. Nice clean restaurant. If the children behave," Champ raised his voice and the bus was quiet except for its noisy engine, a sound they were all used to, "Then we can have a nice lunch. What do you say?"

She said nothing.

"Turnoff to Breezewood is coming up. What you say?"

"I want a hamburger!" Neal shouted and they all laughed.

"Ok." Delie hung onto the rail in front of her as Champ changed lanes to get off.

"When we get back on, we going to get on the Lincoln Highway. You'll see how it is."

He pulled up a hill to a small building with other buses in front of it. The children piled off the bus. "Ladies." Champ made a grand gesture as he handed first Em and then her sister off of the bus. He didn't let go of Delie's delicate hand. She shivered inside her gray fox wrap. "Yeah, your coat is for Georgia winter. We got to get you something better for this up north cold."

"It's something. Isn't it?"

"There's bad and good in life. You'll see." He opened the Post House door for the women and let them in. A young girl with perfectly marcelled hair and a pressed gingham apron stood in front of them. She smiled and Champ was glad.

"May I help you?"

"We have eight. Please, ma'am."

"Certainly. This way."

Delie was definitely wowed. He wanted to laugh, but he didn't. If she was wowed at the Post House, imagine how she would be in some of the fancier restaurants and clubs he could take her to…after the fight. He would buy her a fur coat and show her what high living was about, after the fight. When he won.

Delie and Em had given the bad eye to the children. They were considerably calmer than before. The woman gave them all menus and walked away. "I'll be back to get your order."

"She was nice." Em said in wonder.

"She was." Delie's heart-shaped face was very sober. What was she thinking about?

"What you want to eat, HB? Kids? Dee? I'm having a hamburger and fries. Maybe some pie."

"That's what I want!" The utterance came out of Neal's mouth and Delie put a firm hand on his arm.

"Quiet." She hissed and the boy was still. Champ had similar energy with his mother, but he had always behaved well. Mostly.

"What else does everybody want? Dee? Em?"

"Sounds great to me, Champ." Em put the menu down, unread.

Delie just nodded. When the young woman came back, he put in the same order for all of them.

Delie shook her head. "Folks in Winslow would not believe this."

"It's something ain't it? Listen, up here, all they care about is green. Money."

"And money will make them be nice?"

"Yes indeed. She sees a big party of eight like this, she want a nice tip. She be nice."

"It's a shame it takes money to be nice."

Champ shook his head. "It's worse when they won't be nice even if you have money. I like it up here better. Even if it is cold."

In short order, the young women brought their hot food. Delie stayed a hand while they all clasped hands and prayed. She prayed about safe journeys and the promise land. She prayed about opportunities and chances. Champ began to understand what made her feel deeply. All of this was new and frightening to her. No more fear for her. She deserved better.

The waitress brought them new plates and served them a whole apple pie. Delie cut the slices and put them onto plates. "This is wonderful." She sighed as she put her fork into the spicy, tender apples and flaky crust.

Champ had already finished his.

"Care to make me a pie sometime?" Champ had an arm around the booth part where she sat next to him.

"I would do it if you wanted it." Delie leaned back into his arm. A warm feeling speared through him where they touched. "Would you eat it?"

"I would. You made them good steaks, you might could make a pie."

"I could try."

Em clapped her hands. "Yay. I would help teach you."

"That would be nice, sister."

Delie insisted they leave the table clean.

"Dee, it's their job."

"All the same. I don't want them thinking these kids are barbarians. They aren't. We aren't."

Delie wiped at a spot where Roy had spilled a little Coke. "We'll make a bathroom stop and then hit the Lincoln Highway."

When Delie came out of the bathroom with Bonnie in tow, she whispered. "There's paper towels in there."

"All kinds of wonders up north. I'ma have to show them all to you, little country girl."

Delie shook her head. "You all big time now. Let's see how you look when you meet the family."

Champ stopped short and brought the boys around. "Let's get on the bus."

"Hmm. Hmm. Not so big now."

"Come on, girl. I'll stand up to anyone who try to say anything to you, Dee."

"All right then."

Still, the burgers, fries and pie made a bit of a rumble in his stomach at the thought of the Bledsoe sisters all lined up to get him.

He was fine with that.

If it meant showing her how much he cared, he would face much more than mean sisters for Delie's sake.

Lincoln Highway was so smooth. Delie laid back on the seat for a little nap. The sounds in their ears the entire trip had been the rattling nature of the bus and the bumpy small town roads they traveled upon. Now on Lincoln Highway, the other sound was gone. On to better things.

And the smooth highway lulled her to sleep.

What kind of cold promise land was this? An incredible one. On promise land ground, she slept and dreamed. This time, she was not screaming. She dreamed about Champ staying and being with her. When she woke up, it was dark. Some of the children were asleep as well. "What time is it?" she whispered into the darkness, knowing her words would reach Champ.

"It's almost seven o'clock," Champ said consulting his watch.

Delie put a hand on her hair pushing it back. "They live in a place called the Hill District."

"I know it well. Remember, I just saw Nettie. She wasn't happy with me."

"I guess not, from the tone of her letter to me."

"And those other sisters of yours."

"They'll be okay. Don't worry about it."

"You gonna fight for me, Dee?" He was half joking but half serious too. What did he want her to do? "Don't let them get me."

"I won't, Champ. I'll be here for you." Her voice quivered a bit, with sleep she supposed. The tremble made her sound as if she was responding with some marriage vows or something. She cleared her throat.

"Good. I knew I could always count on you."

Could she count on him? He had brought them all here. They were in Pittsburgh because of Champ. He wasn't a young boy any more. Instead of sniping at him, she stayed silent. No kind response came to her mind.

Champ drove further into the city. The streets became increasingly narrow. Soon, there were street lamps lit. Even in the darkness, Delie could see professional, proud and well-dressed Negroes walking around in big coats. She remembered how proud everyone was from when she was here years agoe for Nettie's wedding.

The pride was still evident despite tough times and she was happy to see it. People walked looking out ahead of them. They weren't hanging their heads down. She would be one of them. And maybe, according to what Champ said, she could get a job and go back to school. A thrill ran up her arms. There were possibilities here. For her. For Neal. For the children and Em. Even for Champ. What an opportunity. She could decide. This was what freedom was like.

Soon Champ slowed down and pulled in front of a familiar row of row houses. Mags and Ruby lived three doors apart in this row of row houses. Champ had sent a telegram to Asa's newspaper office to alert them they were coming, so it was no surprise when Delie saw Mags and Nettie hurry out to the curb wrapped in shawls, clapping their hands against the cold.

Champ opened the door and Delie ran off the bus into their arms. Mags smoothed Delie's marcelled hair after pulling her away to look at her.

"Oh, sissy. Delie grew up so pretty. Isn't she pretty, Net?"

Delie could see Nettie's eyes were misty. "She's the one of us who looked the most like Mama."

"A young, pretty Mama she is. Look at her." Practical Mags said. "And here are the children. Oh and there's Neal. I know him anywhere."

Delie had counted on how welcoming her sisters would be to the children and they were. They both embraced all the children as their nieces and nephews and made no difference. They marveled over how well Em looked. Delie and Em started crying. They should have made more visits over the years. She never realized how important her sisters were to her.

Champ stepped off of the bus. He brushed at his pants and took off his apple cap. Nettie and Mags stood apart for a bit, encouraging the children to go inside to get warm and eat warm food.

"Hello, Mrs. Evans. Mrs. …" Champ greeted Nettie as his most charming self and put a hand out to Mags.

Mags did not shake his hand.

Delie blinked. Was this Mags? She was the kindest sister with the best heart among them—even better than Nettie, who was a pastor. It was obvious by the way Mags held her swan-like neck with dignity, she was not happy.

"Caldwell." Mags rewrapped the shawl around herself and kept her hands tucked at her sides. This was going to be worse than she thought.

"There he is." Nettie folded her own hands at her sides. "Yep. MIA. The boxer my husband sponsored turns coat and runs back South. Lord, I tried to tell Jay."

"Tell him what?" Delie inserted with an upraised cry.

"Not to sponsor this boy. He's not trustworthy. He's always running off." Nettie asserted.

"Now, ma'am. I had my reasons."

"Certainly. What were they?" Nettie crossed her arms and Mags matched her stance. Although Mags was a shade taller, they always did look like one another—female reflections of John Bledsoe.

"It's mighty cold and we been traveling a long way with the children. Mind if we go inside?" Champ intoned without any shakiness in his voice. Good for him.

Nettie turned to Mags. "It's your house. What do you think?"

"Mags. Nettie. Please, let us go in." Delie interjected. Champ squared his shoulders and helped her up the few stairs of the stoop in front of Mags's house. She recognized that stance. He was ready to fight.

"Let's go." Mags gestured. Delie could see her taking note of how Champ guided Delie with his hand hovering at her waist. His hand there was a warmth against the February chill, for sure.

"I'll be in in a minute. I'm gonna get the bags. You should go in and get warm." Champ told her in her ear.

"Thank you. I appreciate it." Delie squeezed his cold hand, wishing she could make him feel better at this scrutiny. She turned and watched him opening the bus doors to get the bags, a burning feeling at this rejection rose in her arms.

Mags's home was warm and friendly, but the cold wind blowing from the two women were not. "Here's the parlor." Mags guided them to the parlor room up front. "We can speak in here without the children hearing."

The noisy children were in the back in the kitchen and Delie's heart rejoiced at hearing the children helping themselves to warm drinks and cookies. The deep male voices she heard were Mags's older boys showing them where everything was. She had not seen her nephews and nieces in a long time and longed to give them hugs and kisses.

But that was not possible now.

The three of them went into the parlor and Mags slid the doors closed.

"Where's Asa?" Delie asked, trying to keep the mood light. She wanted to know where her reasonable brother-in-law was. He would help her.

"He's still at the office. He should be along shortly."

"And Jay?"

"Him too. It's better we get this all sorted out before he gets here."

A converted man of God now, Jay had a checkered past and Delie did not care to see it resurrected against Champ. Champ came clumping into the parlor and sat on the davenport next to her. He seemed large and foreign against Mags's beautiful dark brown oaken carved davenport. Delie longed to put an arm around him, to take the sad look off of his face, but there was no easy thing for him. He would have to face the fire as he could. Mags and Nettie stood. "Explain. Before Ruby gets here." Mags put a hand to her hips.

"I don't know what you mean, Mrs. Caldwell."

"She means, why were you in Winslow when you are supposed to be training and getting my husband's money back?" Nettie's voice echoed loud in the parlor.

Delie did not like Nettie's accusatory tone, but as the baby, she always had a hard time standing up to her big sisters. They seemed like giants to her in all of their exploits and adventures. And now, with the way they lived, they were like fairy princesses in this special wonderful kingdom just for Negroes. She was about to speak, but at Nettie's words, Champ was on his feet.

His stance was the old fighting one. Ready for battle. *Go, Champ. Battle on. Give him strength, Lord.*

"This ain't about the money. I know what this is. And look, I don't expect forgiveness from you all for what I did when I left Winslow. But I didn't know. I didn't know about Delie. I didn't know there was a baby after I left."

"How could you not know? Your mother—"

"Told me nothing. Not about Delie. She just said she left Winslow and went to school. When I left, I was trying to improve my prospects. I was trying to be better for her. I didn't leave her right, but that's what I was trying to do."

"Effie told you nothing about this baby who looked just like a Bates coming back to Winslow with my parents?" Mags's elegant face was all wrinkled up in a mask of confusion. "Neal was born up here and when the time was right, I brought him down to Winslow myself for my parents to raise. There was plenty of talk about where that baby had come from."

Champ twisted his cap in his hands. "She doesn't think Neal is mine." He sat down, already defeated.

"She doesn't what?" Nettie threw herself down on her knees behind the big stuffed chair and began to mumble in prayer. Mags did not blink an eyelash at this dramatic behavior. Delie was not surprised. Nettie was always the most religious one out of all of them.

"She got you convinced?" Mags blinked.

"She's my mama, Mrs. Caldwell. What am I supposed to do? I know she don't say the right things and our mamas always fought, but she brought me up."

"Delie," Mags's voice boomed out in her parlor, "is the one you said you loved? When I think of her up here, big and pregnant, just a baby herself, crying out in her labor over you, scared and alone but for her us. Lord, Lord, Lord." Mags whipped out a handkerchief and wiped at her eyes.

It had all happened to her, and there was a slight painful prick behind her own eyes, but she didn't cry.

Nettie stopped her praying and stood to face them again. "Are you training now?"

"Ma'am. I haven't stopped training. I'm still doing it. Matter of fact, I'ma leave here in the morning for the train and go back south to finish."

"To your mother?" Mags whispered.

"I don't have no place else to go." Champ gripped his cap again and Delie wanted to hold his hand. He looked so helpless. She had to admit, some of this was very interesting to hear. Especially about Effie Bates.

"Good. Get on back to Winslow then. He's going home." Mags turned to Nettie and Delie could see she was trying to calm herself. And Nettie. And the almost meaning of her words, Delie knew. *He just drove them up here. There's nothing happening between them anymore.* And Mags treating it as if that were the reality, seemed to make it so.

Nettie shook her head. "I might see, but Ruby…"

And almost as if they conjured her, the doors slid open and Delie's oldest sister, the lynchpin of the Bledsoes, stood right there in front of them. Delie's knees quivered a little as she rose to greet her older sister. She had to reach down to hug her. Ruby wielded the most authority of the sisters, but she was barely five feet tall.

"It's good to see you, Ruby!" Delie exclaimed.

"Baby sister. Praise God, you made it in safe. She looks like Mama, doesn't she?" Ruby's smooth and unlined cream-colored face had barely changed. Delie knew her oldest sister was on her way to forty, but did not look it. She was as beautiful as ever. She pulled Delie back from her. "Where is Em?"

"She in the kitchen with the children. Making sure they all eat something warm and good." The maternal Mags put in. What else would she be with seven children of her own?

"You're home, you hear me, baby sister? Home now. We're going to help you. Who is this?" Ruby linked her arm through Delie's so they could stand side by side.

"Champion Bates." Nettie intoned every syllable, which rang throughout the room. Her voice dripped with sarcasm. Shocked at Net's tone, Delie barely noticed her brother-in-law, Adam Morson come behind his wife Ruby. She had had a crush on him when she was little and they always shared a special relationship. Adam would always be a big brother to her. They embraced warmly and Delie stood next to him.

"Do tell." Ruby said. Delie could not see the look on her sister's face, but she sure didn't like the tone of her voice.

Good thing Champ stood again.

"Yes. He took Jay's money for training and went south with it to meet up with baby sister again." Nettie pointed out in an accusatory tone.

"Do tell." Ruby folded her arms across her chest. "What for?"

"To let her know I was ready." Champ spoke up.

"For what?" Ruby's clipped two-word responses were making Delie shake. Adam kept a firm arm around her and Delie was glad for the support.

"I had made it in the world and I was ready to come and be with her."

"Oh. I thought you said you was ready to claim your son." Ruby's tone was light. Delie was a little relieved. Until old holy roller Nettie stuck her nose back in.

"Effie Bates does not believe Neal is Champ's son." Nettie said in the same slow, maddening sarcastic way she had spoken before.

"What?" Ruby's head turned all the way around to face Delie and back to Champ again.

"That woman was something to deal with." Mags shook her head. "She never wanted Mama to have a place in the church. You was gone after she started taking over First Water. Now, she has it complete with no Bledsoes down there. God bless them."

"Mmmm. When Mrs. Bomead died, she came on in. I remember hearing about it." Ruby's gaze stayed on Champ. "And you believe your mother?"

"I don't know what to believe anymore, Mrs. Morson."

And the parlor was awfully quiet. Delie couldn't even hear the children in the kitchen, almost as if they knew something terrible had come down. This was Mags's house, but Ruby had the final say.

"If you don't know baby sister would never hurt a flea and never tell a lie, you best get on out of here. If you got some place to be training, better get on with it." Ruby's dictate came down hard and everyone in the room was silent. Champ grabbed the cap off his head to move to the door where Adam and Delie stood.

"I'll see you tomorrow." Champ's gaze on her was firm and sure.

Delie smiled back, "Okay."

"Good night. Good night, Mr. Caldwell." Champ said to Adam.

"This isn't Mr. Caldwell." Delie said. "This is Dr. Morson, Ruby's husband."

"You don't know him?" Nettie's voice came loud in the silence of the room.

Champ kept gripping his hat. He backed out toward the door. "I can explain, ma'am."

What did all this mean? Delie turned to Nettie. "What are you talking about?"

"As a condition of the training money, he was supposed to go to Adam and get a check up. Has he been to see you?" Nettie asked.

"I'm afraid I have not met the vaunted Mr. Bates before, Nettie. I certainly have not had him as a patient."

"So in addition to being a lowlife, he's a thief." Ruby put the word down. End of the line. *Please, God.*

"I'll just be going." Champ made his way through the door.

"Oh my." Mags said. Delie could feel a victory slipping away. She had almost won Mags over.

Neal came out of the dining room and went down the hallway. "Champ, where are you going? We got cookies, and they got hot chocolate here."

"I'll see you all tomorrow, little man. I got to go now. Delie." Champ's gaze locked on hers. Things looked very dark now, but she smiled at him, just a little bit, to encourage him not to give up hope. Why hadn't he gone to Adam as Nettie said? Adam would have only helped him. She wanted to ask him about it, but Champ slipped out the front door and shut it.

She let out a breath and Adam's arm pulled her to him again. She would try not to worry about it. Champ said he was coming tomorrow. He would be back.

Wouldn't he? Now the tears, the ones that had threatened before, came forward stinging and slipping down her face. Things had changed. She had changed. And she thought he had too, but what did Nettie mean about going to see Adam?

Champ was strong in his body and strong in his mind and heart. Why did he have to see a doctor?

Please, God, help Champion be strong. I don't know if I can live without him.

CHAPTER FIFTEEN

Champ specialized in the knockdown. He had never known any other way but to take the other boxer completely out. He might have suffered some collateral damage over the years, but he had come out on top as the best—most times. But those fights had been no match for the awful confrontation he had just endured.

The cold February air pierced his lungs with the sharpness of a knife, but it was better to be out here in the sharp cold air than inside with that wall of sisters treating him as if he had done a great wrong to Delie.

Well, he had.

And he was paying for it every day of his life. Especially now. But he would make it up to her. He walked up to the bus and got on, just sitting in the driver's seat.

Where was he going to put this big old bus? For how long? And where could he go?

He had been generous with Jay Evans' training money and his funds were running low. And now that Nettie had seen him, he was not liable to get any more. There were several hotels in the Hill District, not at all hard for a Negro man with some cash to find a place to stay. The Crawford Grill had some places to go.

Well, he would fix both problems by finding a place to put the bus and stay on it. Cold in February on the bus in Pittsburgh was not at all the same as cold in February in the Bledsoe barn, but he would do what he had to do. Still, he shivered inside his clothes. He started the bus up to keep warm and tried to think of large tracts of land in the Hill District where he would be able to stay close to Delie and the kids without running off.

With the bus halfway warm, he was about to pull off when there was a rap at the door. Jay Evans. He put the bus in park and opened the door. A gust of the February cold intruded into the warmth of the bus. "Hey there."

"Mr. Evans. Good to see you."

"So, you back in town. How's the training going?" Jay Evans climbed up to the first seat without invitation and rearranged his long and elegant limbs.

"I've been training. Your wife doesn't think so."

"Nettie's intense, more than some other folk. She has a high standard. Don't worry. It's going well enough, right?"

Champ nodded. "I've never been more ready for anything in my life."

Jay inspected him closely. "Got something to prove?"

"Your wife's family thinks I am a lowlife."

"Wow. Tough stuff. Hey, they didn't approve of me much either at first. It has taken me some time to get to know them."

Champ turned around in the driver's seat to face him. Jay Evans? A hard time? "They gave you a hard time?"

"Oh yes. Especially Ruby."

They both chuckled together. Then Jay grew serious. "Nettie told me a lot after I saw you at the bank. You the father of Delie's baby?"

"I guess so."

A smile tugged at the corner of Jay's lips. "I think you better be a little more firm. One thing I have learned about the Bledsoes, they don't take kindly to anyone saying or suggesting bad about their own."

"I didn't say anything bad. I just said I didn't know. I was gone. She never told me anything about a baby. When my mother wrote me, she said Delie had gone to school and gotten a baby there, proof positive that Delie was fast. I just thought she had found someone else. Plenty of fellows were always interested in her."

"And you stayed away?"

"Yeah, because I was young and stupid. I been working hard, trying to make myself into something. Guess it didn't work. They think I ain't nothing."

"Hey. I believe in you. I funded your training."

True. Champ swallowed the rising gulp in his throat.

"But you know what else? God believes in you too."

"I been knowing He in my corner for a long time."

Jay shook his head. "There's knowing. Then there is believing. You got to believe. Then, it don't matter what Ruby say. All that matters is what God wants. And I believe God wants you to get in the ring and win. To show we can win."

"Oh, I'm going to." Champ's words came softly.

"But?"

"I want Delie to be proud of me. I want her with me."

"Brother, all you got to do is bow your head and get to work. It's all in the doing. God is there. Believe in Him. He'll see you through." Jay adjusted his elegant coat around his shoulders. "Delie, if she loves you, she'll come around and forgive."

"I hope so."

"But don't let it affect your training."

"I'm not. I know I got work to do."

"Wonderful. Where you staying tonight?"

"Gonna go up to the Crawford." Champ swallowed. He really didn't know.

"Too noisy. Come on home with us. You can have Goldie's room."

"Your wife don't want me at your house."

And as if to prove it, Nettie came bustling out of the house with Adam and Ruby in tow. Nettie gave the bus an evil glance and Jay beckoned to her. "Let me handle this."

When Jay Evans rearranged his elegant frame and bent low to get off the bus, Champ had no doubt in the outcome. The angry look on Nettie's face softened and Jay went over to talk to her. Nettie started gesturing and pointing and said words that sounded like, "Thief," and "Lowlife." Ruby glared at the bus too.

But, Jay said something like, "Matthew 7:1."

Nettie was silent. Champ couldn't help it. He chuckled low in his throat.

Jay knocked on the door. "Changed the plans a bit. Nettie says you didn't go to the doctor, but you can go with Adam and Ruby now. Adam will examine you and they will put you up for the night. Come on by the bank after the appointment and we can decide where you want to stay for the rest of your training. I've got some ideas. Fine?"

He had no choice but to agree. He didn't know what was more terrifying, staying in a house with Ruby or knowing what Adam would say to him and knowing he would tell Jay and lose his chance at the fight.

Please, God. This is the only chance I got to get Delie back. Please, let it be alright. "Good enough."

"See you in the morning." Jay escorted his wife down the street, almost as if the February cold didn't impact either one of them. They were in their own little world.

Ruby glared at him. "Bring your grip. We just live a few houses down. Did you eat dinner?"

The hamburger seemed a long time ago, but he didn't know what to tell her. He just shook his head.

"He's training. We can give him some protein." Adam gestured to Champ. "Four houses down."

"Thank you." Champ hoisted up his grip. "What about the bus?"

"It'll be fine there. Come on, you must be exhausted." Adam gestured and stood against the cold.

Champ appreciated Adam's warm and welcoming ways. His wife was another matter.

As they entered the house, Champ could see it was twice as large as Mags's house, nearly palatial. He shouldn't have been surprised. Adam was the last living son of the Winslows. Champ knew from Delie, he got money from the mill somehow. The mill had fallen on hard times because of the Depression, but still, Adam was clearly doing well for himself as a doctor.

A maid came to him and picked up his grip to take it upstairs.

"Take him up to Solomon's room and then when Em comes she will stay in Maisie's room with her." Ruby grumbled to the maid and stomped off down the hall.

Adam faced him with a smile and offered to take his jacket as he stepped into the warm foyer. "Welcome. I'll let you eat tonight and get some rest. We can conduct the examination in the morning."

"I appreciate it."

Adam regarded him more closely. "Thank you for getting Delie, Em and the children here safely. Quite the trip for you, surely. You'll have to tell us all about it sometime."

"I'm sure Mrs. Morson doesn't want to hear about my exploits."

Adam shook his head. "According to Jay, you're about to embark on a great mission for our people. That matters. And it matters to Ruby." He waved a hand as he gestured toward the kitchen, the same place as where it was in Mags's house. "She's mad at you because of her baby sister. Who, I have to remind her, is not a baby anymore, although I remember those days when she was."

"I first met her after you left Winslow."

"Ah yes. And you've loved her ever since. A very long time."

Champ nodded.

"Keep loving her. She'll come around." Adam stood to attention when he heard Ruby's mary jane's clicking down the hall. "Right this way."

Champ appreciated the warmth Adam greeted him with. God had a way of working things out. And for sure, he would pray and trust everything with the examination would work out too. Right after he ate of the crispy fried chicken, sweet potatoes and green beans with cornbread heaped before him. Ravenous, the hot food filled him with not just the knowledge of God's goodness to him, but a belief in love.

Now, he had to be worthy of it.

Champ slept well, but the first thing he thought of looking at the frost-covered windows in the Morson house was Delie. Was she alright? Did she need help with the children? What about Neal? Did Bonnie sleep well? Was Flo shy with the Caldwell children? Were Willie and Roy fitting in?

The best thing to do was get going and face the day. Champ was still amazed at seeing a maid in a Negro home. And the Morsons had hot running water. She asked him what he wanted for breakfast. "A couple of eggs and some bacon."

"Biscuits?" Champ shook his head no. He had eaten enough bread in the past few days. "How many eggs?"

"Six. Same of the bacon."

The maid disappeared and Champ went into his own beautifully appointed oak bathroom to wash and get ready. After breakfast, he would see Adam and check on Delie and the kids and get to the gym. He came down the stairs with his grip packed.

Adam greeted him with a good morning. "Did you sleep well?"

"Very."

"Why the grip?"

"I'll need to be on my way once I see you and then Delie and the kids. I can get a workout in and then leave."

"Weren't you supposed to see Jay somewhere in there?"

Champ had forgotten. "Yeah."

"Please, make yourself at home." Adam gestured and a maid came forward to take the grip from him again. She took it back upstairs. "Our older children are off at college, so things are a little quiet down here. Please, breakfast is ready."

"Champ!" Em smiled at him from the table in the kitchen.

"HB! Good to see you!"

Ruby, who also sat there, raised an eyebrow. "HB?"

"Honey Bun. It's Champ's special name for me."

Ruby slid the platter of fried eggs and bacon to him. "I believe this is for you."

"Thank you, Mrs. Morson."

Champ tucked into the plate of eggs and admired the cure of the bacon. "It tastes like country stuff. I been all over and you only get this from the country."

"It's from our farm, outside of Pittsburgh. Where Delie and the children will stay."

"Yeah." Em was sad. "We have to be in the city away from them. I might not like it much without the kids."

"Why are they getting shipped off?"

"They need the fresh air and the room. It's best for them."

Interesting how this little woman just waved her hands and everyone in the family did what she said. Almost her husband too. Except Adam did go out of his way to be nice to him, and Champ was grateful for his kindness.

"You going to have a good life, HB. Plenty to do here in the city." Champ made his voice bright, but he could tell Em was not happy and her sadness made him a little angry. "What you going to do?"

"I don't know. I been so used to taking care of the kids and helping Delie. I don't know what else to do."

"Sister dear, eat up. You got a lot of skills. You can sew. You can dress hair. They need those skills in the city, not the country."

Champ didn't want to say anything to this woman in her home, but was compelled to speak. "Em should be able to make up her own mind."

Ruby looked at him as if he had sprouted horns. "These are family matters, Mr. Bates. I would ask you to stay out of them."

"Em is like a sister to me too."

"A lot of nerve you have." Ruby stood. Even though she was short, her carriage was imposing. Champ had fought plenty of battles. He was ready for her, but Adam was at the doorway.

"Ruby, I want to get Champion's examination underway before much longer. I may need your assistance."

Her tone completely changed toward him—one of professional distance. "Of course, Adam. Please, take your time with breakfast, Champion. We'll be ready for you whenever you are." And she left the room.

"Ruby's a nurse, you know? She'll take real good care of you." Em put some margarine on a biscuit.

"Yes, HB. I bet she will."

Champ's eggs and bacon wanted to take a little migration North on their own, but he wouldn't let them. So he swallowed hard.

God was there with him and would see him through.

Delie shook her head. Her sisters were losing their minds in their old age. Mags was the sister Delie could always get over on, and she did not expect any less now that she was grown.

Ensconced in a house of love and laughter, Mags was the grand dame of a brood of seven ranging in age from sixteen years old down to the baby girl a few months old. She sure had her hands full. No one would know if she snuck out to see Champ.

"Where you going, Mama Dee?" Bonnie stood in the doorway with her plaits sticking up. Delie smoothed them down with a hand, wondering if Em would be able to help with Bonnie's hair today.

Getting away from the kids was another matter. "Go on now, Bonnie, go play with your cousins. I got to go see about something."

"Is it Champ? What about him?" Neal came in on the other side, asking the question in his loud voice.

Delie turned around from going to pick up her gray felt hat and her wrap. "Okay, I thought I told you to finish breakfast."

Neal shrugged his thin shoulders. "We have. Now, I'm bored."

"You don't want to play with your cousins?"

"They're a bunch of pinheads. Nothing there."

"Yeah." Bonnie said.

"Well, Willie, Roy and Flo seem to be getting along with the Caldwell children."

Mags came into the hallway holding the baby. "What? What is going on here with you, children? What are you up to, Delie?"

Caught. Delie lowered her clutch purse in front of her. "Can you watch these two for a few minutes? I'm going out."

Mags shifted the squirming baby on her hip and faced her younger sister. “This isn’t Nettie’s. You can’t dump children on me and not have me notice.”

Delie’s shrugged her shoulders. “What’s a few more here or there?”

“Please. Were you trying to see Champ?”

“I’ve got to. Please.”

“Yeah, let her go. We can stay here and be good if she brings us back Champ.” Neal said.

“He’s ours.” Bonnie explained.

Mags stepped forward a bit more. “Is he now? And how did that happen?”

Go to it, Bonnie. Delie knew baby cute when she saw it. She had been a long-standing practitioner of baby cute herself. “He drove the bus. He brought us food when we were hungry. He plays games with us. He bought me a hamburger and shake. And when I had a cold, he brought me a little plastic dolly.” Bonnie held up a cheap, naked, banged-up, pink-skinned doll with blonde hair standing all over her head.

Mags leaned down to the girl. “Well, you have made quite a case, Miss Bonnie. What do you say you and your brother come in the kitchen with me and make play clay while your Mama goes to see about Champ?”

Neal smiled, and Delie was glad to see his boredom had gone away.

“Bye, Mama Dee.” Bonnie waved.

“Be good, you two. I’ll see you soon.” Delie faced Mags and mouthed, “Thank you.”

She couldn't tell by Mags's expression, but Delie knew she was rooting for her. She let out her breath into the cold February morning. She had Em and Mags in her corner. Now to work on the other two. Stepping out into the cold Pittsburgh air nearly took her breath away. Goodness, she had thought it was cold in Georgia. How could it be so much worse?

Ruby's house was just four houses down, but she was nearly completely chilled by the time she got there. She stepped to the front door and knocked quickly. There was a stirring around and Em opened the door. "Delie. What are you doing here?"

Delie practically knocked her down trying to get inside. Inside from the cold. Inside to Champ. "I need to know what is going on."

"With what?"

"Champ."

"Oh. He's in Adam's office. Ruby went off nursing and left me to clean the breakfast up until the day maid comes." Em shook her head. "Breakfast was bad. Ruby don't like Champ."

The realization made her sad and Delie wrapped her cold arms around her older sister. "We can win her over, HB. I just know it."

"Maybe. I don't know. Ruby is mighty mad, and Champ didn't look too happy when Adam said she had to do nursing for him."

Delie and Em went into the kitchen and cleaned up while Champ was in his appointment. When they were done, another day maid came. There was nothing to do but go and sit in Ruby's fine parlor, down the hall from the doctor's office that operated out of the side wing of the house. They had not sat down on the fine davenport for a minute when the three of them came out of Adam's medical office.

The congeniality between Adam and Champ had disappeared. Now, they looked like they were going to fight with one another while Ruby's face was—resigned and sad. It all made no sense. What was going on?

Her heart threatened to beat clean out of her chest. Something did not look right here at all. "What happened?"

"Are you going to tell her?" Adam folded his arms and gestured to Delie.

Champ came and stood next to Delie. He put his arms on her shoulders. Warmth came to her through his large hands and fingers. What would it be like to have those fingers working on her? "Come on, let's go see the kids. I been missing them."

"They miss you too. But is there something going on I should know?"

Champ gathered up Delie's cold hand. He was not afraid to touch her in front of Ruby. Why not? Especially after last night. Her hands went even colder, something she thought impossible a half hour ago when she came down here. "Dee, let's go on ahead."

Out of old habit, Delie turned to Adam. He was her big brother. Now, instead of looking mad, the sadness on his face matched Ruby's. "Sister, I cannot say anything to you regarding my examination of Champion. You aren't married to him, and I—"

Her knees went weak and pains gripped her in her stomach. "What's going on here?" Delie fairly screamed.

Ruby stepped forward and grasped her shoulders away from Champ and sat her down on the davenport. "Adam and I can't say anything cause our license to practice could get taken away. You just need to be strong, Sis. Okay?"

Ruby waved her hand. "If you want to take her for a walk, go on."

"I don't want to go for no walk. I want to know what is going on."

On the other side of her, Em started crying and Ruby went over to embrace her. Em didn't know what could possibly be happening, but crying was a typical reaction of hers when she didn't like what was going on in the room.

She didn't like the way the room felt either.

Delie faced Champ, duplicating his stance in the ring. "If you don't tell me what is going on…I'll fight you myself, with my own fists."

Champ sat down next to her, grabbed both of her hands and held them. His touch was always so warm. It sent jolts through her. "Dr. Morson says… Well, he just saying what the other doctor said—"

"Other doctor?" Ruby turned from embracing Em. "You didn't say you had been to another doctor before."

"I didn't want to. I wanted to see what Dr. Morson would say first."

"And he agrees with me." Adam fixed Champ with an intense gaze that made Delie's heartbeat slow way, way down.

"Yeah. You both saying the same thing. Dee, they say if I fight anymore, I could go blind."

The room swam as she tried to take in what he said. The words sorted themselves out. "Wait a minute. You say if you fight, you could go blind."

"Oh, Lord." Em wailed.

"Hold on, HB." Delie gripped at Champ's hands. They were a little slippery with his sweat. Or was it hers? "It means you can't fight anymore. Right?"

"Yes. That's what it means."

The relief in her heart was like a light load. *Thank you, God.* Something she had not even known she had been praying for had come to pass. "No more fighting?"

Delie turned to Adam. "I am afraid not." Adam intoned.

She faced Champ again. "Well, I'm sorry, because you love it so, but now you can move on with your life. You got a whole lot of other things you can do, get that garage going. Help us with the dairy farm. Make another way. I know you love it, but when God tells us something, we got to listen."

Thank you for making it easy.

But Champ dropped her hands and the cold surrounded them again. "I can't give up fighting."

"What?" His little sentence didn't make sense to her.

"I'm a fighter. I got to fight this fight."

Out of the corner of her eye, Delie could see Ruby shake her head. Adam's arms were folded. His lips were pursed.

"I don't understand."

"He said he's not giving up fighting." Adam interjected. "He said the same thing in my office."

Delie faced Champ again and looked into his eyes, those brown eyes she had always admired with fringed long black lashes. They were so beautiful. To think he would not be able to see out of them again if he kept fighting. It made no sense.

"You've got to stop."

"How can I? I've been waiting my whole life for this fight. The purse, it would mean everything to me. I can't buy you no house like this, but I could do something, get something nice for you and the kids on the purse I could win. I could get ahead a little. Do you know what that kind of money means now? When so many are struggling?"

"I know. But Adam says no more fighting."

"I don't mean no disrespect to Dr. Morson or anyone." Champ seemed to be looking at Ruby, whose face was still sad. "But I'm a warrior for God. He's going to take care of me."

"He could make you blind if you fight, Champ. Don't you hear what Adam said?"

Champ stood up, put on his hat and pulled the brim down low. "He don't know what God know. Excuse me."

And he left them all in Ruby's parlor. She sat, frozen in one spot, but not knowing why she should be so surprised. It had happened again. Abandoned again. How many times could she let

Champ leave her and keep her dignity intact? She didn't want to find out anymore.

This was the last and final time.

CHAPTER SIXTEEN

Champ grabbed his grip as he left and pulled his cap down over his head. Since when did a woman get to tell him all about his life? Champ stomped on the bus and started it up, letting it run on in the cold, cold, Pittsburgh morning. What happened to the time when he could do what he wanted, go where he wanted? Why couldn't he go back to his old life?

Delie. Delie had his heart. No, she was his heart.

Ever since they were little, she had always had his heart and now, seeing the crushed look on her face at the thought of his blindness, he couldn't take it. He just couldn't.

Better to be alone.

But, now there was Neal.

God, please tell me what to do. Help me see what I need to do to be a warrior for you. He sat there, thinking, praying Delie would come out of the house and talk to him, to let him know she would stand by him. That everything would be okay and she would support him in the fight.

The bus ran on in the cold for fifteen minutes. Delie never emerged from Ruby's large warm, beautiful brownstone her rich husband provided. Who could blame her? Her sister would take care of her. The kids would be okay out on the dairy farm. He was nothing. He could do nothing for her. He had to do what he could do for himself. Except it wasn't for himself. It was the moment he had trained his whole life for, to be a Bates for.

He had to do it. Now, he would see Jay to tell him what Adam said. If he didn't want to give him what he needed, he would find another way to get his steak and do what he needed. He couldn't let go now.

He went back to the bank. An employee there told him Jay was still at home and gave him directions. By the time Champ turned the bus around and drove up a small hill, he was only about three blocks away from Ruby and Mags's houses. They had all settled so close to one another.

If he lived up here with Delie, he would have to live around those sisters. He sure didn't want to live all piled up with those sisters. They hated him.

And he? He didn't hate anyone. He loved Delie and her sisters were a part of her. He loved Em and wanted to help take care of her too. They had become an important part of his life again, a part he didn't want to lose. He had to fight for this purse to be able to give them what they needed.

Jay and Nettie's house on top of the hill was the biggest one around. To prove the point, the driveway was long. Big enough to accommodate his bus, even with two cars already parked there.

Impressive. Champ went to the front door and knocked on it, expecting a maid here too, but it was Nettie. "Oh. Come on in." Her voice had a new note of sympathy in it.

Nettie's tone was completely different to him. Did she know already what Adam had said? As he entered the house, he had his answer. Nettie and Jay had a telephone. Yes, she probably knew already. "Jay is in his study."

"Thank you, Mrs. Evans."

Nettie trailed into Jay's study, which was off to the left behind him.

Jay turned around in a big overstuffed chair behind a desk. "Champion, I've been waiting for you."

"I went to the bank. I didn't know where you lived."

"Of course. I'm glad you caught us here. Sit down. Make yourself comfortable. Anything to drink?"

"No, thank you."

"Are you sure?" Nettie asked in a too nice tone. Oh yes. She knew.

"Yes, ma'am."

"You've been to see Adam this morning."

"I have. Dr. Morson said if I kept having injuries and blows to my head, I could lose my sight. He recommended I don't fight any more."

It was easier to say the words each time, especially since he had known for months now. What was hard was seeing people's reactions, like Nettie's, who gasped. She said, "Dear God," and began praying.

He could only imagine what his mother would say.

"I knew about this before Dr. Morson examined me. So if you want me to pay back the money I owe you, I will." Champ went on. He had no idea where he would get a job to pay that kind of money.

"So, you aren't going to fight?"

"I am. I just didn't want you to pay for me to fight under these circumstances when you didn't know what you were buying. That was the whole deal with the examination, right?"

"Yes. I was protecting my investment."

"So I'll pay you back."

Jay shrugged his shoulders elegantly. "I'm not sure why. I paid for you to train. You fight and win. An even exchange."

"Jay, I—" Nettie chirped.

"Timothy 1 chapter 4, verse 3."

Nettie went silent. Wow.

"So that's it?" Champ could hardly believe it. Someone in the world was for him, not against him.

"Yes. If you still want to stay with us while you train, there's plenty of room. Bring your grip on in. Nettie can get those steaks fried up for you just right."

And she would probably dose them with poison too. "I was going back to Georgia to train in Winslow."

"Would you be productive there? Are there trainers? A gym?"

No. It was just so his mother could fry his steaks. Now, Nettie would do it. Maybe he should stay and convince Delie to be in his corner. Just as God was. His mother would not be happy, but this was worth a try.

"I can send my mother a telegram." Champ offered.

The first smile Champ had seen from the former numbers runner slipped across his face. "You need to get busy training, don't you? When we go to the bank this morning, Nettie can send the telegram for you."

Whew. What a relief. He snuck a glance over at Nettie to see if she was willing to do these things. She wasn't as rigid as she had been at the bank weeks ago, but she was not smiling either. "Thank you. I can get going now."

"Feel free to leave the bus in the driveway. The gym is only a few blocks away. You can go with us or--"

"I'll walk. It will be good exercise for me. Thank you, Mr. Evans. Mrs. Evans."

Nettie dipped her head, but the expression on her face was completely neutral. She said nothing.

After he left the house, Champ grabbed a few things from his grip that was still on the bus and went down the hill. At the bottom of the hill, he turned in the opposite direction as Jay had described and walked the few blocks to the gym. When he opened the door, he inhaled. It was all there in the gym—sweat, fear, the spice of love and a primal sense of defense. The central place in his world. He belonged here. A little brown man approached him, surveying him up and down. "Champ, name's Bob Grace. Mr. Evans told me you need some support for your fight."

Champ shook hands with the wizened man whose skin was the color of shoe leather. "Thank you, Mr. Grace."

"Not Mister. Just Bob. I'ma work on you like you need to win. Come on."

"That what I come for, Bob."

And, as he knew how to do, Champ stripped down to begin to work the medicine ball. Home.

Where he should have been comfortable. So, why did he feel miserable?

Because Delie was his home. Delie was his heart.

"I can't believe he is going to do it. It's crazy. A Negro man is nothing in this world without his eyesight." Mags said, after Delie, Ruby and Em had arrived back at Mags's house to see to the children.

Delie was in a bit of a haze. Why would he do it? "It's just money. He gets this big purse, says it is enough for a year, maybe more."

"Champ wants to do the right thing to win." Em said defensively. "He going to win."

"He's going to go blind." Ruby said with emphasis. She turned to Delie. "Do you really want to take care of a blind man on top of the children?"

"Ruby!" Mags spoke to her older sister in a sharp tone Delie had not heard before. "For shame!"

"I'm being practical, Mags. Can baby sister handle it? What kind of job will she have? Him? How would they live? Can a blind man work the dairy farm? Come on, it's impossible. Better he go on back to Georgia now if he is determined to do this crazy thing."

Still, the practicality of it was harsh. "Delie loves him, don't you?" Em asked.

And there it was. Em had a way of putting it all out there, plain as day.

"I do."

"Then that's all that matters." Em spoke in a platitude she must have learned from somewhere—maybe a book or a radio show. Mags had given Em a basket full of socks to mend and Em worked happily away in the corner watching the children. If only her life were so simple, as easy as Em's.

"I don't believe this. I just don't believe it." Ruby threw up her hands.

"God asks us to forgive those who have transgressed against us." Delie insisted.

"He didn't say forget about it. He brought you all up here safely. Great. Thanks. Say goodbye and let him go on back down there to that hateful old Effie Bates."

"I been praying about it," Delie folded her hands almost prayer-like. "And praying. And praying. There is something here in all of it I can't put my finger on. And he's got a right to get to know Neal, regardless."

"Even if he thinks Neal don't belong to him?"

Well, that was a bit of a problem, Delie had to admit. "I'll make him see the truth."

"Hard to know how the fight is going to turn out, when he's going blind. He probably came back so you could take care of him."

"Ruby!" Mags repeated in her strict voice.

Delie stood. "This is very hard, but I can't imagine how hard it must be on him. I wish he would come and tell me about it."

"He don't need to say nothing to you." Ruby insisted.

"I just don't want him to suffer. I can only wish the best for him. Neal is his blood and wishing bad for Champ would be the same as hurting Neal. I'm trying hard to forgive him in my heart. I'm almost doing it too. I've got to keep trying for me, if not for the children."

"Beautiful, Baby Sis. The children need to see forgiveness in operation." Mags's face was soft and glowing. Delie knew she was on board with her.

"Yes, I think so."

"You both are crazy." Ruby folded her arms.

Delie came and stood over her short sister. "We may be crazy. But if anyone in this here room knows forgiveness and what it can do for you—it's you, Big Sister. Am I right?"

Ruby lowered her head and nodded, almost as if she were ashamed to remember. "Oh, Dee, my situation was different."

"It was. But it was still about forgiveness. David was your childhood friend, like Champ was mine, and he did you a great wrong. Solomon came out of it. And you forgave him on his deathbed."

One lone tear coursed down the cheek of Ruby Morson. Delie would have rather cut off an appendage than hurt her sister, but she had to make her see what she saw in Champion. "I did. He asked me to. I didn't want to. But he was lying there, dying. I was looking into the face of God. How could I have said no?"

Delie put an arm around her sister as they sat side by side in the big chair. "How did it feel when you forgave him?"

"Like peace. He was a stupid boy who did what his father told him to do when he attacked me."

Delie cringed as she thought of what her sister had gone through. At least Neal had been conceived in a night of love. "Champ was just a stupid boy who was doing what his mother told him. He was so very young."

The doorbell rang and Mags went to get it. Living on a journalist's salary, she had no maid. "Come on in, Nettie."

"What's going on, Nettie?" Delie looked up at her older sister who was holding a piece of paper in her hand.

"I can't stay." Nettie leaned on a chair to catch her breath. "Jay wants me at the bank. I'm supposed to be sending this telegram."

"Telegrams are bad news. What does it say?" Ruby looked up from her reverie of the past, interested.

"I got to send a telegram to Effie Bates to say Champ is staying up here to train. I got to fry his steaks and such." Nettie made a distasteful face.

"You got to fry his steak? What for?" Delie sat up straighter.

"He's staying with us. Jay says so. He don't want him to worry for anything during his training. He told him to keep training."

"Oh, how could Jay do such a thing? I liked him." Delie slapped her thigh.

"He said it is an investment, honestly." Nettie grabbed the paper. "I love my man, but he can be so infuriating."

"Champ wants to fight. Let him." Em said, and again, the plain simplicity of her way of looking struck Delie hard. She tried to make Em see reason.

"HB, we don't want him to lose his eyesight."

"We got to pray. We've got to put God on him. Champ will be alright then. He can do anything." Em hummed as she sewed.

The sisters turned to each other. "Are you sending the telegram?" Ruby asked Nettie.

Nettie threw up her hands. "I do what my husband says."

"Send it on." Ruby put an arm around Delie. "Put some money with it." She reached into a pocket of her housedress. "I got ten. Send the message, but put in another line to tell her to come up here. You put another ten with it and tell Effie Bates to get her big behind up here to Pennsylvania."

"What?" Delie turned to Ruby. "I don't want her here, judging me. I said goodbye to all that last week."

"Hear me out, baby sister. Once she hear about what is going on with Champion, she'll stop him from fighting. He's so good at listening to his mama and doing what she say, he won't do it to please her."

A light dawned. Ruby might have something there.

"Devious." Mags quipped, "But not half bad."

"It isn't devious," Nettie said, and that settled it. "We're letting a mother know about her child. I do it all the time."

"I don't want to see her no more." Delie blurted out. Her heart raced in her chest at the thought of seeing the woman again. No way.

"If she comes up here looking for a fight, you know your big sisters are here. We won't let anything happen to our baby girl." Ruby put an arm around her and squeezed her shoulders.

She was a little reassured. It made her warm inside that her sisters gave her so much love and support. However, something rankled her. Something she couldn't quite name. For Delie, the other part of it was, this was her fight. She should be able to handle Effie Bates. She would have to find some way in her to handle what should have been handled years ago. "I'm glad I can talk to her with you all here."

"That's what we're here for." Nettie said with her brow furrowed.

Whenever Effie arrived, Delie would have to find the strength to talk to her, to help her see what should be done for Champ's sake. She could do it, she knew, because she loved him.

Delie turned to Ruby. "Champ is staying. What do you think?"

"I don't know, sister. Since when does Winslow have the means to support a fighter?"

"I guess it has been years since you all have been down there, but you are right. There's nothing.

It would be the most rudimentary training, just how he used to train when he was young, doing those set up fights to entertain the rich white men in the battle royals."

"Was he any good?" Mags asked. "There might be a story here for the newspaper. I need to let Asa know about it."

"Oh, he's good." She told them all about Miss Irene. "I had no idea until Miss Irene told me this was a special God-appointed work to support Champ. It's about more than a boxing match. How we got to let white people know we are people too. And we matter as humans." The painful prick of tears threatened behind her eyes. "It all could go away if he loses his eyesight."

Silence filled the room.

"On your knees. I got to get on to send this telegram." Nettie intoned and when Nettie said that, they all heeded her. The Bledsoe sisters, one and all, came in a circle on their knees, joining hands.

"God of all mighty. We lift ourselves up to you in the name of our brother. Our friend, Champion Bates. It seems you have put a mighty work before him and he does not know what to do. Please, give him the wisdom and the sight he needs to help him through his time of trial. Stay by the side of our baby sister, God. Help her. Help her to know you are with her and you are in their corner at all times with this terrible, terrible news."

Delie's stomach was all quivery and jumpy with fear. All of a sudden, there were little feet behind them. The feet entered the room—the children. Delie looked up. They wanted to be part of the circle too. They came into the circle and joined hands. Bonnie's little hand slipped into Delie's on one side and Neal sandwiched himself between Ruby and her. She inhaled their wintry little children smell and her heart gladdened.

"We lift him up to you. Give him the healing and yes, Lord, give him the sight to know, to see that you want for him to do what is right. Please, God. We pray for safe journey on the train for Effie Bates. Help her to come here with yYou in her heart. Help her to open her ears and hear Your Word. Most importantly, Lord, help her to be of You, to accept what is before her."

"Help her, God." Ruby interjected.

"Help all of these children to do your will. We got the farm, Lord, and we going to let them live out there in your word, to know what is right and good for them. We going to make sure they're educated and grow strong in Your will. Where they come from, where any of our children come from Lord, doesn't matter. They are here now with us and we love them and we're going to accept them as the gifts they are."

Delie's heart brimmed at Nettie's powerful prayer. She couldn't help herself. "Amen."

"Yes. God, help us to know and understand you have brought us through many trials and tribulation. Many here in this room have endured rough times, but we have always come back to you. And we'll continue to come back to you every time, God, because we can only be sustained and nurtured through You. In your name, God. Amen."

"Amen." Everyone in the room all intoned together and the joint prayer lifted up to heaven lifted Delie's spirit. As they all stood, Delie went over to Nettie and embraced her.

"Thank you."

"Anytime, Baby Sister. Anytime. Let me get on before Jay wonders if he still has a wife."

Delie watched Nettie slip out the front door marveling at how everyone always thought her middle sister would be the one that never married and here she was the most loyal and faithful wife to such an unusual man.

And she? Would Delie ever marry? Who knew? All she cared about was Champ staying healthy and whole. But what was the best way to convince him?

She had no idea. She hoped his mother could help.

CHAPTER SEVENTEEN

When Champ and Delie were young and in school, she was the smartest. Unless it was math, he couldn't do much to help. Delie always was straightforward and said the right things. Well, maybe at the wrong time, but the right things, regardless. She had no filters holding her back. She would speak what was on her mind. Champ missed that voice telling him what he didn't want to hear.

His leaving her changed everything. It had changed her, for the better, of course. She was grown now, a real woman not a baby girl. Instead, she had come to know sadness. He had done that to her, and he had changed her. Better he stay away while he train.

When it came time to spar, he asked the sparring partners to stay away from his head. "How you going to protect your self from the block shots?"

"I figure it out."

The sparring partner shook his head. "I would still want to be ready for the white man if I had the chance, you know?"

Champ bristled at his suggestion. "I be ready. You making me ready."

"If he go for your head, it's all over."

This wise sparring partner spoke truth in a number of ways. But at this point, for Champ, it was about fighting smart, not harder.

Bob Grace understood. He may not have known what Champ's diagnosis was, but when he came out of the sparring ring for some jump rope work, he clapped him on his bare shoulder. "Fight smart, that's the way. Hold back on your energy. The more you let it out, the better hold he have on you. And if he gets all out of control, there's an opening for you."

Champ stretched his body out. What a help Bob Grace was. He had a team. Still, Delie and the children were missing. He needed them on his team. At lunchtime, he went to the sandwich place around the corner and had a couple of roast beefs. Bob Grace frowned at this. "Dinner, you get protein. You need to build your muscle up. No bread. Red meat makes a boxer hungry. Got a woman to fry your steak up?"

"Sort of."

Bob Grace regarded him closely. "Either you does or you doesn't."

"Okay, I do."

He wasn't convinced. "If there is some trouble with her, you better get it cleared up before you step foot in the ring. If you thinking about your woman, that's a way for your opponent to get to you. Get it right afore next week."

"Thanks." Champ tried to work out as long as possible, to avoid having to go back to Jay's house and face Nettie, but the gym eventually emptied out and he was hungry. He picked up his gear bag for the long walk back to Nettie's. Maybe she could tell him something about Delie and the children when he got back.

Sure enough, when the door opened, the scent of frying steak was in the air. It smelled delicious, but Champ wasn't eager for what Nettie was going to fix for him. He walked down the steps in the entryway back toward the kitchen. Little voices. Who was it?

"Champ!" Neal called out in his loud little voice. "We're having steak again. This is the second time I had steak since knowing you!"

Even though he was a little saddened at the truth of his statement, Champ had to laugh. Delie turned around from the stove. Those hairs were loose around her face again. The felled tendrils made her look so dear and so familiar. This was the home he longed for—with Delie at the center of it.

He went to her. Without thinking or even asking her if it was okay, he laid a hand on her shoulder near her elegant neck and drew her to him. As he came near, he could see her eyes were wide in her face, but he didn't care. He had to taste her to know if she tasted the same, after so many years a part. He reached for her, taking her in. Her lips on his were soft and warm. Just as he remembered.

Exactly like he put into his mind over and over again in all of the dark, cold, lonely small places he had stayed over the years chasing a phantom dream. Delie and her sweet, saucy lips were what was real. How could he ever have doubted it?

Delie's special a luscious mix of sweetness and spice melted away all the defenses, all the excuses in this moment as he stood there kissing Delie over the hot hissing stove. He was thirsty, drinking in the taste of her, left out in the desert for so long. He could partake of her again and again, never getting full.

A little giggle erupted off to his right side. Even as he drowned in Delie's delicious taste, a smile tugged at the corner of his lips. He guessed Bonnie would laugh at someone kissing her Mama if she had not seen it before. He pulled back for air before he drowned completely.

"Well, hello to you too," Delie said. His kiss made her beautiful lips more red. He liked that. He wanted his lips to be imprinted on hers, so everyone would know she was his. Still, he expected a little more excitement from her.

A cough sounded behind him. He shifted to his left. Nettie sat at her own kitchen table. Champ had not even seen her there. "Oh. Good evening, Mrs. Evans."

"Hello."

"Since when do you greet me like that?" Delie demanded as she wielded a fork.

"Since I wanted to. I've been wanting to do it for a long time." Champ admitted. It was good he was not in the ring at this moment. Bob Grace was right. Such moments left you open and vulnerable.

"Well," Delie repeated. "Your steaks are just about ready. The children put the silverware on the table. You can just go on to the dining room and have a seat."

Champ walked past her. Her reddened cheeks showed she liked his kiss. Or was it all the heat from the stove? "We'll talk later."

Delie nodded, paying closer attention to the sizzling steak, as if her life depended on it.

He walked out into the dining room where most of the children were giggling and carrying on.

Jay Evans, already seated at the table, regarded him coolly. For some reason, the expression on his face took Champ back to the day earlier in the month when he was asking him for money. He nearly broke out in another cold sweat.

"How's it going?"

He was one smooth cat. "It is going great. Had a great training day."

"Wonderful. Children, please adjourn to the living room for a few minutes."

In all his time with those noisy kids on the road, he had never seen them obey so fast. What was it about Jay Evans? His cool smooth way? His low voice? Whatever it was, he was coolness personified. The only time the man showed a little warmth was with his Nettie. Nettie was the brazier who lit him up. Amazing.

"Champion, I'm glad you are having a great training period. However, you need to make sure you aren't gambling with Delie's heart as well."

Oh wow, that kind of came out of left field. "I see."

"Adam is not the kind to speak on this nor would Asa. Given my capacity as a male figure in this family, as well as your patron, I would caution you to proceed very carefully with her. She has been tremendously hurt before. She can be again. And now there are the children to consider as well. Why would you embark on something potentially dangerous to her and to you? Makes no sense."

The heat rose in his veins and threatened to shoot out of his fingertips. He had always heard there were prices to pay for having a patron. Was this one of them? "I been on the road for a long time, building up my career and my record. I did it all on my own. I never asked a man to put a dime on me until now. A couple of fighters said a patron was the same as selling your soul, and you couldn't call on things yourself as before. I didn't want to believe them. But, Mr. Evans, I been part of this family longer than thewhole lot of you. Delie's my heart. I went back to Winslow to claim it. I couldn't live without her any more. I couldn't exist. And just as I am fighting a white man, I'ma fight for her. No one is going to say to me what I can do now."

"No one?" Jay sat there, cool as ever, regarding him. "Not even your mother?"

"No. Not even her."

Jay twirled a fork on the table. "Good. Something had to be said."

Champ sat back down. "Bob Grace was asking me the same thing today."

"He was."

"Yeah. Told me to get it straightened out."

"And he's right. Get it straightened out. You got enough on your mind. Can't have these problems popping up as well. If she's going to be in your corner, if the children will be in with you, then that's all I ask for. The fact you are staying up here rather than running back to your mama told me a lot." Jay extended his hand.

Champ was not sure why Jay extended his hand, but he shook it.

"Welcome to the family." Jay smiled and so did Champ. "You going to marry her?"

"If she'll have me."

"She will." Jay's voice was smooth and firm. "I was about to make it clear to her she needed the protection of a man on the farm. She had to marry someone. I had several other potential candidates lined up." He kept twirling that fork while Champ's blood went cold. He broke out in a sweat again.

"You did?"

"When we go out to the farm, you'll see. Can't have no woman out there alone. Got to have a man on the farm. You ready?"

"I did farm work all my young life. I've seen a lot. Wouldn't mind returning to it sometime."

"Good. Glad to hear it. Here come the ladies."

Nettie came into the dining room carrying a platter of steak and Delie came in with other bowls in her hand. "Where are the children?" Delie asked Champ as she set a bowl of potatoes and another of carrots down on the table.

"I sent them in the living room to play," Jay said, "while Champion and I had a little man talk. You may call them back in."

Champ's spirits lifted to see them again. Their presence was part of what enhanced his life and made him feel as if he had a purpose in this world. Even after their spat yesterday, Champ did the right thing by coming back to her. Now he was coming to understand, the rewards of the return were many.

Delie didn't know what had just transpired before she and Nettie entered into the room, but the way Champ grinned at her with his pretty teeth was nearly blinding. "Hey, watch the grill." She held up a hand in front of her eyes. It was an old joke of theirs. Delie always liked to tease Champ about his "girly" parts—his gorgeous brown eyes, eyelashes and his beautiful teeth. So much of him was…well, pretty. No other way to describe it.

But when he kissed her a few minutes ago, she had felt his hardened chest next to her and knew without question, this was a man who kissed her, not some untried, practicing boy. How had he gotten so smooth?

Delie started scooping out potatoes. Better to not ask. "It's not as shiny or complete as it used to be."

"I wondered about your teeth." Nettie said stabbing steaks and doling them out to the hungry well-behaved children. Jay had quite an impact on her children. He had them half-scared to misbehave. "How come your teeth are so pretty?"

"I always take care of them with baking soda and hydrogen peroxide."

"No. I mean, how come no one hasn't knocked them out?"

Delie and Champ looked at one another and burst into laughter. "What's so funny?" Nettie said, slightly flustered as she kept serving steaks.

"No, big sis. Champ's teeth was the sideshow while he was fighting in the battle royals back in Winslow. The white men would pay extra for anyone who could get Champ in the teeth. They thought he was too proud."

"Yes. They were a form of bounty."

"And no one did?" Neal chewed on his steak in wonder.

"No. No one did."

"You must have been real good." Willie said, his eyes sparkling.

"Must have been? Still am." Champ dug into his steaks and gave Delie a wink as he did.

Maybe he was too good. She might have hoped in all the time he was away that he would have gotten knocked out a few times, but maybe not. She remembered Adam's diagnosis and guilt rose to her face in the form of a heated blush.

Champ had made some hard choices in his life.

"Did you train well today?" Delie asked picking at her steak, even though it hurt her to ask. Fighting was the thing he loved more than her, and the thing he loved which took him away from her. And Neal.

"It went well enough, Dee. What about you?"

"Me? I didn't train for a fight today."

The children laughed and some of her appetite came back. Champ reached out for her hand. "I mean, your day. How was it?"

"We're trying to line these ones up to get them to school. So we did practice work today and then we'll see when we get them out to the farm about the school they'll be going to out there."

"Tell us about the farm."

"It's a dairy farm. Out in a place called Penn Hills. About twenty minutes ride from here. You won't be in the city all the time, but it'll be enough for us to see each other more regular than years apart." Nettie smiled. "A lot of fresh air. Lots of cows. You'll love it."

"I'm a country girl at heart, I think." Delie sighed and they all laughed. "What did I say?"

"You're just a handful no matter where you are." Champ said fondly and Delie smacked him on his arm. Maybe she shouldn't have touched him. The hard steel feel of his unyielding flesh reminded her of his manliness.

God, help me to do right. Delie breathed out through her teeth, which had a gap in them and weren't nearly as pretty as Champ's.

He loved her, right? She had to try to let him have space for what he loved until she could have her turn.

She was willing to wait. As she did, the days passed companionably. She went to Nettie's to cook dinner for Champ and brought the children after he was done at the gym. With Nettie and Jay there, it was almost like a family situation and she forgot, as the days went by, Effie Bates was coming in. She almost forgot. Until she did.

At the end of the week, they were preparing to go to church, when a telegram came to Asa's office and told of her arrival time. After they all attended Nettie's church, the sisters gathered in the all-purpose room in the back for lunch as Champ tended the children.

"Someone will have to get her." Nettie pointed out.

"I can get her." Delie offered quietly.

Not one of the sisters said anything and Delie could not figure out why. "I'm learning how to drive now that I'm here in the city. I can do it. I have a few things to say to her."

"No doubt." Ruby said, biting into a chicken leg.

"I guess you'll have to." Nettie said resigned. "The Lord will bless you and keep you with that one."

From across the room, Champ regarded her with love in his beautiful eyes. What wouldn't she do if he continued to look at her like that? She was even ready to encounter his dragon of a mother.

"Where will she stay?" Mags asked.

"Sister, you have a full house. She can stay in Goldie's room. So she can be near Champ." Nettie offered.

And away from me, Delie mentally added.

Somehow, she didn't mind. Since she was staying with Mags, Mags did have a full house. Maybe Champ would be able to convince his mother about what he wanted for his life if he and his mother were at Jay's house together.

And so, the next day, in a modest blue dress borrowed from Ruby and altered to fit by Em, Delie figured out how to navigate her way through the busy Pittsburgh streets in Ruby's car and met Effie Bates at the train.

She was sure her stomach was full of big pine knots. She tried to keep at the top of her mind how Champ loved his mother. She stood on the platform watching as Effie disembarked, wearing a great big hat from a far earlier time period that slanted to one side, looking disheveled and greatly put out. Effie tugged on a burgundy dress that was far too tight for her and far too long to be fashionable. Her better than best, Delie supposed.

"Hello, Mrs. Bates." Delie said, waving her over.

Of course, just at that moment, a Pullman porter whistled at her legs. And her heart sank.

Effie's eyes bore into her. "It's cold as anything up here. What you doing standing on the platform in a skimpy dress?"

"Good to see you too, Mrs. Bates." Delie kept her tone light, lest she slap her.

"I didn't get a wink of sleep all the way up here."

"Is your luggage nearby?"

"Yes." She gave her the ticket. The moment she did, a Pullman was grabbing the other end out of Delie's hand.

"Let me take care of that, baby girl."

"Thank you, sir." Delie said loudly, on purpose, to emphasize she did not know the man.

"Hmm. Fast as ever I see."

"I'm a newcomer here. Same as you."

"Why you here by yourself? Where's Champion?"

"He's training."

"He better be. This is his one shot. He needs to get himself home to see about getting some real training in. I'ma take my son home with me up out of this craziness. Should have known he would come up here and get his head twisted around."

Delie followed the porter who gathered the two cheap pasteboard cases and took them to the car, parked illegally in front of the station. Ahh. So, that was where her train money went. Instead of buying a sleeper, she sat up for the whole trip and bought these cheap suitcases. Many of the migrants who came into Pittsburgh never had a suitcase. Effie Bates would not risk looking country, so she bought them. She had enough luggage. It looked like she was planning to stay. She did not want to bother the Lord by calling on Him.

Delie was ready for her, regardless. She gestured toward the waiting car and went around the other side, praying for a steady hand to drive the short way through the city back to the gym. Her driving skills were still very new. 1.

Effie eyed the car with suspicion. "Whose car is this?"

"Ruby, my older sister. She's on medical cases with her husband and didn't need it."

"Looks like a car bought with ill-gotten gains." Effie slid her wide behind down in the backseat of the car.

"Ruby is a nurse and Adam is a doctor." Delie edged herself in across from her. *Please stay by me, God. Help me to stay polite and nice to her.*

"Hmm, I just remember something about some gambling money in your family."

"Jay, Nettie's husband, and Champ's patron, was in the numbers game quite a few years ago. He sold his share of the game out for sports endeavors and is part owner of a Negro baseball team and field here. His backing of Champ is part of his growing sports empire."

"Oh." Effie straightened out. Any one who supported Champ was for her, unless it was Delie. "Sounds like a wealthy business man."

"You'll be staying in his home, with Champion. I hope you don't mind."

"No. It sounds like it will be nice. He married Nettie, you say?"

"Yes."

"Yes. Nettie was always all right by me. She's someone who knows the Lord God." A sly implication that Delie did not.

"We sent you to come here, Mrs. Bates, because we got some disturbing news about Champ." Delie leaned forward a bit.

"Oh, dear God. What is it? I knew there was some reason why my baby was not coming back. They cancelling his fight?"

"No, ma'am." They passed a billboard, talking about the fight. "Far from it." She pointed up. "There's an advertisement for it. It'll be in Philly."

"I gotta get a new dress then, if he ain't coming back to Winslow. Oh. This is his chance, I just know."

"Dr. Morson, who I just told you about, said Champ is having vision problems. If he keeps fighting, he will go blind." Delie never, ever believed in delay. What was the point?

"Blind?" Effie shifted in her seat.

"Yes." Delie gripped the seat as they navigated the narrow streets of the Hill District. "I had hoped you could help me tell him not to go ahead with the fight." Delie wondered how the woman didn't blink an eyelash at this terrible news of her son.

"Have you lost your mind? This is his chance. He ain't going to blow it for anyone. Especially not you."

And in her cruel response, all of Delie's hopes went straight out of the proverbial window. She was on her own. Abandoned. Again.

CHAPTER EIGHTEEN

Bob Grace was not being especially complimentary today. Champ did not look for compliments usually, but this close to the fight, he liked to have a little encouragement. And now word was getting around about the historic nature of the fight, there were visitors to the gym. Jay came all the time on break from the bank.

At some point in today, Asa Caldwell would come. He got to know Delie's brother-in-law pretty well. Since Asa was a journalist, he started writing articles about Champ at Jay's encouragement. Other visitors started to come and watch his practices, even long-legged females.

The distraction made focus more difficult, but he had to remember what this was all for. To get Delie back into his life and to make a home with her. A real home. A home where she wouldn't have to suffer and work so hard. Her happiness was all he had wanted for years.

And to get a chance. Just one shot to show what he could do.

Dear God, was that his mother coming into the visitor's bleachers? How could he have expected she would stay down in Winslow when he did not come right back as he told her he would? Always a price to pay. He held up a fist to his sparring partner, took out his waxen mouth guard and went over to where Effie Bates sat.

"Hello, Ma." Champ put his arm around her and gave her a big smack on the cheek. "Long time no see."

"I should be mad at you for sneaking out from home, but Delie showed me all of these people who are behind you, son. Isn't it wonderful?"

His mother squeezed him extra hard.

"Where's Delie?" Champ looked beyond her. His heart lightened every time she came into the gym, even though she did not come that often.

His mother let him go.

"She's with the car or something. I ran ahead. You ain't glad to see me, son?"

"I didn't say anything, Ma. Just trying to make sure everyone is all right. I'm looking at Bob Grace now. He ain't too happy about all this attention cause he think it makes me train worse."

"Oh, I'm sure that can't be true. Hello!" His mother waved at Bob Grace, who was frowning in the opposite corner of the ring where they were standing and talking during his impromptu break. Bob Grace got up a big mouthful of spit and put it in the bucket. His bucket. Champ wasn't happy about that. Bob Grace wasn't the one fighting, he was.

"Did she tell you what the doctor said?"

"She said something about some doctor saying you going blind." Effie Bates waved her hand as if she were waving away a fly.

"That's what one doctor say around Christmas time. Dr. Morson agrees with him."

"What do a doctor know? He just a man. Leave it to God. God will take care of you."

True. Still, it would have been nice to have his mother worry about it more. "Ok. I got to get back to training."

"I'ma sit right over here."

"Fine, Ma." Champ still had his eye on the door, but squatted down a couple of times to loosen his leg muscles up.

And there she was. Delie came through the door in what was probably another one of her sister's outfits made over for her. Maybe it was one of Ruby's dresses. He could tell, because the dress was a little shorter than it should have been and afforded a nice view of Delie's fantastic legs. Lord have mercy.

Delie sat on the bleachers next to where Asa sat with his amputated leg thrust out. Champ gestured to her with his wrapped fist. Delie looked over to where Bob Grace sat and waved a hand. She knew to check Bob Grace's attitude. But, hey, he was the fighter. Delie came to him as he beckoned her.

"How doing?" Champ's words slurred around his mouthpiece.

"Fine. Been better."

"Take her to house."

"She was not having it. She wanted to come here to see you, especially after she saw the billboard as you come into the Hill."

"Get her out of here."

"I will. We can stay until lunch and then I'll use lunch as an excuse to get her out of here. Do what you have to do." Champ looked into those jewel brown eyes of Delie's and his heart warmed to see how the little fuzzy tendrils of black hair escaped from the edges of her bun. Her beauty never failed to stun him.

"Yes, ma'am. Kiss me?"

Delie made a face so contorted, he threatened to spit out his mouthpiece and laugh.

"No, you drool when you have your mouthpiece in." She started to turn away and then looked back at him with a wink. "I'll make it up to you later though."

"I be looking forward to it." Champ put on his gloves and smacked his fists together. Ready to go. His blood raced with intention. Delie and the children had made him want to win this fight like no fight he ever had. Ever since he had seen her on Main Street in Winslow, his belly was lit up like a steel furnace.

Best to get down to work so he could buy bolts of beautiful fabric for Em to make Delie a whole new wardrobe. Em would have something to do and he could feast on Delie wearing green, the color he liked best on her. No gray.

Yep. He had a lot of fight for.

Delie stepped around all of the dirt and trash in the gym back to the bleachers. She tugged on the skirt just a little more. Why was Ruby so short? She needed to buy some extra material to add to this dress. Em could put it on as a banner. Everyone wore banners on their dresses these days, no disgrace in that. She purposely ignored Effie's withering gaze of disapproval on her. Better to sit next to Asa. Still, though, she needed to do the Christian thing so she waved for Effie to come over to the other side of the bleachers.

"I'm keeping my eye on my son." Mrs. Bates spoke in her shrill voice and pointed to Champ. Effie was being defiant because her side of the bleachers was closer to where Champ practiced in the sparring ring, and she could see him up close much better.

Delie wanted to snicker. If Effie knew who Asa was, she would have been over on the other side of the bleachers like a shot. "Asa, I want to introduce you to Champ's mother, but she won't come over here on this side."

"I would go over there, but my leg is kind of twitching today. Might be a thaw on the way."

When she was little, Delie thrilled to the way Asa would forecast the weather by the twinges, aches and pains in his legs. When he had first come to Winslow as an investigative journalist in the cotton mill, she was the only one who was not afraid to ask him about his leg. Everyone else acted as if it would be rude.

Delie jumped up. "I'll tell her who you are. Watch her practically fly across the room when she hears you are a newspaper man."

Delie moved back toward Effie. "Hey, Champ's trying to get his sparring going on. I want to introduce you to someone over here."

"He needs to focus on his work and can't do that with you switching yourself around here in your short dress. And I'm trying to cheer my son on, if you don't mind."

Actually, Delie didn't care about what she wanted and would have said so. *Lord, help me please.* And of course, God obliged her. "Asa

Caldwell over there is my brother-in-law, Mags's husband. He's the journalist who has been writing articles about Champ. He'd like to talk to you."

She opened her mouth to get the words out of her mouth but Effie stood and walked in the open area, around Asa's leg. "Oh, oh my, Mr. Caldwell. How are you today?"

A smile tugged at the corner of Delie's lips, but she kept her lips from twitching. She walked around too and noticed Champ watching her as she did so. What was he looking at? Probably the same thing his mother noticed — her dress was this much too short. She pulled on the dress again. Going to introduce Asa to Effie Bates, she detected Champ giving a wolfish grin around his mouthpiece. Devil Man.

"Mrs. Effie Bates, may I introduce you to Mr. Asa Caldwell? Mr. Caldwell is my brother-in-law and a writer for the Pittsburgh Courier."

"Good to meet you, sir. We are always reading the paper down in Winslow."

"Well, yes ma'am," Asa turned on the charm. "I have been wanting to talk with you about Champion. My photographer will be here shortly. He might take a couple of photos as well for my next story, do you mind?"

Effie looked as if she had been struck sideways. "My picture…in the Pittsburgh Courier? All over the country."

"Yes, ma'am." Asa rubbed his leg. "I would have gone over there to talk with you, but my old war injury is acting up again."

"You a war hero too? My goodness. I would have never expected so much of my trip up here to Pittsburgh. What do you want to know, sir?"

"Well, ma'am, many readers will want to know about his name. I'm sure many people express surprise when they hear it. Can you tell us a little more about his name?"

Delie knew this story already and was about to tune Effie out when she realized she had not had an opportunity to hear the story from his mother. "My husband's family, the Bates, had been long standing boxers. They were the ones who, back in slavery times, were the boxers."

"It was their job?"

"Why yes. Down there at the Suther plantation, when you was a Bates, you were a boxer. It was in their blood. First, people thought it was cause the Bates were mean, and they would stand to the end of the fight. Then, it got to be they had the best bodies. They was bred for fighting. Old Harvey Suther, he wanted only certain strong female slaves to be with a Bates, to have them be big and strong. Even when slavery times ended, the Bates were real careful about who they married and had babies with to keep up their boxing bloodline. So, when I was a girl and Earl Bates came around, I was happy."

"Happy?" Delie asked.

"Yes, girl. Earl Bates was a fine looking man with a broad strapping chest." Effie's hands went waving in the air to show just how broad Earl Bates was. "A beautiful, beautiful man." Yuck. Delie colored a bit at this fond reminisce from

Champion's mother. She did not need to know how Champ got into the world. And the way Effie was smiling was not reassuring either.

"When we had our son, Earl said to name him after the great Jack Johnson. He said our son would continue the line of great boxing men. So I called him Champion Jack Bates, after the heavyweight champion of the world."

"I see," Asa said and his mustache twitched a bit.

"I'da had more great boxing sons for him too, but he was working out in the fields one day and he just fell over and died. Champ was only three months old."

"He what?" Delie sat up now. She had not known how Champ's father had died. Blood rushed in her ears and made her face and neck warm.

Effie peered at her as if she had a few screws loose and maybe she had. "That's how my Earl died, in the fields. We ain't had no mule plow, and he was plowing himself. My Earl died in a harness."

"Did the doctor say why he died?" Delie asked.

"Ain't no doctors going to come for no colored man when they dies, girl. What's the matter with you?"

"I just hoped he got medical attention."

"This short time in the north done turned your head. His heart just give out." Effie gestured largely with her hands and for all the world, looked like Neal. Delie gulped.

She ventured another question to the crotchety woman. She would apologize if she was taking up Asa's time. "His heart? How old was he?"

Effie squared her shoulders. *This is a wound*, Delie thought. She had to probe it though. "We was young. We had just had Champ. Earl was 'bout twenty-two years old. I was twenty-one."

My God. Delie was sure the blood drained out of her face to her fingers because they tingled.

"Had to be mighty hard to have to raise a boy by yourself at such young age, ma'am," Asa said, as he wrote something down.

"I know. It was. I ain't going to lie. It's mighty hard to raise a boy by yourself when you just a little girl yourself. But Earl knew, before he went on from here. He told me how to raise my boy to be a champion, to grow to be strong. He told me about the Bates boxing history and how he chose to be with me because I was a big boned girl. Never thought Earl Bates would look my way. But when he told me why he wanted to be with me, I was proud."

Delie covered her mouth to keep her horror inside, some reason to be proud when a guy wants to be with you for your big bones. Still, Effie's words struck her just as hard too. Was Neal's problem one he had gotten from his grandfather? She had never heard about Earl Bates before. If they had been from Winslow originally, people would have talked all about it, but Effie moved to Winslow when Champ was about nine years old. Delie was the first one in town to make friends with the new boy.

She uncovered her mouth. “I never heard about him before.” Delie voice came in a new whisper.

“I tell Champ about his daddy. He’s for us to talk about. I don’t talk about him to no one else hardly.”

Delie ignored this bit of rudeness as typical Effie. “Are there any more Bates folk down by the Suther plantation?”

“No, I don’t think so. I moved back to Winslow where I had people because there was a bad flood. Couldn’t get the crops in and I heard about jobs in the mill.”

“You had to bring the crops in by yourself?”

“Don’t know who else would have done it.” Effie straightened out her big body as much as she could. “It was my job to raise my child.”

“Yes, I understand that.”

“A fascinating story, Mrs. Bates. I know many will draw strength from your story.” Asa reassured her.

Effie half laughed and waved her hand. Her laugh was a strange sound Delie had not known before and now she understood why. “Negroes don’t have a choice but to do what got to be done. I put my hand on the plow and my faith in God. I just do as He told me to do.”

“Praise God.” Delie said softly again. “Did you take Champ to a doctor to see about his heart?”

“One of the reasons I come to Winslow was cause I heard there was a Negro doctor who might see if Champ was like his daddy. It wasn't true, though. Every time he be fighting in those battle royals, I get on my knees praying to God to deliver him and that he don't get hit in the chest cause of his heart. One Christmas, we went to Atlanta and I took him to the hospital there. Plenty of doctors there, they tell me he was okay in his body."

Delie drew a visible breath of relief. His eyesight was problem enough. She didn't know if she could take it if something was wrong with Champ in his body. "I pray the same thing for Champ's eyesight, ma'am. I pray he will be alright."

"He'll be fine. You got to have faith in God and lean on Him more. He gone take care of Champ. It's His will Champ be ready for this mighty fight. I know it, just like I know I am sitting here."

To Delie, Effie Bates stood in a new light. She wanted to grasp her hand and get some reassurance, but she knew she would be rebuffed and Delie did not think she could handle a rejection right now.

"Your faith is an amazing testimony, ma'am." Asa said, his voice grave as he wrote more notes.

She had to put it out there. They had never spoken this extensively before, but she had to say it. "One reason we came up north is so my son Neal can get an operation."

"One of all of them kids needs an operation? It is mighty costly having all those little ones, girl. I don't know how you do it."

"Yes." Delie fixed her with a very direct look. "For his heart."

Would she react in any way? Did it even register with Effie the problem with Neal might be the very same problem with Earl Bates? Did Effie even care? But the woman's eyes did not flinch in one direction or another. And in that moment, Delie knew she was a Christian. God was right there with her, because Delie could have really resented her for her lack of reaction.

What did she expect? That Effie would open her arms and say, "Praise God, I have a grandson?" No. Nothing happened. Delie's revelation never shifted the look on her face. *God, grant this woman peace and love.* Champion's mother had endured hard times in her life and God should grant her those two things, even if she were not able to love.

"I'll pray for you and your children, girl."

Effie might have said the same to a stranger on the street. Not even her name. Not even a moment of kinship to show they were both women who had sons they were raising on their own and worried about. Delie lifted her chin and slid off the bleachers, blinking fast. "I'll take all the prayers I can get, Mrs. Bates, thank you."

The fast blinking worked and she did not shed one tear. *Thank you, God.*

Asa sensed the tension and struggled to his feet. Delie gripped at her short skirt. She never knew if she should help him in moments like this. Mrs. Bates started to fuss as if to help him herself, but Asa stood up and smoothed down his pants leg. "Oh no, ma'am. I'm fine. My photographer is here.

Mr. Harris will take some photos in the corner of the ring. Let me see if this is a good time for Champ to stop for his lunch break."

Asa went halfway to Bob Grace, who had a more satisfied look on his face since his charge had been working hard and gave him a hand signal. "It's okay. Mrs. Bates, come on over next to Champ in the ring. You stand here. Mr. Grace?"

Delie had not ever been a large size, even when she had carried Neal, so she did not know someone with girth could move so fast, but Mrs. Bates slid down off the bleachers and went right over to Champ. Asa gave them all directions so they could pose and be ready for the camera. They all looked great. A great spread in the newspaper for Champ and his mother. Time for lunch with the children. She turned to get ready to leave when Asa called her name.

She went to her brother-in-law quickly, so he didn't have to meet her halfway with his leg.

"You aren't going to get in the picture?"

For once, Delie had no words.

"Come on, Dee," said the mouthpiece-free Champion. "You come on this other side."

Out of the corner of her eye, Effie Bates gave her the evil eye. Too bad.

Champ had asked for her.

She stood on the other side of Champ. He put a sweaty arm around her shoulder. He had his mother at his other side and Bob Grace stood in front of Champ, since he wasn't very tall. Mr. Harris snapped several photos in quick succession, popping flashbulbs as he did so, causing Delie to blink. "Ok, folks it's a wrap. Thanks for the help. We'll check in on the training session tomorrow."

"Mama, I know Delie will take you for a nice lunch and I'ma see you later for dinner." He kissed his mother on her fleshy cheek.

"I would much rather stay and see you train."

"No more women around today." Bob Grace said with particularly bad grace and Delie smiled. She liked him. He was like her in some ways.

"See, Mama. I got to do what my trainer says."

"You sure do. I'll go where ever she takes me and wait until dinner time."

"Thank you, Ma. Thanks, Dee." Champion's gorgeous thick lips touched her too briefly on the side of her face. Coward. If he hadn't just dealt with his mouthpiece, she would have laid on him as he did the other day. He didn't dare kiss her as he did the other day in front of his mother.

Asa stood next to the ring scribbling and came up to them. "Got to identify Delie for the picture. What you want me to say, Champ? For the picture."

"What you mean?"

"I've got to put down. "Mrs. Effie Bates, mother, Mr. Bob Grace, trainer, and Cordelia M. Bledsoe…"

She didn't know why, but there were knots in the pit of her stomach. What would Champ say?

But she knew. They had been connected by the heart for more than twenty years and she knew. "Cordelia May Bledsoe," Champ said with the funny emphasis he put on her middle name to make her sound country. "My fiancée."

And the room got light and airy all of a sudden and was nothing like a sticky, stinky gym anymore with closed air.

Champ had called her his fiancée.

In front of his mother.

And she didn't mind he had not asked her directly at all.

Well, not really.

CHAPTER NINETEEN

Although the two women he loved most in the world were at Jay Evans's house, ready to welcome him home, Champ was not eager to walk through the door after his workout in the gym.

He was dreading it.

The sweat pouring off of his body now came from dread, not the punishing workout he had just endured. He tried to put the disastrous picture from earlier out of his mind. Asa Caldwell had said, "Fiancée? I didn't know I was going to get a news scoop on the family as well today."

And, Delie's cool response, "Was that a marriage proposal?"

And, his completely messed up way of responding, "Yeah."

"Well you need to come at that again." And Delie had walked out of the gym while he looked after the way her short skirt swayed back forth enticingly.

Then there was the satisfied smirk of his mother.

And Bob Grace frowning. "See, that's why I don't want women in the gym."

Oh boy. What was he going to do now? He already owed Delie big time, since she had to keep company with his mother and entertain her all day long, something she had not done before and would, doubtless, have to do until the fight next week. Bob Grace had an idea, but he knew neither one of them would like it.

Move camp to Philadelphia where the fight was so he could get used to the city and its food and water until the fight. And leave the women out of it. Leave one more time.

Delie would not like this at all.

His mother would be unhappy. He brightened a bit. He had not asked her to come here. What was she doing here anyway? First, he needed to get at the bottom of why she was here, and then unravel what had happened with Delie. His nerves calmed quite a bit. It was always best to have a plan.

But, this would be a long night. Champ knocked on the door to Jay's house and was surprised to see the tall, elegant man answer his own door. "I knew it was you. Come on in the study."

Oh no. Not more trouble.

Champ followed Jay into the study. "I made a little trouble at camp today and I was trying to get it straight here."

"Get your thoughts straight first. You want to marry her, right?"

"I do."

"Then ask her the right way. Delie doesn't seem much like the dress-up type, but you at least got to ask her right, man."

Champ gripped at his head. "I know, I know. I really messed up."

Jay shook his head. "Bob does not like all this drama in camp. He called a bit ago and told me he wanted to move camp to Philly."

"And?"

"I think it is a good idea. With your mother here and all now. Those Bledsoes. Lord, those sisters. I sure didn't think your mother should be up here. All Nettie had to do was say you were staying up here." Jay shook his head back and forth. He wasn't mad, just amused at his wife's antics. Look at what love did to a man.

"I think they thought Mama was going to talk me out of fighting. Goes to show they don't know her well. She been raising me for fighting my whole life long."

"And you going to do it?" Jay regarded him evenly.

"Absolutely." Champ and Jay shook hands on it. The door to Jay's study creaked opened a bit. They both looked at each other with curiosity as the door shut hard.

"Excuse me." Jay did a bizarre looking tiptoe to his own study door and opened it a crack on the other side. "Ah ha!" Jay pulled a startled looking Bonnie into the study. "A little spy."

Champ grinned at the incongruous picture of teeny Bonnie, looking up at Jay scared out of her mind. Jay was the tallest of any of them. Champ coughed and spoke to Bonnie in his deepest tones. "What you doing here, Bonnie?"

Her eyes got big and round as they stared up at Jay. "They made me come here to see if you was in here, Champ. Willie said he heard the door."

"And?" Jay folded his arms and regarded the little girl very harshly, but Champ could see the amusement twinkling in his eyes.

"I sorry. I won't do it no more." Bonnie worked the end of one braid between her fingers. The sound of her scratchy hair echoed in the quiet throughout Jay's study.

"Do you know what happens to little girls who dare come into my study uninvited?"

"No. No, Sir."

Jay regarded her and laid a long finger on Bonnie's head, directing her behind his desk. "They get a peppermint stick." Jay pulled one out of a drawer and Bonnie's eyes went extra wide at the treat. "But you cannot have it until dinner is over. Go and take it to your mother."

"Thank you, sir."

"You're welcome, child. Go on ahead. Let her and Miss Nettie know we will be out in a minute. No more spying."

The two men grinned at each other after Bonnie closed the door. Champ couldn't help but chuckle. "Those kids have been so scared of you." He completely understood. He had been in their shoes not so long ago.

"Yeah, I know. It's been fun teasing them." Jay looked wistful. "I have a girl too, you know. I remember what it was like."

Champ remembered hearing about his daughter who was away at school. He hoped he would get to meet her some day. He guessed he would if he were in the family. "They are something."

Jay was all business. "Get on to Philly. Tomorrow. You do that and win the fight. I will spring for the ring. I'll be in Philly next Thursday." He clapped a hand on Champ's shoulder.

"Thanks, Jay. Mr. Evans."

Jay extended a hand to him. "Jay is fine. You going to be in the family now. No more running off from my little sister. You have a problem, you come and talk to me about it." Champ knew he was serious.

Wow. What an interesting thing in his life.

To have another man— a brother, a friend to talk to in times of trouble. Someone who understood.

In this moment, he had never known that kind of companionship and it came to him, he had been lonely for a long time. "Thank you, Jay, for all you have done."

"Now, let's go in and get all of your woman trouble straight. Got to do as Bob Grace says."

"Yes, sir." And there was the dread again.

"Lord a mercy." Nettie waved a hand in front of her face to cool it in the hot kitchen. "Me and Jay was rattling around in this house by ourselves and then the whole lot of you come up in here. Even got the Mama here."

"We'll be moving out to the farm soon." Delie soothed her sister.

"I know." Nettie gave a half smile as she stirred the beef stew. "And I'll probably miss you too. You going to the fight?"

Delie's face took on a stubborn expression of crossed eyebrows. She turned up her nose. "I don't know if I should."

She peered all around and there was Effie Bates, the High and Mighty One herself, in the dining room, trying her best not to engage with any of the children. "I have had enough of her and she wouldn't miss it for anything."

"Well, maybe."

"I have the children." Delie sliced up some bread to go with the stew.

"We can take care of them here. Em can help out."

"He didn't ask me."

"Girl, God put something in front of you and you afraid to rise up and take it. Like you don't deserve it. You're a Bledsoe. Take it."

"I don't want anyone who don't want me." Delie said with her lip poked out, baby girl cute style.

"Grow up, Dee. Be a woman. He'll see you and be a man."

She stopped pouting. "Really?"

"Try it. You'll see." Nettie grasped the stew pot with the towel in her hands. "I hear Jay and he's going to be hungry. Let's go."

Delie picked up the platter of bread and followed Nettie into the dining room. The children all sat with their flatware in place, milk poured in their cups.

Nettie spoke to Champ's mother with unfailing politeness. "Welcome to our humble dinner, Mrs. Bates. I'm sorry it isn't fancier, but it's all we have at our welcome table."

"Oh, please, Sister Evans, it is my pleasure to dine with you and your wonderful husband. He has taken such good care of my son. I'm so grateful to you both."

Delie put the bread platter down by her space.

Champ sat next to her, but she did not look his way. Not one little glance.

Nettie went around and sat by Jay. "Prayer, wife?" Jay asked.

"I'm going to pray," Nettie said.

Delie saw Willie roll his eyes. She wished she were closer to him to smack him upside the head, but fortunately, he didn't say anything.

Nettie cleared her throat. "God, our Father. Please watch out for the health and safety of every one at this table. Take care of us, Lord. Shelter us in Your presence. And please, help these ones who need Your guidance to reach for it and grow. Let them grow up and show their hearts so they may walk in Your righteous path. God, we ask you to bless this food and to help us everyday in Your name's sake. Amen."

Everyone said amen in unison. Delie opened her eyes to see Effie Bates dabbing at her eyes with a worn handkerchief. "So beautiful, Sister. Your preaching is just beautiful. I hope I can attend church while I am here."

"You're more than welcome to my tarry service tomorrow night. And again on Sunday."

A light in Effie Bates's round face made it appear as if some special honor had been bestowed on her. Maybe it had. Nettie did pray beautifully, no matter what Willie thought.

The only sound in the dining room was the scraping of stew onto plates and the quiet thank you's as the bread was passed around. More quiet except for chewing noises.

Champ spoke. "Bob Grace wants me to go to Philly to train. Tomorrow."

She might have known. What was wrong with training here? Even though she had just swallowed a bit of a potato and said nothing, he responded as if she had spoken the words.

"Bob said I got woman troubles and I need to train away from trouble for the fight next week."

"Son, you got to follow what he say. Mr. Grace knows what he is doing and he going to tell you right." Effie Bates ate of the beef stew with loud grunting noises that made the kids giggle.

"We'll miss you, Champ," Neal's sweet face took on a sad shadow. His sadness tore at Delie's heart.

"I'll miss you too, Little Man. But, I've got work to do."

"You could just stay here and help us move to the farm." Delie covered her mouth with her napkin. Sometimes, inappropriate Delie still made an appearance.

Oh. No. What had she just said? What was wrong with her?

The entire table looked at her. She sat up. Nettie gave her an encouraging half grin.

"We moving to the farm?" Bonnie asked.

"We got to get started sometime."

"I got the fight. I…"

Delie waved her hand and let it all out. "I know. I know. You've got to go to Philly and lose your eyesight. I know all about it."

Champ's fork clanked against the wood table as he set it down, "Delie."

"Well, excuse me. I don't mean to be harsh. But if you thought I was just going to stand by and let you lose your sight without me saying anything, you're crazy. You know I always say what is on my mind."

Effie leaned in, grabbing up some bread. "Son, if she won't support you, I will. Don't you worry about it. Eat your stew. It'll be alright."

Champ drew in a breath. Out of the corner of her eye, his wonderful bulky chest rose and fell at the deep breath he drew. Beautiful. "Mama, I'm wondering if you won't be more comfortable back in Georgia listening to the fight on the radio I bought you."

"What? There is no way I am going to miss the fight. I've looked forward to this since you were born. Your daddy, God rest his soul, he died for this chance. I'm going nowhere."

"Then you got to go and know Delie is going to be there. You got to be nice to her. I love her. I have loved her since I was nine years old. I thought I could stop. I chased what was out in the world when God knew I had left my heart in Winslow. I ain't leaving her no more. Never."

Had she lost the ability to breathe? Champ had never made such a speech to his mother. She was stunned, like a wooden plank had hit her in the head.

"Yeah, Champ!" Neal said in his loud voice. Delie bit her lips, hard, to keep the laughter in.

Effie wiped at her mouth with a napkin, obviously savoring the last bit of beef she had scraped up in her spoon. "My goodness, Champion. What will Sister Evans think of you being so disrespectful to your mother and not honoring that commandment about your mother and father? Really now, son."

Champ reached over and grabbed Delie's hand and put his big hand on top of hers. "I'm speaking what is in my heart now. Sister Evans won't fault me for that. I've been too quiet. Now, I'm saying what I got to say. You got the decision, Mama. You welcome to come, but you got to be nice."

"I'm always nice."

"No, Mama. No talk about her clothes and stuff. Her name is Cordelia May and you got to say her name when you speak to her."

The warmth of his hand covered hers and spread up her arm to her cheeks, both of them.

"Champion, I don't want you to get all upset. I'm going to do whatever you need to support you, son."

"Fine. I'll get you a room at another hotel. I don't want you saying anything to us when we spending our honeymoon in Philly."

"Goodness in the Lord, what are you talking about now?"

"We getting married. I told you today. I just didn't ask Delie proper." Champ tugged on her shoulder, forcing her to face him. "Delie, honey.

I'm sorry I didn't ask you right today. Asa shouldn't have been the first to know. You should have. Please say you'll marry me."

Now that they were facing one another, Delie saw all the seriousness in his face and all the love he had for her. It would be so easy to just say yes, to do what everyone wanted and give in.

But there was one more thing. Only one more thing. One more and Delie was going to have to be inappropriate to get it. She cleared her throat of beef stew. "Champion?"

"Yes, baby?"

"You know Neal is yours, don't you?"

He seemed surprised. Hmm. "I believe what you say, Dee. I always believe you. All of the children will be mine. I love them all. I'ma be their papa. "

Why did he have to sound like a praying man about it? Either he believed her or not.

"Yeah!" Neal shouted, "I got a dad!"

You always did. And all of the children came and started embracing them, knocking over their uneaten beef stew and hugging them. Delie hugged them too, but she wasn't happy.

Champ knew what she had meant.

Even worse, Effie Bates knew too.

Effie Bates sat there, wiping her greasy lips with Nettie's fine linen napkin, chastened at having been told off by her son. But still, there was a small smile of pleasure on her shiny lips because Champ had not said the words of ownership of Neal.

Well, she had wanted someone to take on all of them. Someone who would not make a difference and still see Willie and Roy as his sons, just as much as Neal was, and would understand that he had daughters, Bonnie and Flo. A complete family.

That's what she had.

God, help me in my heart. Help me to be satisfied with what has been put before me.

But she wasn't happy and it wasn't in her to pretend to be.

CHAPTER TWENTY

Champ thought he had trained hard before, but when Bob Grace got him in Philadelphia, he was in a whole different world.

By the end of the day, he ached where he found new muscles. However, Bob Grace did not own his thoughts at night, and his mind kept wandering to Delie and the children.

How were they? Had any of them gotten sick? What about Neal? Had they moved to the farm? Would they wait until he got back? Would he even be able to help them when he got back?

Of course he would.

Pray. God, please keep me whole and help me fight smart and not disturb my head. Keep my head on straight.

On the last day of practice, a different guy came in to watch him. Champ could tell he was a boxer, with his tapered waist and broad shoulders. The new boxer disturbed the trainers who all started whispering about him.

Now, Champ was a little disturbed. This was his camp. Who was this slick-haired Negro stranger with sloed eyes? Champ was the one they usually whispered about.

God, you telling me I'm on my way out? This here is my last fight. I'm all washed up.

But I can move on with my life if they're talking about someone else.

Nerves got to his stomach at the thought of his next step in life. Strange thing was, though, he could hardly wait.

"Who's he?" Champ asked Bob Grace.

"Boxer out of the Midwest, name Joe Louis. They say he looking for a white fight."

"He looking at my guy?"

Bob nodded. A sheepish look crossed Bob's face and Champ wanted to laugh. Bob Grace looked cross so often, it was funny to see him look just shy of mad.

"That's all right. He can have the scraps when I'm done."

"That's the way I like to hear you talking."

"I'm cutting out to get Delie at the train station."

"I told you to leave that woman mess in Pittsburgh. Now you shipping it in? Lawd a mercy. You best be glad I'm done with you today. And get Mama a room of her own."

"I did, both of them. I got my stuff to do. Never you mind."

Bob and Champ shook hands at the end of the session. Champ walked down the stairs out of the ring and made his way back to the locker room. Something told him to go up to that Joe Louis character and introduce himself. There were a couple of trainers talking to Joe, but when Champ approached him, tying his robe, everyone got quiet.

"Hey there." Champ offered his hand. "Hear you looking for a white fight."

"Yeah. Just about that." He seemed an affable guy.

"Great. Hope it goes well for you."

"Thought your guy might do."

"You won't want him when I am done with him."

"Why not?"

"You wouldn't gain any points fighting him."

"At least he's willing."

Champ nodded. "Sure. But when I knock him out, others'll come trying to prove it was a fluke. Might want to take a look at those."

"I didn't come all the way to Philly to look at a fluke."

"Well then. Hope you enjoy the fight." Champ nodded at him and walked off.

He had to go get his girl.

Joe called to him. "Hey. Your name really Champion?"

"Yeah it is."

"That's what your mama call you?"

"She did. You can ask her yourself at tomorrow's fight."

"I just might, partner."

"See you later. Going to get my sweetheart from the train station."

"Hope it works out well for you."

"Thanks. Enjoy the fight."

This Joe Louis character seemed kind of young and out of his element, but Champ had an eye for these things. Joe had good hands. He might be able to get a white fight.

A few years back, he would have been fighting a young one like Joe. Now, he was fighting this white fight to get out of boxing.

He fairly danced around the ring at the thought of doing it.

Delie had thought the Pittsburgh train station was big, but she and Effie were not prepared for the vacuum of space in the train station in Philadelphia. How would she find Champ in all of this with his mother biting at her heels? But just as soon as she climbed the steps, Champion stood right there in a black suit tailored to fit his magnificent body.

If Effie Bates had not been right behind her to catch her, she would have fainted in a swoon at the sight of her sweetheart. He took her breath away.

Thank you, God. I dressed so he isn't ashamed of me.

She walked over to him in her new suit of black and white with deep cuffs and a symmetrically cut collar. She had on a black and white cloche to match. And they matched. What a fine-looking couple they made.

"Champ, we're here. Thank God."

Champ embraced her right away, in front of his mother and everything. He put his lips to hers and kissed her, right there in the middle of the station and Delie kissed him back with everything she had. She had him groaning low in this throat.

"Oh, baby, I missed you so much." Champ pulled his lips away so they could breathe but kept his face close to hers, their foreheads touching.

"Me too, Champ."

Effie Bates usually chimed in at these key moments, but she stood to the side just looking at them with a resigned look on her face.

Well, Champ's little speech last week worked really well. Effie had been much better, and had even tried to make friends with the children, even though they were still afraid of her and really did not like her much.

"Ma. Welcome." Champ reached over and kissed her on the cheek.

"This is certainly a big station," Effie Bates seemed cowed for the first time in all of her life. Amazing.

"Jay's going to get our luggage and escort us to the hotel."

"Did Nettie come?"

"No, she and Em are taking care of the children. They say they are going to listen on the radio. It's the biggest thing in Pittsburgh."

Champ took Delie's arm and put it through his. "And after the fight, our wedding. I can't wait."

"I've waited seven years. I guess I can wait a day more. But, it'll be hard."

Delie waved over Jay who had a porter.

Her brother in law came over with the porter stared at all of them as if they had two heads.

Champ wrapped a protective arm around Delie. "He's not used to seeing Black folk dressed up as we are. Come on. The hotel has a good dining room. We can eat dinner there."

"Good, I'm starving," Delie slid her hand through Champ's and squeezed it hard, Miss Irene style. It was so good to be with him again. She held onto him so he couldn't get away from her, not any more.

"I want a kiss goodnight."

"Bob Grace is going to come out of his room and attack you."

"A kiss from those sweet lips is worth fighting for."

Champ and Delie sat in the hotel lobby after dinner. The lobby was the only place where they could see one another, decently, as Effie Bates insisted Jay pay for one room and she and Delie could share it. No use in wasting money, Effie pointed out and Delie said she was right. Champ wanted her to have her own room, but he could see how that might cast some suspicion on her, so he let it go.

Jay had used his money to pay for the finest hotel in the colored section of Philadelphia and it certainly was fine. Only five years old, the hotel was beautifully decorated in an ornate Art Deco style with mirrors and chandeliers and hand-carved wooden chairs.

Champ and Delie lounged in the lobby, holding hands. Joe Louis walked by with a male friend, ready to go out for a night on the town, he guessed.

"Hey." Champ called out. "Taking part of the nightlife?"

Joe turned around, came back and shook his hand. "I don't have no fight tomorrow like you. Only coming in to watch the bill."

"Probably training though."

"True, pal, true. But we've all got to have fun from time to time." Joe took a look at Delie. Champ did not like his look. Not at all.

"This here is Delie. She's going to be my wife when the fight's done."

"You don't say? Congrats then. Name's Joe Louis. I'll just shake your hand. Can't have Champ here wasting his fighting mojo getting me cause I kissed the bride-to-be."

She shook Joe's hand in a firm, but distant manner.

Champ wanted to laugh. Delie was not impressed by him. "Good to meet you, Mr. Louis."

"Yes, indeed. We'll be keeping on. I know you be in bed soon."

She slipped a protective arm through his. "Champ has a great work to do tomorrow. He needs his rest."

"Good to have your lady in your corner."

"Yeah, it is." Champ was a little bit stunned.

"Good night. I be looking forward to the fights."

Joe and his party headed on out the door of the hotel.

Delie shook her head. "Who is he?"

"He's looking at my guy, trying to get the next white fight."

"He can't have one, too."

"Well, if I walk away after this is done, they won't let it be the end, sugar. They going to want to prove they still got fighters on top. They'll have to find someone else to take Tom on. When I walk."

Delie turned to him. "Are you going to?"

"I said it to you and God. I meant it. This is the end of the line for me. I got to move on from here. I'm God's warrior and I'm under his protection. But I'm not going to stretch my luck. My time is done."

"Good, I'm glad."

"God asks us to do hard work. Just like… Well, see Joe? He's going out on the town. Probably spend a lot of money and get into some club and drink and find a lady friend. I got the hard work to do, sitting here with you and getting ready for bed."

Delie punched him in the arm. "I can't believe you. It's hard having to room with your mother too."

Champ got quiet. "I'm all she has."

"If she would embrace me and Neal, she could have more."

"She got to embrace all our family. You said she was getting better."

"Why don't you say Neal is yours? Why Champ?"

"I thought you didn't want me to treat any of the kids any better than the other, doll. If I said it, then Flo and Willie and Roy and especially Bonnie might be sad."

"Ok. But your Mama tried to act like I'm some kind of whore of Babylon who slept around on you after you left. Champ, there was never anyone else. I never did that with anyone else. Ever again."

Champ patted her hand. "I know, baby. I know."

The tears rose in her eyes and surprised him. "When he was born, I cried out all night. I was in such pain because you weren't there to see your son be born."

Waves of guilt washed over him as he remembered the way Delie's sisters talked about it. When he thought about it in any way, he wanted to beat somebody, mainly himself. But, that was an impossibility.

He had to keep his spirits up high for the fight.

Delie went on. "When I named him, I remembered something I heard. I wanted to name him after you, but I knew with such a name, people might expect a lot out of him and he was kind of puny when he was born. I didn't want to put it on him. So I did it a different way. I looked it up in the dictionary book. Neal. It means Champion. I could name him after his father and have it be my own secret."

God, what did I do to deserve such a clever and beautiful woman?

"Look at how you used all of that education you got at Spelman. Thank you, sugar."

"You welcome, Champion."

Champ held her face tenderly and put a small light kiss on her lips. "I'm going to bed to focus on the fight and what I have to do. Then, I can think about our wedding the next day, alright?"

"I hope you ain't going to be beat up too bad," Delie said to him. She was really thinking something else.

He hoped so too. *Please, God. Be my strength and shield tomorrow.* And the answer was peace in his heart. He knew God would be there for him. He had no doubt at all.

Where is this place? Oh please, don't let us be late.

Delie tried to walk faster, but Effie would be left behind. A tempting thought, but she couldn't do it. They had missed the first streetcar, and taken the second one, but in the wrong way, and now they straggled into the staging hall where the fight was to take place.

"Oh, you're going too fast. Why are you walking so? My feet…I can't." Effie's breath came in alarming short puffs.

Delie grabbed Effie by the arm. She very rarely touched her, if she ever had, and bolstered her up. "You can do it. For Champ. We got to be there so he will see us."

Because he wouldn't see them anymore after the fight, if he were taken down.

Dear, God. Please don't let it happen. Let him be well. Let him be okay.

When they entered the hall, there were Negro fighters who were clearly in a smaller weight class fighting one another. Another bout. *Thank you. We made it.*

Delie made sure Effie was seated in a row close to the front. Walking to the back, Delie saw Joe Louis and his crew sitting up a bit higher, laughing and talking with no women amongst them.

They were there about business, despite their light-hearted looking approach.

What an attention gatherer. He surely seemed to like the limelight. Must have been brought up in the North. There's no way any Negro man would like too much spotlight on him. What Louis did was probably on purpose, too. She passed by them and Joe Louis made an exaggerated hand wave at her. She waved back, but kept moving. Yeah, he had noticed her. Good luck to him. He would need it.

She made her way to the locker rooms and started knocking on them. Once she had knocked, fair warning, right? She opened doors, seeing all kinds of men on the bill in various states of inappropriate dress. If she had not been so determined to find Champion, she might have laughed out loud at how some of them reacted to her boldness. But, she did not care. She continued to search for her Champion. The fifth one she opened, Bob Grace stood before her.

Looking up at her, the petite trainer swore.

"That's not a nice word, Mr. Grace. If your mama heard you saying that, she would be so disappointed."

"My name is Bob and my mama been gone nigh on thirty years. My fighter needs to focus. Don't need no woman here."

Since she was taller than the short, wizened man and in much better condition, Delie pushed her way in. "I only want to see him for a minute. Stop being such a grub nose."

Dressed in his fighting reds, Champ looked resplendent. Her heart skipped a beat. "Dee, you got here."

"Yeah. Should have taken a cab. Trying to save money, like always, but I'm glad we made it in time."

"Jay here?"

"He came separate, for some reason." Delie looked around the bare room and was surprised Jay wasn't there, protecting his investment.

"Oh. Well, thank you."

"I wouldn't miss it, for the world. Champ?"

"Yeah, baby?"

"Do you want to pray with me?"

His face lit up like a new dawn sky. "I thought you would never ask. I was waiting to pray with Jay, but he hasn't come yet."

"I'll pray with you."

Delie came and stood next to Champ. With her heels on, she was as tall as he was. They joined hands. "Dear, God, please bless Champion in this fight today. Stay by his side. Help him to do the mighty work ahead so everyone will know we matter in this your world. In your name. Amen."

Champ squeezed her hands and the wrappings on his hands cut into hers, but she didn't care.

They looked up from bowing their heads and smiled at each other, lips just a little bit apart. "I'm not Nettie."

"It'll do. Thank you, honey. And, I got to tell you before I go out there. I know Neal is mine. And I'm sorry, so very sorry for all the pain I have caused you all this time. I came to an understanding about why this part of me, of us, is so very special. It has only been for you, all this time. I wanted to be worthy of you."

"What?" The sharp tang of tears began like a headache behind her eyes. She couldn't believe it. "All them years you were traveling, you had some other lady friends."

Champ gave a little snort. "I ain't said they didn't try. I just, maybe it's why I had a good record. All my heart was in my boxing. I came to know how empty all was without my wife, my God-intended wife with me. When the doctor told me about losing my sight, I had to come back to Winslow, to see your pretty face one more time. Just like I am now."

Oh. The tears flowed freely down her face and threatened to clog up her nasal passages.

"I'm here. You see me now, right?"

"I see you. You're beautiful. And, I love you."

"I love you too, Champ."

His beautiful chest expanded under his red robe. "Tell Neal I love him. No matter happens, I always will. And Bonnie. And Flo. And Willie. And Roy. And even if I'm an invalid, I can still help you. I'll be a good father."

That's when Delie knew. They were protected. God's peace welled in her heart. He had them in His hands. Champ would be alright. The fear left her as if the emotion had wings and gladness replaced it. "You would never be an invalid. Not in any circumstances."

"We'll see."

"Time to get her going." Bob Grace muttered.

Their heads pressed together, Champ pouted out his beautifully round lips to meet hers. One little kiss. Not a lingering one. Quick. Too quick.

Bob Grace grunted from the little corner where Delie had pushed him, disapproving of this small kiss they snatched.

"I love you." Delie said again because she wasn't quite sure what to say.

"Keep praying, honey. God is on our side."

They let go of each other. Delie hated the sound of the sharp click of her heels as she walked away from him. The silence had meant she was with him. Now, she wasn't.

When she was on the other side of the door, Bob Grace closed it right on her tailored bottom. Well…of all the nerve. Delie didn't have a handkerchief. Just as she used to when she was a tomboy, she wiped her face with the back of her hand and kept going.

She emerged from the basement where the locker rooms were into the opening of the arena looking for her seat, but seated in a row up front was Jay Evans's tall figure poking up amidst a bunch of children. Children? Her children? The back of Neal's curly head was her focal point as she sprinted in her heels down the concrete steps.

Not caring about how she looked, Delie threw herself into the crowd of children accepting hugs and kisses from her wriggly ones. "What are you all doing here?"

"We come to see Champ, Mama." Neal said in his loud voice, which rang out, even in the large room.

"You brung them?" Delie said to Jay, as he climbed over some steps back to some other rows where Nettie, Em and Effie sat together.

Delie followed him and embraced her sisters. "We all here, honey. To support you." Nettie's firm grasp was reassuring. Even if she couldn't say Champ's name, Nettie's support meant a lot to her.

"Thank you." Delie mouthed to Jay.

"You welcome. Is he back there?"

"Yes, he's been looking for you. Fifth door."

Jay's elegant figure slipped down the steps into hallway that led to the basement.

As Delie sat with the children, boys on one side, girls on the other, she would never forget his kindness.

"I want a snack." Bonnie slipped a small hand into Delie's.

Delie waved at her sisters. Nettie and Em went to a concession stand and purchased bags of peanuts to pass around. On the other side of the ring were a lot of reporters shouting and waving their arms. All the attention twisted Delie's insides. She was no Joe Louis. She just wanted all of this to be over and Champ in her arms again for good.

"Y'all eat them peanuts and stop that squirming." Effie yelled down to the children.

A wave of seasickness, or what she imagined it would be like, rolled around in her stomach. How could the children eat peanuts in the midst of the stink in an arena of sweat, the metal tang of blood and thick, acrid smoke? Still, Delie heartened a little bit at her future mother-in-law's efforts to discipline the children from four rows back. Yeah, she was nervous too.

Turning her head forward, Delie saw a small blond woman with a Marcel,, just like hers, only it wasn't as neat, dressed in a worn brown suit. The woman kept wringing her hands and whipping out a handkerchief from her purse. She was the only white woman in the arena in a sea of white males, reporters and spectators who crowded the spaces around the ring.

There was a connection between them, she knew, because Champ was going to defeat her man and because her suit was not new like hers. Despite all of that, they were sisters in all of this, twins in the battle. She became fascinated with the blonde woman and couldn't take her eyes off her, watching her nervous reactions as the janitor swabbed out the ring for the fight. She was the other boxer's woman, most likely.

Was she his sweetheart or his sister? Delie judged her to be about the same age as she was, in her mid-twenties. *She's praying to God too, same as me. Only, her man isn't in the same position as mine. I got to pray harder. I got to pray louder. I got to pray stronger.*

After the janitor cleaned the ring free of blood, sweat, spit and loose teeth. He rung a bell and a tall thin white man breeched the rope and stepped into the center where a microphone dangled overhead. With his height, he easily grabbed it and spoke into it. "Now for the draw. This is the one you all have been waiting for. In this corner, in the blue, Tom McCasson."

The blond woman started applauding as if someone would take away her hands if she didn't clap as hard as she could. She sat up straighter to get a look at this man as he came in. A man with the chest the size of a barrel in trunks of blue came down the aisle past her and the children. His entire body seemed to be coated in brown coarse hair. The man seemed otherworldly somehow. Where did they get such a big, hairy man to fight her Champion?

The knot of fear in her throat would not be gulped down. But she kept trying. This man was Champion's deliverer, one way or another. The crowd noise was so loud and went on so long in support of Tom McCasson. Champ had to have heard how the crowd of mostly white males was cheering for this hairy boxer.

How to help Champ struck her. "Link arms!" Delie shouted above the relentless din that went on and on for McCasson.

They would make a wall, a long wall of protection so Champ would see they all were there for him when he came in to the arena. Before she knew it, her sisters, had scrambled down to join her and linked arms with the children. Even fat Effie Bates struggled over the bleachers, but eventually she came down to Flo's end and linked her thick arm through Flo's on the other side.

"Pray!" Delie shouted over the din. "We got to pray as hard as we can."

And their heads all went down. Nettie shouted a prayer. "God, help our Champion. Help our Champion."

The children began to chant Champ's name, over and over.

The irritated voice of the announcer came without fanfare or build up. "In this corner, in the red, Champion Bates."

The children stamped their feet and hooted. Champ came past them on the side where Jay Evans had linked arms with Willie. She worried a moment at the way he blinked his long eyelashes trying to adjust to the bright lights. But as he breeched the ring, his focus was tight, not looking left or right.

His posture made Delie glad, but he had to know, despite the silence of the crowd who did not cheer for him, that there was a wall of love for him.

"Champ!" Neal shouted and this time, his little voice rose above the din and carried through the arena.

Neal spoke it it in his loud child's voice, one by one, they all joined in. Now, they were all saying his name. *And a little child shall lead them.* Isaiah. The improbable made reality. Delie understood for the first time in her life. The time for this to happen was now. It was time for their people to get a fair chance in this world, to get a fair shot in life. It was time.

And Champion, her Champion was the spark of it all. She was so proud of him. All of a sudden, she swam in a sea of wetness. Nearly every pore of her body oozed moisture at what she was witnessing, her man making history. Would it be fair, just or right for Champ to pay with his eyesight? Would he have to sacrifice himself in that way to have this chance happen? *Please, God, let him remain your warrior, whole and complete.*

Champ slipped off his robe and stood high above them. Delie's heart beat nearly through her chest. She slipped her eyes up to look at him. Her face was drenched with moisture. Tears or sweat, she didn't know which. She didn't care if her drenched face scrunched up ugly-like. Her arms were linked with Bonnie and Em, so she couldn't wipe at her face to clear it of the stinging salt and blurriness.

I love him so. Please, let it be alright. Let it be alright. The bell rang.

In a flash, so fast and so quick, Champ gazed down at her.

Just at her. Everyone else in the arena went away.

He winked.

And her heart went back to its normal beating rate.

He would win.

How long would it take him?

Delie sat back to keep track of the time. She hoped it wouldn't be long. She had a wedding to get ready for tomorrow.

CHAPTER TWENTY-ONE

Tom McCasson was not the fighter Champ had asked for.

They got him this Irish guy instead.

Probably because there was no respect for him as an Irish man either. They faced prejudice as well, so McCasson knew what was what.

Still, he was the biggest man Champ had ever seen and the hairiest. Brown-red hair all over the place. Was that McCasson's defense? His body hair? Would it cushion him from Champ's blows? The moment Champ turned to face him, he wanted to laugh, but he didn't. He couldn't.

Please, God. Help me do this.

When they went into the center of the ring, he could see the desperation in Tom's eyes.

And in McCasson's blue eyes, he saw–was that possible–a small frisson of fear? At what? Champ's big fists? The gleam of his bare chest under the lights in the ring? His thick thighs poised ready to take McCasson on? What was he afraid of? He was a man, just a man who was fighting for his family, his little family all lined up down below him. Neal himself looked like he wanted to get into the ring and do battle with McCasson. Yeah, he was a Bates.

But Champ knew he didn't want to hurt him. He didn't want McCasson to hurt him either.

Fight smart, not wild.

Bob Grace's words took on extra meaning in his mind as he circled McCasson, who still didn't even want to be touched.

They parted at the ringing of the bell and went to their corners. He came out fighting. He didn't know what McCasson was there to do. He didn't care. No way was this hairy giant getting near his head, cause if that's what the doctor's said would protect his sight, he would protect it.

Block.

Block.

Block the head. Nearly got close. He'd make him pay.

Uppercut.

Right cross.

Left cross.

Down.

And like a cut tree in the piney woods of Georgia, the very place Champion didn't ever want to go back to and harvest turpentine, he fell to the center of the ring. Hard.

McCasson.

Shades of David and Goliath.

Champ did not even have time to draw sweat.

He stood over his opponent, looking down at McCasson, whose blue eyes were crossed in his face. McCasson shook his head, trying to clear the daze from them.

The announcer, who had been so lackluster about saying his name, barely had time to arrange himself into his corner. He had to be summoned forth again to assist the referee.

"Ten, nine, eight."

Tom turned over and Champ stared into his blue eyes.

"Seven, six, five."

More fear there. *Please, don't hurt me again,* Tom's eyes seemed to plead with him. Champ was not in the hurting business. He wouldn't. All McCasson had to do was stay on the mat.

"Four, three, two…" The announcer was taking a long, long time about it. As if he didn't want to say the result.

Tom's eyes closed. No more blue looking up at him.

"One. He's out. It's a Knock Out!"

The loudest din came from Delie and the kids, who stood up and cheered.

Champ undid the laces on his gloves with his teeth. He threw down the gloves in the ring and breached the ropes. He jumped down to his sweet Delie in the crowds, swept her up in his arms and kissed her as if he were a thirsty man emerging from the desert. Her lips were so soft and tasty. He could kiss them forever. If only God would let him.

Her reaction surprised him.

"Is he okay?" Delie peered over his shoulder with worry reflected in her eyes.

Something that never occurred to him before. Think of the other man. Better make sure he hadn't killed him. *Please, God. Help Tom up off of the mat.*

The little blond woman from the crowd bent over Tom McCasson and rang her hands in sorrow. A doctor joined the two of them in the center of the ring.

"Just a minute."

Champ breached the ropes again. At his reentry into the ring, the crowd fell silent. He approached the group in the center of the ring, tentatively. The doctor, the woman and Tom, whose eyes were open again, seemed startled to see him.

Champ repeated Delie's question.

"He's going to be fine, boy. Go on ahead, now." The doctor's voice was edged with impatience and disrespect.

The blond woman stared up at him with anger in her own blue eyes. "What kind of beast are you anyway?" Her squeaky voice came across as a scold.

Tom spoke. For the first time, a deep voice resonated from his opponent. "Leave him be, Jeannie. It's one of them old boxing tricks. Only the best knows how to do it. Just be glad I don't have to face him no more."

"You giving up on boxing too?"

"Too? You leavin'?"

"My gloves are in the ring." Champ gestured to them, the age-old gesture of a boxer who was done with the life, never to return again.

McCasson sat up and the crowd clapped politely. And just as Champ had done, he pulled at his glove laces with his teeth and pulled the big overstuffed gloves off of his hands and threw them into the ring, one after the other.

Champ reached out to Tom, offering to help him up. Who else would do it? Not petite Jeannie or the short doctor.

McCasson reached up, unafraid to touch Champ's bare hand, and Champ pulled him to his feet. McCasson stood up next to him, towering over him by about three or four inches. Rather than letting go of Champ's grip, he took Champ's arm and raised it high into the air.

Completely unexpected. Some in the crowd clapped. Others made low hissing and booing sounds. Several photographers took their picture. McCasson let go of his hand and Champ tapped him on his hairy shoulder.

"Thanks. God bless you." Champ said and shook the man's hand. More flash bulbs at that. Might as well give them what they came for. He turned back around and breached the ropes one more time. One last time.

This time when he came out, Joe Louis stood at the bottom with Delie and the kids, regarding him with respect. He thrust his hand out to Champ. He shook it. The kid had a good grip on him for sure.

"A good fight. Guess your Mama knew what her boy baby was, huh?"

"She did. I come from a long line of fighters." He put his wrapped hand on Louis's shoulder. "It's all yours."

"Thanks," Joe didn't miss a beat. "But with you walking away, I'm always going to wonder if I could have taken you or not."

At that, Champ let go of Joe's hand.

Champ surveyed his little group of support all gathered there at ringside: Delie, his mother, Jay, Nettie, Em and the children all clustered in little groups. There was so much future in his people. He was more than ready to go meet it.

"It would have been a knock down drag out, Joe. And one of us would have won. But the fight we have ain't with each other. It's out there. Go out there and K.O. it, hear?" Champ turned from him toward his family. His legs got weary all of a sudden.

But Joe called to him, "Hey. If I ever need any help, do you have a contact?"

"You can reach me at Smithington Dairy Farm in Penn Hills, Pennsylvania." Champ waved at Joe as he left with his family.

At that point, he fell into the arms of his mother, who greeted him with a warm hug and a kiss. But as soon as she let go of her hold on him, he reached down to Neal and Bonnie and took each one of them into his arms and gave them a kiss. "You going to be our papa, now?" Bonnie asked him.

"Yes, baby girl. I'm going to be the one telling all your dates they can't take you out until they treat you real good."

"I'm so glad. I prayed real hard, Champ." Neal's words were just for him, small and nearly silent.

Champ turned to look into the eyes of his son. He had Bledsoe eyes, just like John Bledsoe, a deceased man who embodied decency. But Neal's hair was his and the shape of his small face, so much like Effie's. "I love you, Neal." Champ told him. Instantly, he turned to the little girl in his other arm, "And you, Bonnie."

He stood and reached for Flo. "Pretty Flo, I love you, and thoughtful Roy. And funny Willie."

"This the best time ever." Em enthused.

"You sure are right, HB."

His eyes met Delie's. Her luminous brown eyes shone with pride. Concern. Love. "You looking at me mighty hard, Cordelia May. What you want?"

"I have waited for this day for a long time and it's better than I had hoped."

"It is? You think it's better than our wedding?"

Delie shook her head back and forth fast. He had to laugh at her disagreement. "Maybe not."

"Well, let's go see. I can't wait for tomorrow." Champ led them all out down near the locker room, ready to shower and change to go eat anything but steak. But first he had a telegram to send to Miss Irene, to let her know of his victory in the two most important fights he had ever fought in his life.

"Do. Not. Get. Married. There. In. Philadelphia. Stop. If. You. Do. I. Will. Never. Speak. To. You. Ever. Stop." Ruby's telegram practically flamed up in Delie's hands, and she wanted to laugh at Ruby's uproarious anger.

"She pretty mad, huh?" Champ twirled his fingers about one another, clearly relishing the new cool metal feel of the shiny band on his finger.

She fingered the pretty blue stone and gold band on her hand. "She'll get over it. Ruby is so bossy."

"When I see her, I'm going to tell her it was all your idea." Champ threw up his hands. "I'm done fighting. No more."

Delie kicked her shoes off and threw herself on the bed next to him sliding a possessive hand along the lapel of his navy blue wedding suit. "Coward. Ruby would be nothing after your hairy opponent. Is that why you knocked him out? You didn't want to fight?"

"Aw, now you sound like the reporters and such."

"Well? Why?"

Champ fingered the side of her face with his touch. She shuddered with joy. "I prayed to God. I asked him to please show me the way to avoid getting hit up in my head. I done fallen to the tarp too many times to count, risking my sight. I had to be able to see your beautiful face everyday."

"I would want to be with you, no matter what happened, blind or not."

"It's good to know in case it ever happens." Champ's face turned sober and she drew a shape on his rounded lips.

"I love you. I don't care."

"It's mighty hard for a man to make a living when he's blind."

"Well, you worked it out. You on the dairy farm. Me at school, teaching somewhere. We'll take care of these kids. We'll be okay."

"I'm just saying. I got things to do. I got to make the dairy farm go and maybe a garage someday."

"I know you will do well."

"I appreciate it, honey." He reached down and traced a shape on her lips.

"And I'm glad your Mama wants to help us."

Champ gave her a mischievous grin, speaking in a slow way. "She's your Mama now too."

"Yikes!" She tried to jump up but couldn't. Champ had a firm grasp on her waist.

"It's just been us two for so long, but Mama had to change. Listen, Cordelia May Bates," Champ lifted her chin with his finger. "Any time she making it hard for you, and you can't take it no more, let me know. No more hurt for you. Cause your hurt would hurt my heart. And I love my heart."

"And I love you, Champion Jack Bates." She could barely get the words out in his haste to reach out for her. Delie slid herself into the circle of his arms, every bit as eager to partake in what God had intended for only the two of them to share.

Time melted away.

They were both eighteen, back in the Bledsoe barn again, picking up where they had left off.

Author's Note

I hope you enjoyed *A Champion's Heart*. My quest in writing this book began when I read an article about *The Negro Motorist's Green Book.* First published in 1936, *The Green Book,* as it was more commonly known, was published by Victor Green, a postal worker, as an annual guide to let African Americans know how and where they could travel safely throughout America. It was good to learn about such assistance. What was even more striking was Green's insistence that he looked forward to the day when he wouldn't have to publish such a guide. So this story was my way of using several of the stories told by African Americans in talking about how they traveled before *The Green Book*—especially in that last year before it became available in 1935.

I was also compelled to think about Joe Louis as an underappreciated civil rights leader in the 1930's—something I had learned about as an undergraduate. The question rose in my mind: who paved the way for Louis to get his first fight in 1937? That's where Champion came from. Anyone who is familiar with *Invisible Man* by Ralph Ellison knows about the battle royals that talented young Black men were forced to fight. So, thinking about that particular concept of entire families bred for sporting greatness, I developed the "Born to Win Men" series. Champion and Delie are book one in this spin off series from my "Migrations of the Heart" series. Look out for future stories about Champion's cousins, King Bates and Duke Bates and their encounters in the sporting world.

These are a few of the sources that helped me write *A Champion's Heart*:

Black Genesis: The History of the Black Prizefighter by Kevin Smith
Bustin' Loose
Cinderella Man
The Green Book:
http://digitalcollections.nypl.org/collections/the-green-book
Rocky
The Sundowners: The History of Black Prizefighters 1870-1930 by Kevin Smith
Unforgivable Blackness: The Rise and Fall of Jack Johnson

About the author:

Piper G Huguley, named 2015 Debut Author of the Year by Romance Slam Jam and Breakout Author of the Year by AAMBC in 2015, is a two-time Golden Heart ®finalist and the author of the "Home to Milford College" series. The series follows the building of a college from its founding in 1866. On release, the prequel novella to the "Home to Milford College" series, *The Lawyer's Luck,* reached Number One Amazon Bestseller status on the African American Christian Fiction charts. The first book in the series, *The Preacher's Promise* was named a top ten Historical Romance in Publisher's Weekly by the esteemed historical romance author, Beverly Jenkins and was a semi-finalist in the Writer's Digest Self-Published e-book contest in 2016.

Huguley is also the author of "Migrations of the Heart," named by *Book Riot* as one of 10 Excellent Historical Romance series. Book one in the series, *A Virtuous Ruby* won the Golden Rose contest in Historical Romance in 2013 and was a Golden Heart® finalist in 2014. The three-book series is published by Samhain Publishing:

Piper blogs about the history behind her novels at http://piperhuguley.com. She lives in Atlanta, Georgia with her husband and son.

71177801R00187

Made in the USA
Columbia, SC
04 June 2017